Praise for the Bromance Book Club series

"This is a lovely and sweet story, an honest and hopeful portrayal of the hard work of marriage."

—*New York Times Book Review*

"Lyssa Kay Adams hits a home run when it comes to the most inventive, refreshing concept in rom-coms this year."

—*Entertainment Weekly*

"Adams's words help you believe that the right people find the right people."   —Shondaland

"A fun, sexy, and heartfelt love story that's equal parts romance and bromance."   —*Kirkus Reviews*

"Adams weaves in humor, complex emotions, and excerpts from the motivational story itself to create a satisfying courtship."

—*Publishers Weekly*

"Sweet and funny and emotional."

—Nstselling author

"*The Bromance Bo*   of *Intercepted*

"The perfect mix of laugh-out-loud and swoony moments—every town should have a Bromance Book Club."

—Evie Dunmore, author of *Bringing Down the Duke*

Crazy Stupid
Bromance

LYSSA KAY ADAMS

JOVE

New York

A JOVE BOOK
Published by Berkley
An imprint of Penguin Random House LLC
penguinrandomhouse.com

Copyright © 2020 by Lyssa Kay Adams

Library of Congress Cataloging-in-Publication Data

Names: Adams, Lyssa Kay, author.
Title: Crazy stupid bromance / Lyssa Kay Adams.
Description: First edition. | New York: Jove, 2020. |
Series: Bromance book club ; 3
Identifiers: LCCN 2020016133 (print) | LCCN 2020016134 (ebook) |
ISBN 9781984806130 (trade paperback) | ISBN 9781984806147 (ebook)
Subjects: GSAFD: Love stories.
Classification: LCC PS3601.D385 C73 2020 (print) |
LCC PS3601.D385 (ebook) | DDC 813/.6—dc23
LC record available at https://lccn.loc.gov/2020016133
LC ebook record available at https://lccn.loc.gov/2020016134

First Edition: October 2020

Printed in the United States of America
1 3 5 7 9 10 8 6 4 2

Cover art and design by Jess Cruickshank
Book design by Elke Sigal

To Gerry,
my husband, best friend, and dirty-joke maker-upper

CHAPTER ONE

Noah Logan always knew the day would come when he officially morphed into someone he no longer recognized, and apparently his thirty-first birthday was going to be it.

But only if he didn't put up a fight.

And, hell yes, was he going to fight.

He folded his arms across his chest, adopted a *you wanna say that again* stance he'd learned from his military father, and clenched his jaw beneath the scruff of his beard. "No. No way. Not in a million fucking years."

His friend Braden Mack stuck out his bottom lip. "Come on, man. It'll be the best birthday present ever."

"It's *my* birthday, dipshit," Noah grumbled. He threw his hand out wide to gesture at the large circle of men and one woman who gathered around a table near the empty dance floor in Mack's country and western dance club, Temple. "And you can save that pouty thing for them. It doesn't work on me."

Which was a lie. Mack's pouty face was how Noah got here. At first, he'd been honored and humbled when Mack asked him to stand up with him in his upcoming wedding alongside his other close friends. But then came the bottom-lip thing, and the next goddamned thing Noah knew, he was doing all the shit he thought brides were supposed to do. Apparently, Mack's fiancée, Liv, had turned all planning over to Mack, who in turn had deemed it only fair that his male buddies get a small taste of what society usually required of women.

Which, hey, Noah was all for. But Christ, in the past eight months, he'd helped Mack pick out flower arrangements, considered lighting schemes, debated the mixed messaging of a particular Bible verse, and gotten into one singularly heated exchange with another groomsman over whether Mack should abandon the outdated tradition of tossing the garter. The wedding was next month, and Mack had officially reached epic levels of groomzilla.

And today? Oh, today they were *crafting*. Mack wanted a handmade archway at the entrance to the reception hall.

Which is why they were all gathered at his club at three o'clock in the afternoon on a Thursday in October to make about five hundred paper flowers. But clearly, it was all a ruse to drop the latest *what the fuck*.

Mack wanted them to perform a dance routine at the reception. A *dance* routine.

"Let me put this in words you understand," Noah said. "Fuck. You. I'm. Not. Dancing."

Mack glared with all the frustration of a kindergartner who'd been denied a second chocolate milk at snack time. Behind Noah, the scruff of shoes on the well-worn wooden floor told him that Mack was about to get backup. Seconds later, a calloused hand clapped him on the shoulder. Noah pitched forward, and his thick, black-framed glasses slid down his nose.

"We dance for Mack," said Vlad Konnikov, a hockey player they all just called the Russian because he was, in fact, Russian. His heavy accent dipped into the *or else* territory.

Which sent Noah's voice higher into the *oh shit* range as he tried another tactic. "What about Liam? Your brother lives in California. How's he going to learn the dance routine if he's not even here?"

"I'm sending him a video to learn on his own."

Noah pushed his glasses up and turned around and found an entire table of upturned faces watching him in anticipation of his inevitable defeat. "You all agreed to this?"

"Friends don't let friends embarrass themselves alone," said Del Hicks, a player for the Nashville Legends Major League Baseball team. His thick fingers were surprisingly nimble as they folded a piece of tissue paper into something that remarkably resembled a carnation.

"My wife threatened me with bodily harm if I didn't do it," added Gavin Scott, another baseball player whose wife, Thea, happened to be Mack's fiancée's sister. Del smacked Gavin upside the head. Gavin winced and quickly amended his statement. "I mean, I'm happy to do it."

The sole woman in the group snorted and dropped a pink tissue-paper flower into the box next to her chair. Sonia was Mack's long-time club manager and the crankiest person Noah had ever met. "Give it up, Noah. If Mack can convince me to *craft*, you can set aside your ego enough for one dance."

It wasn't ego. It was self-preservation. Yeah, he still wore his hair too long and his clothes too casual, but even with his man bun and geeky comic book T-shirts, his former hacktivist pals would never recognize him today. The man who'd once been arrested by the FBI for attempting to hack into a university research center was about to become a tuxedo-wearing dancing monkey at a million-dollar, Pinterest-worthy wedding alongside the rich and famous.

True, Mack and the rest of the guys were nothing like the war-mongering scumbags he used to try to bring down with his computer skills. In fact, these men were the most decent people he'd ever known. But still, he'd come a long way. He was a successful businessman now, the owner of a growing computer security company catering to celebrities and other high-profile clients. He was officially respectable. A millionaire before he was even thirty. He was finally fulfilling his father's last, dying wish. *Do something with that genius brain of yours.*

A cheesy-assed groomsmen dance was definitely not what his father had in mind.

He grasped at his last, best excuse. "Dude, how do you even think Liv will respond to this? She hates this kind of romantic stuff."

Mack shrugged. "But she loves to laugh."

"So the point is to humiliate ourselves?"

"No. The point is to allow ourselves to be vulnerable in front of the women we love."

Mack said the last part with a pointed emphasis that made Noah squirm. It was a low blow, and Mack knew it. But Mack never missed an opportunity to harangue Noah about his relationship with his best friend, Alexis Carlisle. Mack and the guys couldn't understand why Noah had kept things platonic with Alexis, and he was damn tired of trying to explain it.

Noah reached around to squeeze the back of his neck where his bun had become loose. He jerked out the ponytail holder and quickly twisted his hair back up.

"Alexis will love it," Mack said, eyebrow raised. "You know she will."

And just like that, Noah let his arms fall limply to his sides. His next words came out in a defeated sigh. "What do I have to do?"

"Just show up Saturday to start learning the moves. I've hired a choreographer and everything."

"Oh yay."

Mack pounded Noah on the back. "This means a lot, man. And you'll see. It's going to be fun."

More like torture. Noah trudged behind Mack back to the table and dropped into his seat. Sonia slid a stack of pink tissue paper toward him. He mumbled a thanks, but then returned his glare to Mack. "But I swear to God, if there's twerking involved, I'm out."

"Dude, no one wants to see the Russian twerk," snorted Colton Wheeler, a country music star who'd gotten his start in one of Mack's four Nashville nightclubs and was now a friend to them all. He was also Noah's newest client. And he happened to be right about the Russian. The hockey player was big, hairy, and had a tendency to fart in public.

"What is twerking?" the Russian asked.

Colton dug out his phone and quickly found a video. The Russian's face turned beet red, and he returned his attention to his paper flowers. "No twerking."

"Speaking of your birthday," Mack said, bending in his seat to grab something on the floor. He sat back up with a plastic bag and passed it to Colton, who handed it to Noah.

Noah peeked in the bag and groaned. A paperback book stared

up at him with the title *Coming Home*. The cover image was of a man and woman embracing, and the man held a football in one hand.

Noah tried to hand it back to Colton. "No. It's bad enough you're making me dance."

Colton pushed the book back at Noah. "Trust us. You need this."

Noah dropped it on the table. "No, I don't."

"But you'll like it," Mack prodded. "It's about this professional football player who comes back to his hometown and discovers that his old girlfriend is still there and—"

"I don't care what it's about. How many times do I have to tell you that I am *never* joining your book club?"

Noah was the only guy there who was not part of the Bromance Book Club, Mack's male-only romance-novel book club. The guys believed romance novels held all the answers to relationships. And while Noah couldn't argue with their results—Mack was happily engaged, and nearly all the other members had saved their marriages using the lessons from the books they read—Noah had rejected all of Mack's literary advances to lure him into the club.

Mack propped his elbows on the table. "All you have to do is read and listen to us, and we can fix this little problem for you."

Noah ground his molars. "My relationship with Alexis isn't a problem that needs to be solved. We're *friends*."

"Sure," Colton snorted. "Just friends. You only spend every other minute with her, go running whenever she calls, play some stupid word game with her on your phone—"

"It's called Word Nerd."

"—have a nickname for her that no one else uses, and hang out with her even though you're allergic to her cat. Did I miss anything?"

"I'm also allergic to Mack, but I still hang with him."

Mack slapped a hand over his heart. "I'm hurt. Truly."

Colton raised his hands in surrender. "I'm just saying that I don't understand why you're friend-zoning yourself on purpose."

"Leave him alone," came a calm but commanding voice from the other end of the table. It belonged to Malcolm James, NFL player, resident feminist, and Zen master. "Men and women can be friends without it needing to be sexual."

"Except in his case, he actually wants to have sex with her," Colton said.

Noah clenched his fist against the table. "Watch it."

"Yeah, dude," Mack said, shaking his head. "That was uncalled for. We don't talk about women like that."

Colton shrugged sheepishly and mumbled an apology.

Malcolm spoke again. "The so-called friend zone is nothing but a social construct designed to give a man an excuse to justify why a woman might not want to have sex with him. It's a bullshit lie, and we all know that. So leave Noah alone about his relationship with Alexis. We should be commending him for proving that men and women can truly be friends."

Like a class that had just been chastised by their favorite teacher, the table fell silent but for the crinkle of paper.

It didn't last long. Mack finally looked up with a sigh. "All I'm saying is that maybe she's ready, Noah."

Noah felt something pop in his brain.

"It's been eighteen months since—"

"Don't say it," Noah snapped. As if he needed Mack pointing out the calendar. Noah knew exactly how long it had been since

7

he'd met Alexis. It wasn't the time that mattered. It was the circumstances.

And they weren't right. Not then. Not now.

Maybe not ever. Which was as depressing a thought as the idea of dancing.

Noah stared at the plastic bag on the table. He didn't want it or their help. And he sure as shit didn't need romance novels to remind him that he was currently a walking romantic disaster. Unrequited love made for a pathetic happy ever after.

But when things broke up an hour later, Noah took the book with him. Because if he had to pretend to read a damn book to get Mack off his back, so be it.

CHAPTER TWO

This was it. Alexis Carlisle could feel it. This was the day the shy young woman was finally going to talk to her.

For a full week, the woman with the long brown hair and rotating collection of sweatshirts had been coming into the ToeBeans Cat Café—the coffee shop Alexis owned—to sit quietly in a corner with a book, alternating between petting one of the café's resident felines and shooting nervous glances at Alexis.

But today, she didn't have a book. Today, she simply looked around, her gaze lingering on Alexis whenever she thought Alexis wasn't paying attention.

In the eighteen months since Alexis had come forward as one of more than a dozen victims of sexual harassment by celebrity chef Royce Preston, Alexis's café had become a gathering spot for other survivors of harassment and violence. Nearly every week brought a new woman to the café in search of a supportive ear, an understanding hug, or guidance on how to get out of a bad situation. Alexis didn't choose this, but it had become her responsibility.

Along the way, she'd learned to spot the signs of a woman ready to talk.

She turned to the barista—her friend and fellow Royce survivor, Jessica Summers. "Can you handle the counter for a little while? I'm going to try something."

Jessica nodded, and Alexis jogged into the back and through the kitchen to the closet where she kept the box of gardening supplies she used to maintain the brick landscaping beds that flanked the front door of the café. They were in desperate need of weeding and pruning, and this idea could maybe kill two birds with one stone. She lugged the box through the café, pretending to struggle more than she really was with its weight. As she approached the door, she wedged the box against the window and once again pretended to struggle as she reached for the handle.

The act worked. The young woman approached with a tentative smile. "D-Do you need some help?"

Alexis schooled her face into what she hoped was gentle friendliness and hid the fact that her insides were skipping rope and singing a summer-camp song. "Thank you, yes," she said, hoisting the box against her chest. "I need more hands."

The woman reached around Alexis to open the door and then took another step back to allow Alexis to walk outside.

"Chilly today, huh?" Alexis said, bending to set the box on the sidewalk.

The girl let the door swing shut. She pulled her hands inside the cuffs of her sweatshirt as she answered. "Yes. I—I didn't expect it to be this cold here."

"You're not from Nashville?" Alexis crouched to pretend she was looking for something in the box. She wanted to keep the conversation going but didn't want to be too aggressive. The last thing the women who found their way to her café needed was someone prodding them to talk before they were ready.

"Huntsville," the woman said. "It's still a lot warmer there than here."

Alexis found her gardening gloves and stood, as if that's what she'd been looking for all along. "I've never been to Alabama. How far of a drive is that?"

"Only a couple of hours. That's why I thought maybe it would be the same weather here."

Alexis shoved her gloves in her pocket. "We're just having an early cold snap," she said, keeping her voice as light and casual as possible.

"Maybe." The young woman bit her lip.

Alexis extended her hand. "I'm Alexis. I've seen you come in a few times, but we haven't formally met yet."

The woman swallowed nervously before accepting the outreach. "Candi," she said, curling her fingers around Alexis's. "Well, Candace, but everyone calls me Candi."

"It's nice to meet you, Candi." Alexis nodded back toward the door. "Can I make you something to drink?"

"Oh, no." The girl shook her head almost frantically.

Disappointment silenced the camp song. But then Candi swallowed and said, "I mean, yes. I came for something to drink, but you seem busy, so I can just go to the counter."

"I'm happy to do it." Alexis smiled. "And then maybe you can keep me company while I try not to kill these plants."

Alexis held her breath until Candi offered that hesitant smile again. "Sure. Yes. That—that would be fine."

"Cinnamon chai latte?"

The smile grew. "You already know my order?"

"Have a seat," Alexis said, nodding toward one of the outdoor patio tables. "I'll be right back."

Alexis kept her gait as natural as possible as she walked back inside. She caught Jessica's gaze behind the counter. "I need a cinnamon chai latte," she said with a furtive glance behind her.

"She finally talked to you?" Jessica asked, eyes lighting up as she started to prepare the drink.

Alexis grabbed a muffin and a scone from the bakery case. Food had a way of breaking the ice and giving people something to focus on when eye contact became too painful. Many a secret had been softly revealed to Alexis over a plate of pastries crumbled by worried fingers.

She returned to Candi and set the plate and latte in front of her. Candi pulled a wallet from her pocket. "How much—"

"On the house," Alexis said, walking back to the box of gardening supplies.

"Oh, I can't," Candi rushed.

"Consider it a *Welcome to Nashville* gift." She tilted her head. "Have we met before?"

Candi's eyes widened for a split second before she once again shook her head. "No."

"You seem so familiar to me."

Candi blinked. "Familiar how?"

"I don't know. Something about your eyes, I guess."

Candi went still. Like a stunned rabbit caught in the act of eating grass.

Alexis grabbed her pruning shears and went after the worst of the potted mums, which had started to wilt from neglect and the growing chill in the air.

Alexis snipped off a deadhead. Waited. Snipped another one.

The quiet clink of the mug against the table was the only sound save the clip of her shears.

When the silence dragged on, Alexis finally said, "I want you to know that you should never feel pressured to talk. If all you want is someone to sit with you, I'm here whenever you need me."

"O-Okay."

Another deadhead dropped to the ground. "Many, many women just like you have come here looking simply for someone to sit with."

Candi's swallow was audible. Alexis lowered the shears into the box and rose. Candi followed her with nervous eyes as Alexis took the seat across from her at the patio table. From her apron pocket, she withdrew a business card reserved only for women like Candi. "My cell number is on there. You can call me anytime."

Candi studied the card as if Alexis had just handed her a one-hundred-dollar bill.

"I know how hard this is," Alexis said. "It's a suffocating secret to keep."

"I—I do need to talk to you."

"Whenever you're ready."

But then a screeching voice interrupted. "Excuse me, but I have a bone to pick with you."

Candi's eyes widened as she turned to look over her shoulder to watch Alexis's nemesis storm up the front sidewalk and march to the table.

Alexis tried to keep her voice calm. "I'm sorry, Karen. I'm in the middle of something. Can it wait?"

"It absolutely cannot."

And just like that, Candi blanched, shot to her feet, and stumbled backward. "I—I can come back."

"Candi, wait." Alexis tried to reach for the girl's arm to stop her from fleeing, but Candi slipped from her grasp and disappeared down the sidewalk.

Alexis gathered the dirty plate and coffee mug and stood. Ignoring Karen, she turned toward the door, walked inside, and approached the counter. She set the dirty dishes into a plastic bin beneath the counter and wiped her hands on the towel tucked into her apron before turning to face Karen again. "Something I can help you with today?"

"You haven't been exactly helpful before, so I seriously doubt it," Karen responded.

Alexis forced her muscles into some semblance of a smile. "I'm sorry to hear our previous encounters haven't been satisfactory to you. Would you like to sit and talk? I can make you a cup of tea on the house."

"I wouldn't eat in here if you paid me."

"Then how can I help you?" Her attempt to remain calm wasn't for Karen's benefit. It was for her own. If she'd learned anything in the past eighteen months, it was that people were going to believe what they wanted, and few of them were worth the emotional effort it took to try to change their minds. Besides, Alexis was used to dealing with Karen Murray. The owner of the antiques shop across the street had been a thorn in Alexis's side since the day she'd come forward with her accusation against Royce. Karen had never even spoken to Alexis before then, but now her complaints were a weekly annoyance.

Karen whipped an overstuffed baggie from her purse. "You can help me with this."

She dropped the baggie on the counter, and Jessica leaped back with a screech as its contents became clear. Two tiny dead eyes stared out through the plastic in a silent plea from what had once been a rat in life.

Alexis stepped closer and lifted the baggie by one corner. "I appreciate the gift, Karen, but I'm a vegetarian."

"Everything is a joke to you, isn't it?" Karen hoisted her purse higher on her shoulder. "That thing was left on the welcome mat outside my store this morning."

Alexis dumped the baggie in the trash can beneath the counter. As soon as Karen left, she'd have to empty it and hose the counter down with bleach. "I'm not following," she said. "Why is that rat my fault?"

"Because your cat left it there!" She said that part with a disdainful point and glare at Beefcake, the rescue Maine coon who was sound asleep on the cat tree by the window.

Alexis forced her lips into a smile. "Karen, there is no way Beefcake did this. He goes home with me every night, and he has been inside since we arrived this morning."

Jessica began squirting the glass countertop with industrial cleaner. Karen took a massive step backward, her purse clutched tightly against her stomach. "You know, it was bad enough when we only had to put up with your weekly cat adoption events, but now we have to put up with this too?"

Karen waved her hand toward the dining area, gesturing at the tables full of women who were deep in conversation—some gleefully, others tearfully.

"I'm afraid I don't understand," Alexis said. "You're mad that I have a lot of customers?"

"These women aren't just customers."

"They all buy food. They look like customers to me."

"You know what I mean. These women fill up the parking lot and never visit any of the other stores on the block. It's not fair that you take up all the prime parking spots for your little crusade."

Alexis crossed her arms. "By crusade, I assume you're referring to my attempt to offer a supportive, judgment-free environment to women who are survivors of sexual assault and harassment?"

Karen rolled her eyes, which said more than words ever could. "Just because someone claims they were a victim doesn't mean they were. For all we know, these women just want attention."

"Yes, because nothing garners positive attention for a woman like reporting sexual harassment against an employer."

Karen's face turned a disturbing shade of red. "I will take this up with the city if I have to."

The old Alexis might have been intimidated by the threat, but that version of herself had disappeared when she finally went public with what her old boss had done to her and a dozen other women. It took a lot more than Karen to scare her now. "Be sure to say hello to the council president for me. Let her know that I'll be putting the pumpkin spice scones back on the menu soon."

Karen turned on one high heel and stomped toward the door. It opened from the outside just in time, and Alexis laughed openly when she saw who was on the other side. Her best friend, Liv Papandreas, stood back to let Karen walk out, but then she made an obscene gesture behind the woman's back.

Alexis gave her a scolding look but loved her for it. She wouldn't have survived the past year and a half without the support of her friends.

"Do I need to throw hands?" Liv asked, coming to the counter. She carried a garment bag slung over her shoulder.

"*I'm* going to throw hands soon," Alexis said, tugging the trash can from beneath the counter.

"Now *that* I would like to see. It's about time you fought back against that woman."

"I don't think my therapist would call it a healthy coping skill, and it wouldn't make a difference, anyway." She looked over her shoulder and nodded toward the back for Liv to follow her. "Whatcha got there?"

Liv nearly skipped. "I have a present for you two," she said in a singsongy voice. She paused behind the counter to fist-bump Jessica. The three of them were bonded for life after working together to expose Royce.

"Bridesmaids dresses?" Jessica asked, grinning.

"Yep. They finally came in."

Liv followed Alexis through the swinging door that separated the dining area from the kitchen and Alexis's small office. As Alexis emptied the offending trash can into the dumpster by the back door, Liv hooked the garment bag over the top of her office door. She unzipped it just as Alexis returned. Liv pushed open the sides to reveal two floor-length strapless gowns made of ruby silk.

"Wow," Alexis said. "They're even prettier than I remember. Mack did a good job picking these out."

The fact that Liv had turned all wedding planning over to Mack was all anyone needed to know about their relationship. He was the romantic one. Liv was the *Let's elope to Vegas* one. And Alexis loved them both.

Liv stood back with a cheeky smile. "I can't wait to see Noah's reaction when he sees you in this."

Alexis's cheeks warmed. Her friendship with Noah Logan was a constant source of speculation and teasing among their group of friends.

"Look at you," Liv laughed. "You can't seriously expect me to believe that you and Noah are just friends."

But it was true. They'd met during the crazy fallout of the Royce incident, and they just clicked. Next to Liv, he was her closest friend. He was funny, smart, kind, and, above all else, safe. With Noah, she felt like more than the two-dimensional caricature crafted by the media of a woman scorned. There might have been a time when she'd longed for more with him, but he'd never let on that he felt the same. And Alexis was still too skittish about men in general to risk ruining the healthiest relationship she'd ever had with a man by pushing for something more now.

The kitchen door swung open suddenly. Liv laughed again. "Speak of the devil."

CHAPTER THREE

It didn't take a genius to know when you were being talked about. And even though Noah was, in fact, a genius by IQ standards, he could tell strictly by the pink on Alexis's cheeks and Liv's grin that he had just walked in on a conversation about himself.

He strode through the kitchen door and held out the white paper bag that was his reason for stopping by the café. "Am I the devil?" he asked.

Alexis's eyes went wide. "Not if that bag contains what I think it contains."

"It does," he said, moving forward. Alexis made a sound of pure lust and lunged for the bag. He laughed as she tore it open and pulled out a foil-wrapped vegetarian taco from the Mexican food truck near his office building.

Alexis scarfed down half a taco and then set it down on the counter next to Liv. "Don't touch that," she warned Liv.

"Where are you going?" Noah asked as she disappeared into her tiny office.

She emerged with a wrapped box and handed it to him. "Happy birthday."

He accepted the gift with a half smile. "I thought we weren't celebrating until tomorrow night."

"I know, but I couldn't wait to give this to you. It arrived this morning."

She clapped as he tore off the paper. His eyes bulged out of his head. "Holy shit. Are you serious?"

Alexis squealed. "I know! Can you believe I found one?"

In his hands was an impossible-to-get, limited-edition *Doctor Who* Lego set. "Where the hell did you find it?"

"I've been battling some dude on eBay for a week for this thing."

Noah turned the box over in his hands. "It's still in the original box?"

"Yes!"

"I don't even want to know how much this cost," he said, looking up.

She waved her hand. "Doesn't matter. The only question is, are we going to leave it in the box or build it?"

"Build it," he said, nodding reverently. "And we can watch that documentary on how purple dye was discovered."

Liv snorted and slid from the stool where she'd been sitting. "Okay, this is the nerdiest shit I've ever seen."

Noah made a *psh* noise. "This isn't even in the top ten of nerdy shit we do."

Alexis nodded as she took a massive bite of her food. After chewing fast, she said, "Last weekend, we attended a lecture by a Vanderbilt professor on the history of female Viking warriors."

Liv mouthed the word *wow* and then leaned in to give Alexis a quick hug. "I gotta run. More dresses to deliver." As she walked past Noah, she grinned. "Did you survive today?"

Noah groaned and put the LEGO set on the counter. "Your fiancé is out of control."

"Go easy on him," Liv said. "He's been planning his dream wedding since he was a little boy."

Liv rose on tiptoe to peck his cheek before sailing from the kitchen. Noah watched her go before turning back to Alexis, who greeted his glance with a teasing smile. "What crazy idea does Mack have now?"

"We have to learn a dance routine."

Alexis tipped her head back and let out a laugh that made everything worth it. He'd endure any humiliation known to man to make her laugh, because he remembered far too clearly when laughter was a hard-fought victory. She was literally crying when he first met her. It was just hours after they'd exposed Royce Preston for the predator he was. They were at Mack's house, celebrating, when she suddenly slipped out the back door.

"Alexis."

At the sound of his voice, Alexis jumped and turned, wiping madly at her face.

He held up his hands in apology. "I didn't mean to scare you. I saw you run out here and wanted to make sure you were okay."

Alexis wiped her cheeks and shrugged. "No, it's fine. I—I was just . . ." She waggled her fingers in front of her puffy eyes. "Letting out some tension."

"Adrenaline crash."

"Is that when your body says oh my God what the fuck have you done?*"*

He chuckled quietly. "I think that's exactly what it is."

She sucked in a steadying breath and held out her hand. "You're Noah, right?"

He closed the distance between them and accepted her handshake. Her fingers were small and warm within his. "Noah Logan."

Alexis pulled her hand back. "Thank you for what you did. Helping us, I mean."

"I should be thanking you for what you did."

Alexis hugged her torso. "I should have done it a long time ago."

"There's no expiration date on the truth."

"How about humiliation?"

Noah felt the first stirring of something he didn't recognize. Something equal parts respect and longing. "I hope we're talking about his. Because you have nothing to be humiliated about."

She looked away as if she didn't believe him.

"So, what's next?" he asked.

"I have no idea. I've been living with this secret for so long. I don't even know what life looks like or feels like without it. I think I'm just ready for some peace." She blinked then and studied him. "I have no idea why I'm dumping all this on you."

"Because I'm here?"

She snorted. "Lucky you."

Little did he know then how lucky he truly was. In a million ways, Alexis was the best thing that had ever happened to him. And he had no idea how to tell her that without ruining it.

The sound of crinkling paper brought him back to the present. Alexis leaned against the counter next to him and opened her second taco. "Thank you. You have no idea how much I needed this."

"I had a hunch that you would have forgotten to eat again."

"It's been nuts in here today."

"The girl come back?"

"Yes." She said it with an annoyed groan.

"What's that noise mean?"

Alexis swallowed. "It means she looked like she was finally going to talk to me but then Karen marched in."

Noah reached over and plucked a stray piece of cilantro from the corner of her mouth. "What's she pissed about now?"

Alexis launched into a story involving parking lots and a dead rat.

"It couldn't have been him," she said of the part cat, part demon that was one hundred percent terrifying. "He's been inside all day."

She gestured toward a cat tree by the front window. Beefcake flexed his paws, and Noah's life flashed before his eyes. He'd never been high on the cat's very short list of people he tolerated, but things had taken a turn for the worse a month ago. The vet put Beefcake on a diet, and now the cat stared at him like a platter of BBQ chicken. He had an unkempt, murderous look about him, as if he'd just gone a few rounds inside a clothes dryer and liked it. His hair stuck out at wild angles with spiky tufts atop each ear. Over his eyes was a unibrow of dark, unruly gray fur that gave him the look of a perpetually pissed-off cavalry man in old Civil War tintypes.

"Anyway," Alexis sighed with a stretch. "She said she was going to take this up with the city, and then she stormed out."

"What the hell does she think the city is going to do? Change parking ordinances? You're not breaking any laws."

"I'm a dirty slut, remember? That's the only law she cares about."

Noah stiffened. "She said that?"

Alexis brushed a curl off her face. "Not in so many words. But her meaning was clear. We're just a bunch of lying harlots."

Noah scowled. "I hate it when you say shit like that."

"Just repeating what everyone else is thinking."

"No one decent thinks that."

"I think you overestimate human nature."

Noah snorted. "I've definitely never been accused of that before."

Five years in the hacktivist community had left him with little hope for humanity. But she was also right. The months following the Royce incident had introduced him to a depth of human depravity he hadn't known existed. His blood boiled just remembering some of the voice mails and emails Alexis had received from Royce's fans. Even with a dozen credible accusations against him, his most rabid fans still refused to believe that their precious hero would do anything wrong. The women must have been lying. They were just disgruntled former employees or spurned lovers.

Noah had helped Alexis set up a new email filtering system that blocked the worst of the messages, but he knew she still received some of them. She had gotten good at just deleting them, but sometimes she still shared the most egregious with him. She'd shrug and say she was used to it, but Noah could read her body language like a favorite book. Her lips would flatten, and she'd have to swallow before talking. It bothered her. A lot. But anytime he suggested she do more to fight back, she would say it wasn't worth the time or effort. Her life was about finding peace now.

Noah felt her gaze on him and glanced over. "What's up?"

"Huh?"

"You're staring at me. Do I have something on my face?"

"Yeah, this," she said, reaching over to scratch his beard. "What do you look like under all that scruff anyway?"

He waggled his eyebrows. "You don't want to know."

"Wow. That bad, huh?"

"No. That good. I have to scruff myself up, because the level of male beauty under all this is more than mere mortals can handle."

"So it's a public service."

"Absolutely."

Alexis swallowed another bite. "Is Zoe going to be there tomorrow?"

They were going to his mom's house for dinner to celebrate his birthday. His sister was supposed to be there, but . . . He shrugged. "Who knows? It's Zoe. She does what she wants."

"Marsh?" Alexis asked casually.

"He'll be there too."

She offered him a sympathetic smile, because she knew there was nothing else to be said. His relationship with his father's old army friend, Pete Marshall—or Marsh, as everyone called him— was complicated. Noah wouldn't be where he was today without Marsh's help and guidance, but his support came with strings attached. The kind that were a constant reminder that Noah would never be the man his father once was.

Noah stood and raised his arms in a stretch with a loud yawn. "Need any help cleaning up after yoga tonight?"

One of the many things Alexis did for the women who came to her café seeking help and support was a monthly yoga class designed just for survivors of sexual violence. The class was tonight.

"I think Jessica and I can handle it, but thanks."

"Damn. I was hoping to have an excuse for getting out of going to Colton's."

"Why?"

"He opened another phishing email and screwed up his entire system."

Alexis laughed sympathetically. "Want to start the LEGOs tomorrow night after we get back from your mom's?"

"Hell yes." He held out his pinkie finger for her to grasp. It was their own secret handshake. "See you then," he said, turning to leave.

"Hey," she said behind him.

He turned around.

"Ask your mom what I should bring for dinner tomorrow."

He walked backward as he spoke. "You know what she'll say."

"'Just yourselves.'"

He grinned.

"See you tomorrow," she said.

And the clock in his brain immediately started counting down the minutes until then.

CHAPTER FOUR

"We're going to run out of space soon," Jessica said, tugging her hair into a ponytail several hours later.

They stood by the counter to survey the room. Tables and chairs had been pushed to the side and stacked to make room for yoga mats and—if everyone who'd RSVP'd showed up tonight—the nearly twenty women looking to reclaim their lives through the power of mindful movement.

"Maybe we should start looking for another place to host the class?" Jessica suggested.

Alexis nodded absently, because she didn't want to commit to that, if for no other reason than to not give Karen the satisfaction of thinking she'd driven the class and the survivors away.

"We'll figure something out," Alexis finally said, crossing the room to hang a sign on the door that read CLOSED FOR PRIVATE EVENT. She shoved a wedge under the door, though, so women could still get in. She'd taken Beefcake home earlier, because two of the class regulars were allergic to cats.

The instructor, Mariana Mendoza, arrived first. She greeted Alexis and Jessica with breezy air-kisses followed by fist bumps. The class had actually been Mariana's idea. She'd approached Alexis at the café several months ago, and Alexis was sold immediately. Mariana was a licensed counselor as well as a certified yoga instructor. The concept she proposed wasn't a new one; survivors had been using yoga to reclaim their lives and their bodies for a long time. But there wasn't anything like it yet in Nashville, and Alexis knew she had to be the one to host the first.

Their initial class four months ago had just three participants, including Alexis and Jessica. But once word spread, more and more women began to trickle in every week until they'd filled every inch of space. Jessica was right. They were going to need to find another location soon if they wished to allow as many women as possible in the class. Something else to add to her to-do list.

While Alexis and Jessica changed into their yoga clothes, several women arrived and began stretching on their yoga mats.

Mariana approached Alexis quietly near the front. "And how are we doing?" Mariana always spoke in the royal *we*.

"Good," Alexis said with a shrug. "Busy, but good."

"We look tired. Are we sleeping well?"

"Yes," Alexis said, but she must have said it with a bit too much gusto, because Mariana narrowed her eyes.

"Anything you need to talk about?"

"Nothing a good yoga session can't work out," Alexis said, carefully sidestepping both the question and the questioner. "I'm going to say hello to some people."

Alexis greeted a few of the regulars, introduced herself to the new ones, and then took her place on a mat in the front row. She always saved the last row for folks who weren't yet ready to be fully seen. It took confidence just to show up sometimes, and even though the class was meant for yoga beginners of all fitness levels and all shapes, it could still be disconcerting to women who were there for the first time to practice a downward dog in front of a room full of strangers.

It was still hard for Alexis sometimes. She felt exposed every day of her life. Not as much as when she first came forward with the truth about Royce, but the anxiety was still there. When she went to the grocery store. When she met new people. When strangers stared at her on the street. She'd catch someone looking at her as if trying to place her face, and her first instinct was to turn and hide from scrutiny. Holding your head up high was easier said than done when your face had been front-page news around the country.

"Okay, friends, are we ready to reclaim our power?"

The class answered her with a murmured *yes*, so Mariana repeated the question. This time, the women responded with a more resounding confirmation.

"We have some new faces with us tonight. We welcome you in peace and healing."

A murmur of quiet greetings rose in response.

"Let's start in Sukhasana pose tonight as we state our affirmations."

The women matched her cross-legged pose on the floor, letting their hands drape across their knees.

"I am strong," Mariana said.

The women repeated it.

"Tonight, I reclaim my power . . . my body . . . my strength . . ."

Alexis closed her eyes and repeated the words, needing them more than she had in a long time. Though she was used to Karen's petty complaints, today's visit was especially annoying because she had chased off Candi. But Alexis soon lost herself in the flow of body, the connection of mind and spirit. The healing power of stretching and pushing her body.

Mariana led them through each pose with calm instructions and encouragement, stopping here and there to assist a newcomer with their body alignment, only putting her hands on them after asking permission to touch them. That was one of the most important aspects of the class—claiming ownership of their bodies once again. Taking back what was once stolen from them.

There was no trauma competition in this room with these women. No one's suffering measured against another's for its devastation or its scope. Every person here had been violated and silenced, and every woman had made the decision to find their voice again.

About ten minutes before the end of the class, the soft scuff of the door against the floor drew Alexis's gaze over her shoulder. She stumbled in her tree pose. Candi stood wide-eyed and red-cheeked in the door as twenty faces turned to look at her.

"I'm sorry . . ." she stammered, hugging a large black bag to her side. "I didn't know this was . . . I'm sorry."

"No apologies, love," Mariana said. "Please join us. Everyone is welcome."

"I'll come back," Candi said, stumbling backward.

Alexis tiptoed out of her line. "Please stay," she said in an urgent hush. "We can talk in my office, if you'd like."

"I'm sorry to interrupt," Candi whispered. "I didn't know you were having a class tonight."

"It's okay. We're almost done." Alexis darted another glance at the class, which had clearly lost its collective concentration. "Let's go in my office."

Candi worried her bottom lip with her teeth but finally nodded. She walked with her head down like a kid being marched to the principal's office as she followed Alexis through the café, behind the counter, and into the kitchen. The *thwap-thwap* of the swinging door was as loud as a firecracker in the otherwise quiet room.

Alexis led her to her closet-size office and motioned to the chair wedged against the wall. "It's small, I know. But would you like to sit?"

Candi stood indecisively in the minuscule space between the desk and the door. Finally, she dropped into the chair but remained perched on the edge, one knee bopping up and down as she gnawed at her lower lip. "That's really cool. The yoga class."

Alexis nodded, sitting in her own chair. "It's been very successful."

"So all those women were, I mean, are—"

"Survivors of sexual violence or harassment, yes."

"Wow. That's terrible."

Alexis heard that refrain a lot, and she had the same response every time. "It's terrible what was done to them, but what they're doing tonight is a wonderful way to take back their power."

Candi swallowed hard.

"You're not alone, Candi."

"I— no." Candi shook her head. She opened and closed her mouth twice before finally letting out a frustrated breath. "I'm not here about that. I mean, I'm not a . . . a—"

"A survivor?"

"Right. I'm not here to talk to you about that."

Alexis tilted her head, struck again with the fleeting sense of familiarity. "Are you sure we've never met before?"

"You said it's my eyes," Candi said. "My eyes look familiar."

Alexis looked more closely. She was right. They shared the same golden, green-flecked irises rimmed by a darker brown. Inside her, the fleeting sense of familiarity gave way to a more urgent surge of alarm. Alexis had always been told how unique the colors of her eyes were, but this was like suddenly looking into a mirror. How had she failed to notice it before?

"You see it, don't you?" Candi asked, breathless now. "The similarity. I noticed it the first time I saw you at the counter. That's how I knew it was true."

Alarm became a near-panic. "I don't understand. What are you talking about—"

"We're sisters."

Alexis heard the words, but their meaning was so ridiculous that her brain blocked them from registering. She puffed out a small, desperate laugh. "I'm sorry, what?"

Candi's face took on the soft sympathy that Alexis was used to projecting at other women, and when she spoke, Candi's voice now carried the same keep-it-light quality that Alexis had just employed against her. "You never knew your father, did you?"

Alexis stood so abruptly that she shook her desk and sent her pencil cup spilling across the floor. "I'm sorry. Y-You're mistaken. I don't have any siblings."

"None that you've ever met."

"That's absurd."

Except it wasn't. Not entirely. Candi was right; Alexis had never known her father. So the chances that the mystery man had gone on to produce other children after abandoning her mother were high. She'd wondered about it—*him*—from time to time over the years, but she'd never pursued it because why bother? What good would it do to know? He'd never been part of her life and never would. Her mother had been enough.

"My father's name is Elliott Vanderpool," Candi said.

Alexis backed up until her desk chair collided with the wall.

"You know that name, don't you?"

"No," Alexis lied, stepping over the rungs of the chair. Her shoelace caught, and she stumbled. She grabbed the edge of her desk to steady herself.

"He's your father too," Candi said.

"No, I—I don't think that's possible," Alexis said in a voice she barely recognized. "I'm sorry you came all this way for nothing. It's a mistake."

"I know this is a shock."

A shock? Alexis would have laughed at the understatement of the century if she could process any other emotion besides numbness. She wanted to run away—not just from Candi but from the rising panic in the back of her mind telling her to escape. But her feet wouldn't move. She was rooted as firmly as the creeping vine out front. At least the vine had something to cling to.

"I have the DNA to prove it," Candi said.

Alexis focused her gaze. "How do you have my DNA?"

"You took one of those ancestry test things a couple of years ago."

Oh, God. Alexis covered her mouth with her hand and turned around. It had been an impulsive act. A weak moment while her mother was sick. A fleeting urge to connect with her roots before her one and only anchor to the Earth was gone. But when the results came back, she learned nothing she hadn't already known—that she was one hundred percent Eastern European and zero percent descended from anyone historically significant. She'd shoved the results in a drawer and never looked at them again.

"I took one too," Candi was saying from somewhere far away. "And you came back as a possible sibling match."

Alexis searched her brain for words. "Those tests can be wrong."

"Alexis, our eyes are the same." Candi's shoes scuffed closer as she stood. "You have a brother too. His name is Cayden. And two nieces, Grace and Hannah. And a sister-in-law named Jenny. And an aunt and uncle—"

"Stop," Alexis choked. Air became poison in her lungs. She tried to exhale but couldn't.

"There's something else," Candi said, tone fading from gently reassuring to preemptively apologetic.

Alexis forced herself to look at Candi, whose features had settled again into the shy hesitance. "Our father is sick."

Alexis barely had time to react to the phrase *our father* before she registered the two words that followed it. "How—what kind of sick?"

"Kidney failure."

For the second time, Alexis reeled backward as if Candi had slapped her. The back of her legs hit the chair, and she sank into it.

"He was in a bad car accident a few years ago, and it destroyed his kidneys," Candi said, voice shaking. "He's been on dialysis, but his kidney function is not coming back. He needs a transplant."

"So you sought me out because . . ." Alexis couldn't even finish the sentence. Sardonic laughter became the period on the unfinished thought.

"You could be a match," Candi whispered.

Alexis squeezed her eyes shut. How was this happening?

"If you're a match, you could save him. He's been on the donor list for two years."

Alexis wanted to cover her ears and yell *La-la-la-la*. She didn't want to care. Not about him. Not about Candi.

"I know this is a shock—"

Alexis opened her eyes. "How long have you known about me?"

Candi's hesitance was an answer all on its own.

Alexis's tone hardened. "How long?"

"I found out three years ago."

Three years. Alexis exhaled an entire lifetime's worth of unanswered questions, only to inhale another lifetime's worth of new ones. Did that mean *he* had known about her for three years too? Or had he always known about her? Either way, he had obviously not cared enough to reach out himself.

"He wouldn't let me contact you before," Candi said, as if reading Alexis's mind.

So he *had* known about her, at least for that long. Alexis rose slowly. "Maybe you should have respected his wishes."

"I can't. We're running out of time. He's at the top of the donor list, but he's been there twice before, and each time something went wrong with the donor. If he doesn't get a kidney soon—"

"How soon?" Alexis heard herself ask.

"A few months. We don't really know."

Empathy warred with self-preservation. And if that wasn't the story of her entire life, she didn't know what was.

"I know what I'm asking is a big deal," Candi said. "To give a kidney to a total stranger."

Alexis puffed out a joyless laugh and shook her head. Giving a kidney to a total stranger would be easier.

Candi stepped closer. "Do you want me to beg? I will."

No, she didn't want Candi to beg. No one should have to bargain for the life of a loved one. Alexis knew the soul-sucking hopelessness of that, of falling to her knees and promising doctors, researchers, and God that she'd do anything, say anything, give anything, if they could just save her mother. None of it had been enough.

Sometimes, hope was a fool's bargain.

She wouldn't wish it on anyone.

"Please, Alexis," Candi said, resorting to begging at last.

Alexis pressed her fingers into the lines forming on her own forehead. "I need to think."

"But—"

"You've known about me for three years, Candi. I deserve a couple of days to get used to it."

Candi's hands once again disappeared inside the cuffs of her sweatshirt as she folded her arms across her torso. The pose might have seemed defensive from someone else, but Candi was simply resigned. Her throat tightened with a deep swallow, followed by a nod. "Okay."

"How can I contact you?"

Wordlessly, Candi retrieved her bag from the floor by her chair. She dug out a small notebook and a pen and scribbled her phone number on a blank piece of paper.

Alexis folded it into her hand.

"I've been staying at a hotel," Candi said. "I have to go back to Huntsville soon."

"I understand," Alexis managed to say.

Candi's hands disappeared into her sweatshirt again. "So will you call me or—"

"I need some time."

Candi's lips parted as if she wanted to say more, probably to remind Alexis that time was something she didn't have. Alexis would've been a hypocrite if she didn't understand that. Nothing screamed as loudly as the persistent *tick tick tick* of time's cruel clock when every second brought you closer to the last.

Candi nodded woodenly before turning away. Alexis watched her sling her bag over one rigid shoulder and then, with one last look behind her, walk away. Her footsteps were deliberate but dejected.

A moment passed, and then the kitchen door *thwap-thwapped* behind her.

Several more moments later, Jessica appeared in the doorway. "Everything okay?"

Alexis blinked out of her stupor. "Can you and Mariana clean up? I have something I need to do."

Jessica hesitated. "I—yes. Are you sure you're okay?"

"I have no idea."

"Alexis—"

Alexis ducked around her and walked through the kitchen in a fog to the back door. She grabbed her purse and coat. They were robotic functions, as rote and unintentional as the beating of her heart and the constriction of her lungs with every breath. In the alley outside where she parked her car, a group of women walked by in honky-tonk attire, leaning on one another and laughing drunkenly. A detached part of Alexis's mind wondered about them, wondered if they knew how lucky they were to be so carefree, to have just missed the teetering edge of a before-and-after chasm that would forever change Alexis's life. Again. Because no matter what happened, no matter what she decided, life would once again never be the same.

She barely remembered driving home, but suddenly she was in her driveway, car idling with an assaulting silence. When had she turned the radio off? She always drove with it on, preferring the mindless chatter of DJs and news shows to the unending chaos of her own thoughts.

She turned off the car and pulled out the key. Her hands fell to her lap. She knew what she had to do but couldn't get her muscles to do the work this time. She stared at the house, its interior dark but for a single lamp in the window. Her mother had been gone more than three years, but it still felt like her house.

In the first few weeks following her mother's death, she'd vowed to sell the place and move. Maybe to a modern loft downtown, where she could lose herself in the noise and the lights of Honky Tonk Row. But then the idea began to feel like a betrayal. Her mother had worked two jobs in order to buy the house. Her sacrifice deserved more.

And so Alexis had stayed. Eventually, she'd made it her own. Frayed couches made way for new furniture. Walls were painted and cupboards replaced.

It had taken years to stop feeling the ache of loss every time she pulled into the driveway. But sometime in the past year, the ache had settled into its kinder form, the softness known as nostalgia.

Alexis dragged herself from the car and up the front walk. Beefcake greeted her with a yowl from the top of the stairs as she trudged up the steps. Her bedroom was the last room on the right down a long hallway. Inside her closet, she stood on tiptoes to retrieve an overstuffed shoebox.

Cleaning out her mother's things had been the toughest part of her death. The finality of it. An entire life, now relegated to a few items—a crocheted blanket her mother had made, some clothes

Alexis couldn't stand to part with, a stack of mismatched dishes, a collection of mementos.

And this box of documents and photos and cards that Alexis figured she'd find the time and peace of mind to organize one day. She couldn't remember precisely where she'd put the specific card she was looking for.

It hadn't seemed important enough before to put it someplace special; just a simple card attached to flowers at the funeral.

All Alexis remembered was the name.

CHAPTER FIVE

"Hey, have you ever seen the Russian's wife?"

"What?" Noah looked up from the disaster that was Colton's laptop. He'd been working for two hours in Colt's palatial estate and had become grumpy. Not only from Colton's complete inability to stop destroying his own security but from the nagging sense that Noah had officially become a fraud.

Here he sat in a house that probably cost more than most Americans made in a decade, a house large enough for twenty people to live like kings. And while the old Noah would have been raging against an economic system that allowed that kind of wealth to accumulate at the very top, he was, instead, making his own money off it.

So, yeah, he was grumpy.

"The Russian's wife," Colton repeated. "Have you ever met her?"

Noah side-eyed him. "No. Why?"

"I don't think she exists."

Noah snorted and lifted his beer to his lips. "That's ridiculous. Of course she exists."

"No one has ever seen her. I think she's a figment of his imagination."

Noah rolled his eyes. "He's a professional athlete. He couldn't have a fake wife. Just google her."

"I did. There are zero pictures of her. I mean, zip. Don't you think that's weird?"

Noah grumbled again. "Don't you have any friends? I'm working here."

"That hurts, man. I thought *we* were friends."

Guilt forced an apology from his lips. "Fine. But don't you have somewhere to be? I thought famous people had to go be famous and shit."

"Nope." Colt slung a six string onto his lap and whipped out a quick set of chords.

Noah glanced up. "That new?"

Colt shrugged. "Something I'm working on for the next album."

His voice had taken on an almost imperceptible tightness. His friend—and they *were* friends, which was so fucking weird—had a lot riding on his next album. His first two went platinum, but his last release didn't have a single top-ten hit.

"You could investigate it, you know."

Noah peered over his glasses. "Investigate what?"

"The Russian's wife."

"Why me?"

"Because you work for the CIA, right?"

"Yes," Noah deadpanned. The guys were convinced his company was just a cover for something much more exciting.

Colton paused in his playing. "Shit. Seriously?"

Noah hit a few more keys. "No."

"But you've got a surveillance van, man."

"All computer security companies do."

"Bullshit."

Noah sighed and leaned back in the chair at the dining table where he sat. "Clients hire me to test the security of their systems. Sometimes that includes communications and surveillance."

"I think you're lying. I think you work for the FBI or something."

Well, that part was almost true. Or it had been at one time. Consulting with the FBI had been the only thing that kept him out of a minimum-security prison.

But those days were over. Now he got paid millions of dollars to help dipshits like Colton Wheeler protect themselves when they clicked on porn links.

His cell phone buzzed in his pocket. Noah pulled it out and saw Alexis's face on the screen. His mood instantly lightened. He put the phone to his ear. "Hey."

She barely made a sound. "Noah . . ."

His whole body went rigid. "What's wrong?"

"Can you—" She made a choking sound.

He stood and nearly knocked over the chair. "Can I what? What is going on?"

"Something happened. Can you come over?"

"I'm on my way." He hung up and shoved his phone in his pocket as he dug his keys from the other one.

Colton watched him, concern lacing his voice and his eyes. "Everything all right?"

"I gotta go."

Noah drove across town like he was trying out for *Mario Kart*. He whipped into her driveway, killed the engine, and threw open his car door. Her front door was unlocked, so he walked in and yelled her name.

She answered from upstairs. "Up here." Her voice sounded thick.

Noah took the stairs two at a time and then walked down the short hallway to her bedroom. She sat in the window seat overlooking the backyard. At the sound of his footsteps, she turned and looked at him. Her eyes were red and puffy. Her hair was piled on top of her head in a crazy, messy knot, and she wore his sloppy sweatshirt over baggy sweatpants. She looked, in a word, horrible. He would've laughed if his heart hadn't suddenly shattered.

His eyes took in the rest of the scene. A box of papers and photos lay overturned on the floor, and other items were strewn across the bed. He crossed the room in long strides and dropped to his knees beside the window seat. "What's going on? What happened?"

She handed him a crumpled, yellowed card, like the kind that came with flowers.

A name was scribbled in hurried scrawl.

Elliott V.

Confusion pulled his eyebrows together. Noah looked up. "What is this? Who is Elliott V.?"

"*That*," Alexis said, "is apparently my father."

It took ten agonizing minutes to get the full story out of her. The young woman, the one Alexis had been hoping would talk to her for a week, wasn't a survivor at all but was instead Alexis's sister?

Noah attempted to keep his features relaxed and neutral as Alexis filled in the blanks. Inside, however, heartbreak battled with rage. Pure, white-hot rage. The man had ignored his daughter her entire life but now he wanted a kidney from her?

Noah sat back on his haunches. "How do you know Candi is telling the truth?"

Alexis swiped a hand over her nose. "Why would she lie?"

"People lie for all kinds of reasons."

"We have the exact same eyes, Noah. And anyway, she says the DNA proves it."

"Did you see it? The test results?"

"No, but there's this." She pointed to the card. "What are the chances that someone named *Elliott V.* would send flowers to her funeral?"

Noah ran a hand over his hair. "What are you going to do?"

"I don't know."

"Did she tell you how to get in contact with her?"

Alexis reached into the pocket of her sweater and pulled out a piece of paper with a scribbled phone number on it.

Noah set it aside and then rested his hands on top of her thighs. "You okay?" he asked as gently as possible.

Her eyes darted sideways. Another swallow.

"Look at me."

She obeyed, but in the same instant, her back straightened and her face became fixed in a mask of composure.

"Don't do that," he said, squeezing her legs.

She cleared her throat, the effort too forced. "Don't do what?"

"Shut down. Pretend you're not upset."

She shook her head, a nervous back-and-forth shake. "I'm fine."

"You're not fine. You're in shock because your life has once again been turned upside down."

She crossed her arms across her chest, defensive and protective. "I'm fine. I just . . . I just need a minute."

Alexis paused to swallow. He'd seen her do that same thing so many times, and he recognized it now for what it was. An attempt to ward off overt displays of emotion. His mother used to do the same thing, back when his father's death was still raw and new. Noah feared that when the explosion finally came for Alexis, it was going to be hard, just like it was for his mother. And Noah vowed he'd be there to help her pick up the pieces, because he hadn't been for his mom.

He rose and winced at the stiffness in his knees from crouching so long. "I'm going to make you some tea."

"You don't have to do that," she said.

"I know, but I'm going to anyway." He tucked a curl behind her ear. "Maybe I'll splash some whiskey in the tea too."

Her smile was as sad as it was forced. "You're a dream come true."

"I know, right?" He grinned and winked and was relieved when her lips softened into something that looked like an actual smile. "I'll be back in a minute."

Noah jogged down the stairs, leaping just in time off the bottom step to avoid an assassination attempt by Beefcake. The fucking cat hated him. He liked to make himself known in the shadiest ways possible. Usually darting underfoot just in time to make Noah stumble or hiding beneath a chair to declare war on Noah's shoelaces. Beefcake hissed and bounded up the stairs with much more agility than Noah would have expected from an animal whose belly dragged on the ground.

Noah grabbed the kettle from the stove, filled it with fresh water, and searched the cabinet for the chamomile tea.

When the kettle began to shriek, he turned it off and poured the water into the mug. Then he made good on his promise and splashed some whiskey into it. For himself, he went with straight whiskey and a couple of ice cubes.

When he returned to her bedroom, he found her sitting cross-legged on her bed cradling Beefcake.

"He tried to kill me again," Noah said, hoping to coax another smile from her.

Alexis set the cat aside and reached for the tea. "Thank you."

"You want a fire?" he asked, gesturing toward the fireplace along the wall.

"Sure."

He set his whiskey on the bedside table before crouching in front of the fire. A minute later, it crackled to life. When he turned around, she had scooted all the way back on the bed to lean against the headboard.

He toed his shoes off and sat down on the mattress. It dipped under his weight and creaked, and the sound sent an uncomfortable jolt through his senses. In all this time since they'd known each other, all the time they'd spent together, he'd never been on the bed with her. He'd been in her bedroom numerous times. Hell, he'd been the one to bring the firewood up here. But this? Never this.

Alexis sipped her tea and sucked in a breath.

"Too hot?" he asked.

"Too whiskey-ey."

Noah chuckled. "It'll take the edge off."

"And put hair on my chest?"

"I fucking hope not."

She laughed. Finally. Thank God. She took another sip, and this time it must have gone down smoother, because she rested her head back against the headboard. After two more sips, she rolled her head in his direction. "Thank you for coming over."

He leaned back and matched her pose, bringing their faces within inches of each other. "What're friends for?"

"I hope I didn't interrupt anything."

"Just Colton making up conspiracy theories."

She laughed again, and before he knew what was happening, she leaned toward him and rested her head on his shoulder. The top of her messy bun tickled his chin. Her hair smelled spicy, like the essential oil she used on her neck to ward off headaches.

"My mom's birthday is next week," she said suddenly.

"Yeah?"

Her cheek lifted away from his shoulder, and she turned her face up toward his. "Her birthday is harder for me than the anniversary of her death. Is that weird?"

Noah forced himself to hold her gaze. They rarely talked about their parents, even though they'd both lost a parent at too young an age. Her mother died from cancer three years ago, and his father died in Iraq when Noah was fifteen. It was something they shared, a club they never wanted to join but that defined them in ways no one outside the club could understand. There was a loneliness to losing a parent so young. A sense of unfairness that separated you from others.

But probably that's why they *didn't* talk about it. They understood each other without having to perform their grief for each other.

He swallowed. "No, it's not weird."

"What about you?"

"The anniversary is harder for me," he said. But then he shook his head and looked at his lap. "Actually, that's not true. The night before the anniversary is the hardest for me."

"Why?"

"Because I start counting down the hours and the minutes until the moment we found out. I can't turn it off. I can't sleep. By morning, I'm . . ." His voice trailed off as he searched for the right words.

She didn't prod him to continue. She just listened and waited. A quality that he doubted was something she'd learned only from working with survivors but was probably just part of who she was. A good listener. A good friend. A good person.

"Impotent," he finally answered. "That's how it feels. I can't do anything. I can't go back and change things."

She nodded, smiled softly, and then rested her head on his shoulder again.

The fire popped. Alexis sighed. At the end of the bed, Beefcake licked his fur. And somewhere deep inside Noah, an ember caught fire.

It's not like it was the first time she'd ever snuggled up to him. Their standard pose when watching a movie these days was her feet in his lap. And just a couple of weeks ago, she'd fallen asleep leaning against him.

This felt different.

Maybe it was because of the guys' meddling. Maybe they'd planted seeds in Noah's brain that were starting to germinate. Or maybe, *probably*, it was because the guys were right. His feelings for her were real, and seeing her vulnerable like this was making it impossible for him to deny it. But the one thing Noah knew about gardening was that there was a small window of time when roots could grow. He'd missed the window with her. Breaching their friendship now would be crazy. Stupid.

Especially now.

He wasn't friend-zoning himself. He was being a friend.

"Your mom never mentioned your father?"

"Not once. Not by name, anyway." Alexis licked her lips and continued. "She offered to tell me who he was when I turned eighteen, but it didn't seem important. He obviously didn't care about me, so why should I care about him?"

As far as Noah was concerned, that sentiment still applied. The bastard was using one daughter to guilt the other—the one he'd neglected her entire life—into risking her life to save his sorry one.

"What're you going to do?" he asked after a moment.

"I have no idea."

"You don't have to do anything, you know. You're under no obligation to do what Candi is asking of you."

She stifled a yawn.

"You okay?"

"I can't keep my eyes open."

"Then sleep. Your body is telling you it needs time to recover from the shock."

She yawned again. Noah took the tea from her hands. "Lie down. Get some sleep."

"Are you going to leave?" she asked, lifting her head from his shoulder.

Noah dipped his head and kissed the crown of her hair. "I'm not going anywhere."

Alexis scooted down and rolled onto her side away from him. Ten minutes later, her breathing had slowed to a steady rhythm.

It would be hours before Noah's did the same.

Noah couldn't breathe.

A hot, heavy pressure on his chest was slowly crushing his lungs. He awoke with a choking cough and stared directly into the glowing yellow eyes of the demon himself.

Beefcake.

This was it. This was the moment when he died. Beefcake had seen him sleeping next to Alexis and was finally getting his revenge. The cat stood on his chest, claws digging into his skin through his T-shirt. Hate radiated from his eyes.

"Easy now," Noah whispered, glancing sideways at where Alexis slept soundly. "Just be cool."

Beefcake opened his mouth and dropped the remains of a dead mouse on his chest.

"Jesus Christ!" Noah leaped off the bed. Beefcake yowled and dug his claws into Noah's chest before taking flight like a winged gargoyle. The dead mouse fell to the floor with a quiet thud.

Alexis stirred but didn't wake. The dead mouse stared up at him with vacant, mournful eyes. Noah was going to have to clean that up before Alexis noticed. He crept from the room and down the hallway to the bathroom. Under the sink, he found a roll of paper towels and a stash of plastic bags. Beefcake growled from the top of the stairs, and Noah fought the urge to flip him off before soft-footing it back to the bedroom.

Holding his breath, he grabbed the rodent with a wad of paper towel and tossed it in the bag. Alexis stirred again, so he froze. Her chest rose and fell evenly with every breath, and in her sleep, her face was as relaxed as he'd ever seen it. He wanted to crawl back in bed with her and wrap his arm around her waist.

Which is why he forced his feet to move. He carried the bag and dead mouse downstairs. The dumpster was just outside the back door, and after tossing it in, he dragged his keys from his pocket. There was no way he was actually going to fall asleep again, so he might as well make use of the time.

He grabbed his backpack, went back inside, and flopped down on the couch. He did a quick search for kidney donation risks. The first result was a FAQ from the Mayo Clinic, so he clicked on it and sat back against the cushions to skim the key points. *Thousands of kidney transplants were performed every year in the United States . . . higher rate of success when donated by a living donor . . . minimal risks of long-term health problems for donors . . . recovery of six weeks.*

He clicked through several more search results, but all gave the same basic information. Kidney donation was safe with very few risks to the donor, and donations from family members who shared a genetic link could reduce the chances of the recipient's body rejecting the new organ.

Noah closed his laptop and scrubbed his hands down his face. It was all so clinical. He stared at the ceiling and pictured Alexis upstairs. In bed. Another groan brought him upright, and he lifted the lid on his laptop again. He typed in the name Elliott Vanderpool. It took less than five minutes of research to realize that he had a lot more than abandoning his daughter to answer for.

The bastard was the head of engineering for the aerospace division of one of the country's biggest defense contractors, BosTech—a company that had been under federal investigation five years ago for failing to properly report defects in its drone navigation systems, resulting in the deaths of hundreds of Iraqi civilians.

Which meant he was neck-deep in blood.

A man like that didn't deserve to even breathe Alexis's name much less ask for a goddamned kidney from her.

CHAPTER SIX

Alexis woke up the next morning feeling like a hollowed-out pump-kin. And not the perky, freshly carved kind either. She was more like a month-old jack-o'-lantern, empty and soft, likely to break into squishy pieces if kicked over.

She'd fallen asleep on top of her comforter, but at some point, Noah must have covered her up before leaving. She couldn't believe she'd slept all night. It must have been the whiskey.

A meow next to the bed interrupted the pointless direction of her thoughts. Alexis rolled onto her side and stared down at Beef-cake. She patted the mattress for him to jump up. It took several tries before he finally hauled his substantial bulk onto the bed with her. He rubbed his face on hers before settling down with a strong purr. She was the only person he trusted enough to let his guard down around like this. The only person he trusted, period. Her poor misunderstood cat.

Alexis adopted him just six weeks after her mom died. She hadn't been looking for a new cat. She could barely function, and the last thing she'd needed was the responsibility of a new pet. But the shelter had called and said he'd been there for more than three months. Could she at least foster him for a little while? Alexis had taken one look at his angry face and knew he'd be hers forever. She'd never been able to turn her back on a lonely creature.

Lonely creatures were almost always fighting a battle no one knew about.

The morning alarm on her cell phone chimed on the bedside table. Time to get up. She couldn't afford to lounge in bed, no matter what had happened yesterday. The café didn't care that a wrecking ball had crashed through her life.

With an apology to Beefcake, Alexis sat up and lifted the afghan from her legs.

And that's when she smelled it.

Coffee.

It had to be her imagination. But when she slid from bed and stood, the smell hit her again. Stronger now. Like a gift from Heaven. Had Noah programmed her coffeepot before leaving last night? It was exactly the kind of thing he'd do. Something warm and gooey spread in her chest as she walked across her bedroom, but she stopped short when she heard a noise downstairs.

A clink, like coffeepot against mug.

The warm, gooey feeling evaporated as her heart somersaulted. Noah was still there. Alexis turned and stared at her bed as all the air seeped from her lungs.

Ducking into the bathroom, Alexis took stock of her morning face. Eyes puffy from sleep. Cheeks chapped from crying. Hair like a cartoon character. So, yeah, she was super attractive. She quickly tamed her hair into a twist on top of her head and splashed some water on her face.

Her bare feet padded softly on the carpet as she walked downstairs and up the hallway toward the kitchen. She stopped short at the sight that greeted her. Noah stood at the counter with his back to her. He wore the same clothes as last night, but they were more rumpled now. His hair hung loose around his shoulders—full and curly and the kind of hair supermodels paid millions to achieve and maintain. He held a mug in one hand and his phone in the other, his thumb scrolling rhythmically through his Twitter feed.

Alexis stepped into the kitchen and tried to keep her voice normal. "Hey."

Noah turned around and gave her a tired smile. "Hey," he answered through a voice still thick with morning. "You sleep okay?"

She nodded and hugged her torso. "I thought you'd left."

He peeled away from the counter, eyebrow raised behind his glasses. "Like I was going to leave you alone." He nodded toward the table. "Sit. I'll make you some breakfast."

"Thanks, but maybe just some coffee? I'm not sure I can handle food right now."

She sat in a chair and drew one knee up to her chest, propping her foot on the edge of her seat. Her eyes followed his movements—reaching for a mug from her cupboard, filling it with coffee, dumping the right amount of creamer and sugar in it to make it palatable. Then he joined her at the table, claiming the seat next to hers.

He handed her the mug. "You sure you're all right?"

"Mostly I'm just numb. Yesterday doesn't even seem real." Alexis curled her hands around the hot cup and let the heat seep into her skin. "Thank you for staying."

He softly clinked his mug against hers. "What're friends for?"

They sipped their coffee quietly. Alexis smothered a yawn behind her hand.

"Maybe you should take today off," Noah said.

"I can't. I need to be there."

"You're allowed a sick day every now and then, Lexa."

"What's your day look like?"

He lifted his eyebrow again at the obvious change of subject. "A lot of voice mails I don't want to deal with and a follow-up meeting with a potential new client and whatever crisis crops up."

"Sounds exciting."

"It's not. I'd rather stay here with you."

Warmth returned to her chest, followed quickly by uncertainty. What did that mean? "What time do we need to be at your mom's?"

Noah sat back in his chair. "Maybe we should skip dinner tonight."

"No."

"It's too much. We can just hang out, put together the LEGO set."

"I want to go, Noah. I need to go." She offered half a smile. "Anyway, I want to make those stuffed mushrooms your sister likes in case she shows up."

"God forbid we should disappoint Zoe."

Alexis nudged his foot with hers. "You're as scared of her as I am."

"That is absolutely true."

The conversation lulled into a shared smile. Alexis opened her mouth to thank him again for staying, but he cut her off.

"I did some research last night after you went to bed."

Her breath caught. "Research?"

"Into him."

The coffee turned to tar in her stomach. "What'd you find out?"

His fingers scratched his beard-covered jaw. "Most of what

Candi told you seems to check out. He lives in Huntsville. Has two grown children, Candace and Cayden. Works for an aerospace engineering company. I found a link to a company newsletter with a profile of him from a few months ago. I printed it out if you want to read it."

His fingers tapped an overturned stack of papers next to his laptop. She studied it a moment before nodding. Noah slid the stack over, but she didn't pick it up. She'd read it later. "Did you find anything else?"

Noah hesitated. "Didn't you say your mom is from Tennessee?"

"Yeah, why?"

"Elliott is from California, and it looks like he didn't move out this way until 1999."

"My mom lived in California for two years before I was born."

Noah nodded absently, but his eyes had a far-off look to them. "I guess that makes sense, then."

Alexis tugged her eyebrows together. "What aren't you telling me?"

"I dug up his wedding announcement in an online newspaper archive." Without meeting her gaze, he powered up his computer, hit a few keys, and then turned the computer around for her to see. On the screen was a black-and-white photo of a beaming bride and groom with their cheeks pressed together and their hands clasped at the chest.

The room spun in her peripheral vision as her eyes focused on the man. Was that him? Was that her father? The man her mother would never talk about, the man who'd never cared to know his own daughter, who'd abandoned her mother to raise a child all on her own? The image was too blurry for her to study the eyes enough to see if they were truly a match to her own, so instead Alexis tore her gaze to the words beneath the picture.

SAMMONS-VANDERPOOL

Andrew and Ellen Sammons of Redlands are proud to announce the wedding of their daughter, Lauren, to Elliott James Vanderpool of Santa Barbara on March 23. The couple were married at St. Francis Cathedral in Redlands followed by a reception at the historic Mission Inn in Riverside. The bride and groom met as students at UC Santa Barbara, where the groom earned his doctorate in aeronautical engineering and the bride earned a bachelor's degree in education. The groom is employed as an engineer at the Jet Propulsion Laboratory, and the bride is a kindergarten teacher. The couple honeymooned in Tuscany, Italy, and will reside in Pasadena.

She read it twice quickly and then a third time, pausing at key words and phrases that painted a picture in her mind. A picture of prosperity and privilege. Of security and stability. Of health and comfort.

Resentment churned in her stomach. Growing up, Alexis had never, not once, wished for more than she had. And even when she began to realize that they lived differently than other people, her mother had been enough.

But what if her mom hadn't had to work so hard? What if she hadn't had to go into debt so Alexis could go to college for a better life? What if they'd had adequate health insurance and her mother hadn't been forced to spend her last few months worrying about leaving Alexis with unpaid bills?

A sour taste burned her tongue as she pushed the computer away. "I knew he was married. I don't understand what this—"

"Look at the date, Lexa."

Her eyes zeroed in on the date at the top of the page. *April 3, 1989.*

At first it meant nothing.

Until it meant everything.

That couldn't be right. Alexis was born in April 1989.

Her gaze snapped back to Noah's as an inexplicable emotion clogged her throat. "He's not my father."

"It doesn't necessarily mean that."

"Of course it does. How could he be my father? My mom would've had to have gotten pregnant while he was engaged."

Noah gave her a look that managed to make her feel both naive and stupid. She shook her head. "No. My mom wouldn't have had an affair with a man who was engaged to someone else. Not unless . . ."

"Unless what?"

"Maybe she didn't know he was engaged. Maybe . . . maybe he was cheating on his fiancée and my mom didn't know and when she told him she was pregnant, he broke up with her." Her words tumbled out in a desperate rush of justifications. Anything to make this all make sense. Anything to answer the loudest question screaming in the back of her mind. *Why?*

Noah shut his laptop and leaned forward. "We're getting ahead of ourselves." His voice was calm, soothing. "The easiest way to find out if he's truly your father is to get a blood test."

He was right. Alexis nodded and looked at the twisted knot of her hands in her lap.

"Or . . . ," Noah said.

"Or what?"

"Or you do nothing and tell them all to leave you alone."

Her head snapped up. "I can't do nothing!"

"You are under no obligation to get involved."

"He's dying, Noah."

"Which you didn't even know until yesterday. You didn't even know about *him* until yesterday."

"But now I do know."

Noah sat up and shoved his fingers into his mop of curly hair to shove it back from his face. A vein pulsed at his temple, as if unspoken words were literally pounding to get out.

"What?" she said.

Noah shook his head and stood, mug in hand. "Nothing."

"Stop. We don't *nothing* each other. Say what you want to say."

Noah walked over to the island and turned around. He opened his mouth and shut it. Then, with a heavy breath, he said, "It's not your job to save the world, Lexa."

"I'm not trying to save the world."

"Then what are you doing?" Noah set down his mug and returned to the table. He sat down and leaned forward until his knees nudged hers. "You know how much I admire what you're doing at the café. And not just for the survivors but, Jesus, even the cats you find families for."

"But?"

"You're running yourself ragged. And then you add all this shit on top of it? When are you going to stop and just take a breath?"

A lump formed in the back of her throat. She stood quickly to cover it. "I have to get ready for work."

"Hey." He reached for her hand, and the warmth of his fingers in hers made her bruised heart thud with a dull ache.

As he spoke, the pad of his thumb brushed her knuckles. "Just remember that you matter, too, Alexis."

The ache became a sharp, pointed pain. And not just because of what he said, but because of how he said it. Or maybe it was just her imagination. Wishful thinking and all that.

Alexis cleared her throat and tugged her hand away. "Thank you for staying last night. And all this." She gestured at his computer.

Noah leaned back in his chair. "Whatever you need. You know that, right?"

Her nod was more of a tremor.

"I'll leave the stuff I printed," he said, standing. He kept his distance from her, literally backing up to avoid brushing his arm against hers. "You're sure you're okay?"

No. I'm not okay. I'm reeling from the punch of a thousand different fists. "Yeah. Fine."

He raised a single eyebrow.

"Well, maybe not fine but . . ." She sucked in a breath and let it out with a shrug. "I don't know what I am."

His face sobered. "Come here."

With a single step forward, he wrapped his arms around her and pulled her into a warm embrace. His heart pounded beneath her cheek. Strong. Solid. Reassuring. He held her and let her catch her breath, pressing his lips to the top of her head, just like he'd done when she rested her head on his shoulder last night. His hands rubbed gentle circles in the center of her back.

"We'll figure it out," he murmured against her hair. "You don't have to make any decisions right now."

"But I have to make them soon. Candi said he's running out of time."

Noah held her a moment longer and then pulled back. "Call me if you need me."

She folded her arms across her chest. "I will."

"I mean it."

"I know."

He studied her silently for a beat, searching her face. "I'll pick you up at six."

They were silent as he gathered his things. She watched, frozen in place, as he slid his laptop into his backpack. As he swiped his car keys from the counter.

He was reaching for the door when she finally found her voice. "Noah."

He turned.

"I mean it. Thank you."

His smile was as reassuring as his words. "What're friends for?"

Alexis waited until she heard his car back out of her driveway before heading upstairs to shower and get ready for work. A half hour later, she lured Beefcake into his cat carrier. It was just after seven when she pulled into the alley behind ToeBeans. This was late for her, even for a day when she didn't open the shop. But Jessica and Beth had things well in hand when Alexis walked in. A line stretched from the counter to the door. Alexis quickly donned an apron and joined Jessica at the counter while Beth filled a customer's latte order.

Jessica looked over from the cash register and did a double take. "Whoa. You okay?"

"Fine," Alexis lied. She turned to the woman who'd just moved to the front of the line. "Good morning, Mrs. Bashar. How's little Max doing?"

Max was a calico kitten that Mrs. Bashar had adopted just a couple of weeks ago during one of ToeBeans' adoption events. The woman grinned and dug out her phone. "Oh, he is just the sweetest little thing."

She turned around her phone to show off a photo of the kitten sleeping on her husband's chest.

Alexis laughed. "And to think your husband didn't want another cat."

"The tough guys always have the softest hearts," Mrs. Bashar said, returning the phone to her purse.

Alexis quickly filled the woman's normal order, promised to stop by her yarn shop up the street soon, and then fell into the wonderful routine of the morning rush hour. It would last until at least eight o'clock, when it would finally slow down just long enough to restock the pastry display before the next wave hit.

At precisely eight fifteen, Alexis served the last customer in line and then went into the kitchen to load up on more muffins, scones, and apple turnovers.

The swinging door flip-flapped behind her, and before she had time to turn around, Jessica's voice echoed against the stainless-steel appliances. "What's going on?"

Alexis pulled a tray of muffins from the tiered cart against the wall. "Nothing. Why?"

"First you ran out of here last night like you'd just seen a ghost. Now you come back in looking like, well . . . like shit."

Alexis set the tray on the counter. "Gee, thanks."

"What's going on? And don't even think about pretending you're fine. I know you better than that."

Alexis paused, her hands hovering over the muffins. Jessica did know her. They'd been through hell and back together. "I don't even know where to start."

"Try the beginning."

Alexis planted her hands on the edge of the counter and let out a long breath. Words tumbled out with it. "Noah spent the night at my house last night, and I think I found my father."

Alexis might've laughed at Jessica's openmouthed expression if the entire situation weren't causing actual heart palpitations. Jessica closed her mouth, swallowed, and blinked several times.

"So, okay," she said. "We're going to get back to the Noah thing, but first things first. What do you mean about your father?"

Alexis returned to the task of transferring muffins from the tray to a bakery display platter. "That girl last night. She says she's my sister and that my long-lost father is apparently dying and needs a kidney transplant."

"And you believe her, this girl?"

"I don't have any reason not to, at this point. We have the same eyes, and someone named Elliott sent flowers to my mom's funeral. It all adds up so far."

The pinch of Jessica's eyes forecasted an incoming storm. "Where the hell has he been all your life?"

"I don't know." Alexis tasted the sour tang of betrayal at the back of her throat. "I don't know if he knew about me."

The words stung. Was it possible her mom hadn't even told Elliott that she was pregnant back then? Would her mother have done something like that? Would she have purposely denied Alexis her own father?

Alexis shook her head to clear away the thought. No. Her mother would never have done that. The only thing that made sense was that Elliott had simply told her that he wanted no part in Alexis's life because he was about to marry someone else.

Jessica moved closer and softened her voice. "This all feels a little too coincidental, though. This girl just happens to find you through some ancestry DNA test when he needs a kidney?"

Alexis's stomach fired a warning shot. "What are you suggesting?"

"Your face was all over the news last year. Maybe . . ." Jessica shrugged. "I don't know. Maybe this is just some twisted joke or something."

"No one is that cruel, Jessica."

"I don't even know how it's possible that you of all people can still believe that."

Alexis shrugged. "I try to assume the best about people until they give me a reason not to."

"Which is why you are a way better person than I will ever be."

Alexis shook her head and shoved the platter aside to make room for another. "Anyway, Candi said she took the DNA test three years ago."

Tiny bolts of lightning flashed in Jessica's eyes. "Are you kidding me? And she just came to find you now that he needs a kidney? You're not a farm for harvesting."

Alexis winced and looked away.

Jessica immediately softened her tone. "I'm sorry. That was . . . I shouldn't have said that."

"It's true, though, isn't it?"

Jessica chewed on the corner of her lip, a sure sign that she wanted to ask an impertinent question but wasn't sure if she should. A moment later, she let out a breath and blurted it out. "What if you're not a match?"

"I don't know."

"What does Noah think?"

Alexis's cheeks burst into flames.

Jessica tilted her head. "Maybe we should talk about the spending-the-night thing now."

Alexis walked back to the tiered cart to get another tray of muffins. "I was upset last night, and he said he didn't want to leave me alone. It wasn't really that big of a deal."

"Then why are you blushing?"

"I'm not."

"So he spent the night and just left this morning and nothing happened?"

You matter, too, Alexis. The sound of his voice came back, and with it, the tingling in her knuckles where his thumb had caressed her.

"I don't know," she said quietly. "I think . . . he looked at me, and I—" Alexis groaned and covered her face with her hands.

"And what?" Jessica prompted.

"I think maybe he was *looking* at me. Like *looking* looking at me. But what if I was wrong?"

Jessica laughed. "I guarantee that you were not wrong. He's been *looking* at you for a long time. You're the only one who doesn't seem to notice."

Alexis lowered her hands and focused on the muffins. "It doesn't matter. It can't happen."

"Why not?"

"It could ruin our friendship forever."

"Not possible."

"Noah is one of the best things in my life. I can't lose that."

"The best love affairs start as friendships."

"But that friendship is way too important to risk."

Jessica rested her hand on Alexis's arm. "Maybe he wants to take the risk too." At her silence, Jessica backed up. "You deserve to be happy, you know."

"I am happy."

Jessica tilted her head like she didn't believe it. "Can I ask you something else?"

Alexis managed to nod.

"What if you *are* a match?"

Alexis didn't answer and probably didn't need to.

There was no point in trying to pretend that she hadn't already made up her mind.

CHAPTER SEVEN

Lexa's house was the physical manifestation of *her*. The sunny yellow siding and white shutters reminded Noah of a cottage on Cape Cod. She'd decorated the wraparound porch with wicker chairs and bright pillows, and, at one end, a swing that he'd helped her put up at the beginning of the summer. Afterward, they'd sat on it side by side and shared a Summer Shandy until the fireflies began to light up the willow tree that draped lazily in the front yard.

She had recently swapped the summery pillows for deep fall colors and fluffy blankets. Pumpkins, gourds, and pots of mums descended the porch steps in an artfully casual way that was probably unplanned. That was the magic of Alexis. Without even trying, everything she touched was beautiful.

Except for the demon staring out the window beneath a sign that read BEWARE OF CAT.

Beefcake followed with his eyes from the window as Noah walked up the porch steps shortly before six and knocked on the front door. The cat slowly lifted one leg and started licking his nonexistent balls. Noah had never been so summarily dismissed yet threatened in his entire life.

"It's open," Alexis called faintly from inside.

Noah walked in slowly, cautiously, eyes darting left and right for an ambush.

"I'm in the kitchen," she said.

As he passed the living room on the left, Noah glanced at the couch. Beefcake was nowhere to be seen. Noah gulped and did a fast sweep of the room and the hallway with his eyes.

The kitchen was as cheery as the exterior of the house. She'd recently repainted the cabinets a bright turquoise and traded her mother's old stainless-steel appliances for a retro brand in bright red. In the center sat a 1950s-style café table surrounded by red vinyl chairs.

"Hey," Lexa said breezily over her shoulder. Too breezily.

"Hey. Something—" His voice and mind stopped working when she turned around. She wore her hair in a long braid over one shoulder, and she'd wrapped a wide flowery scarf thing like a headband around the crown of her head. Several curls had sprung free and hugged the curve of her cheeks. Dangly earrings hung from her earlobes, and as she walked toward him, the sleeve of her long blue dress slipped down to reveal one creamy shoulder. She tugged it up absently, apparently unaware that tiny flash of skin had just taken a year off his life.

She smiled, but there was a brittle quality to it. "Something what?"

"Huh?" He blinked. "Oh. Sorry. Something smells good."

She shrugged with one shoulder. "I made way more food than I needed to."

"Per usual."

Alexis lived in fear of people starving to death. He'd never once left her house without enough leftovers to last him at least three meals. But he sensed that today's overabundance had more to do with her needing a distraction than anything else. He knew the feeling.

A timer on the stove sent Noah into cardiac arrest.

"The mushrooms your sister likes," she explained.

Alexis pulled a foil-covered dish from the oven and set it on the counter. Then she retrieved something from the warming drawer. "I also made a big batch of cheesy potatoes for your mom. And for you . . . ," she said with dramatic flair as she removed the dome off an opaque cake plate. "Carrot cake with cream cheese frosting."

She'd made his favorite cake for his birthday. The tightness in his chest became a thickness in his throat.

Her smile this time was almost shy. "Happy birthday."

"It—It looks amazing," he rasped.

Alexis held his gaze for a moment before doing another one of those half-hearted shrugs. "What're friends for, right?"

"Lexa—"

She replaced the dome over the cake. "I need to grab my purse from upstairs and feed Beefcake. Do you mind carrying the food out to the car?"

"Sure."

It took him two trips to carry it all out, and then he waited by the front door while Lexa got Beefcake settled on his perch of discontent on the back of the couch. He held her coat for her, a long, red vintage thing that she'd found in a thrift shop. With a quiet thanks, she waited for him to go out first before pulling the door shut and locking it.

"I found some new music for us to try," she said as they got into the car.

He checked the mirrors and then pulled his seat belt on. "Plug it in."

As he backed out of the driveway, Alexis connected her phone to the car's USB port and then hit play. A folksy, twangy sound filled the car—a harmony of banjos and fiddles and acoustic guitars. After a moment, his thumbs began to beat the steering wheel in time to the banjo.

"I like it," he said.

She grinned at him. "Good. Because they're going on tour and coming to Nashville in a few months, and I bought us tickets."

He laughed. "What if I'd hated them?"

"You'd be too polite to say so and would then endure a horrible concert on my behalf."

"Accurate."

She turned up the volume. "This one is my favorite."

Out of the corner of his eye, he saw her lean her head against the seat and close her eyes. Alexis didn't just listen to music. She existed in it, lived in it, let it run through her and merge with her cells. The first concert they went to together, he'd spent more time watching her dance than the show itself. Hips swaying and arms raised and eyes closed as if she were alone in the world, dancing without a soul in sight. Which is why she was right; even if he'd hated this new band, he would've taken her to the concert. But he wouldn't have had to endure anything. Just watching her enjoy it would have been enough for him.

The front door flew open almost as soon as Noah pulled into his mom's driveway. A blur of bright red hair flew down the porch steps.

"Zoe dyed her hair again?" Alexis asked, affection in her voice.

"I've forgotten what her natural color is at this point," he said.

Zoe bypassed his side of the car and instead skipped over to the passenger door.

Alexis opened her door, but before she could even get out, Zoe ducked down with a desperate expression. "Please tell me you brought food."

Zoe was a vegetarian too.

"Stuffed mushrooms?" Alexis asked.

"Dear God, I love you."

Noah snorted and told his sister to help them carry in the food. His mom greeted them in the foyer, balancing a large tray of raw steaks. "There you two are," she said with a warm smile.

Noah bent to kiss her head. "Hey, Mom."

She handed him the tray. "Just in time, birthday boy. Take these out to Marsh, will you? He's out back fighting with the grill."

Noah traded her the cake for the steaks, and then his mom extended her free arm to Alexis for a hug.

"It's so good to see you," she said, drawing Alexis in for a quick squeeze. "I'm so nervous, because I made that spaghetti squash recipe you sent me, but I'm sure it's nowhere near as good as you'd make."

"I'm sure it's amazing," Alexis said.

"She made stuffed mushrooms," Zoe said with as much lust in her voice as Mack talking about centerpieces.

His mom looked over her shoulder at him. "Go on," she said with a shooing motion. "Get those steaks on the grill. We girls have to do some talking."

Alexis met his gaze and tried but failed to hide her smile. He'd just been dismissed from his own birthday party.

Noah turned left into the formal dining room and walked through the kitchen. His mother had lived there more than ten years, but it still felt like a strange house at times. Probably because he'd never actually lived there.

No, that wasn't it. His father had never lived there. His presence was there in photos, but it wasn't the same. Maybe that's why his mom wanted to move. Her memories were harder than his. At least in this house, she didn't have to think about the sight of a military car in the driveway. Didn't have to remember looking out the window and seeing a uniformed marine and a chaplain walking up the sidewalk. Didn't have to recall how her legs refused to work when the doorbell rang.

"Don't answer it," she whispered, her back pressed to the wall, arms crossed over her chest.

Noah went cold at the look on her face. "Who is it?"

"No one. It's no one." His mom said it quietly, frantically, as if wishing it to be true. And then her hand flew to her mouth.

Zoe clutched a throw pillow and drew her feet up onto the couch as if waiting to spring into action, climb the walls, fly straight out the window, anything to escape the fate that was now on the porch.

Noah trudged on wooden legs to the door and pulled it open.

Even then, Noah knew that some details would eventually fade. But he also knew that he would never, ever forget the sound of his mother's scream as she collapsed to the floor.

The sliding glass door scraped across the aluminum track as Noah walked out back. Marsh stood at a rusty propane grill that was held together with duct tape and nostalgia. He wore faded jeans and a Nashville Legends T-shirt. He looked over his shoulder and bypassed any form of greeting. "Come help me with this thing."

"Hi to you too."

Marsh fiddled with the burner and hit the ignite button. It made a clicking noise but nothing else. Marsh swore and swiped his hands over his graying high-and-tight haircut. "Damn thing belongs in a scrapyard. Why the hell won't she buy a new one?"

Noah bristled. "You know why."

Because that was the grill they'd bought as a Father's Day gift for his dad. The one his dad never got to use. Noah set the steaks down on the patio table and took over on the grill. He got it started on the first try. "You have to let the gas run for a minute before trying to ignite it."

"Dinner is saved," Marsh said dryly.

"Alexis brought enough food to feed the Airborne, so we could've eaten that and been fine."

The sky-high arch of Marsh's eyebrow meant he'd said too much. Marsh was always giving him shit about his relationship with Alexis.

Noah stabbed a raw slab of meat and threw it on the grill. Marsh swatted his hand away. "Not yet, dumbass. You have to let it get hot first. Haven't you ever grilled a damn steak before?"

Noah rolled his eyes and stepped back.

"Grab us a couple of beers," Marsh said, nodding with his chin to a cooler by the back door.

Noah grabbed two, twisted off the caps, and handed one to Marsh.

Marsh took a long drink and then belched. "You sleeping with her yet?"

Noah coughed and wiped the spittle of beer from his lips. "What the fuck, Marsh?"

Marsh chuckled and took another drink. "That's a no."

"My relationship with Alexis is none of your fucking business."

"Hey," Marsh snapped, pointing his beer like a weapon. "Watch your mouth."

"Alexis and I are friends."

Marsh threw a steak on the grill. "No such thing as friends between men and women."

"If you're trying out for Misogynist of the Year, you just won."

Marsh tossed another steak onto the grill. "It's biology. Men want to sleep with women, not hang out and talk with them."

"Really? Does my mother know you feel that way?"

Marsh's face hardened. "Watch it."

"You get to give me shit but I can't reciprocate?"

"My friendship with your mother is a helluva lot more complicated, and you know it."

Yeah. Complicated as in neither one of them would date other people but had never dated each other because it was the ultimate betrayal of his father, and so no one was happy.

Marsh took another long drink.

"I signed a new client a couple of days ago," Noah said.

"Anyone famous?"

Marsh was always hung up on the fact that Noah worked with celebrities. "Probably no one you know. He's a young country singer."

"Good money?"

"Enough."

"You meet with that financial planner yet?"

Noah winced. This was a regular fight with Marsh. He couldn't make the old man understand that Noah had no interest in meeting with *his* financial planner. Noah preferred his own investments, the kind that weren't tied to propping up the fossil fuel industry.

Noah had tried to explain it once, that there was a growing industry of socially conscious investing, but Marsh had scoffed, called it
leftist bullshit, and told him he was throwing his money away.

"I've made some progress," Noah said simply, keeping the details to himself. A petulant part of him wanted to ram his most re-
cent earnings report down Marsh's throat. Or maybe the *paid in
full* note on his mother's house. Or the zero balance on Zoe's tuition
bills. She would earn her Ph.D. next spring without a penny of debt.

That was enough for Noah. He didn't need Marsh's approval
as long as he had theirs.

And Alexis's.

Through the glass door, he could see her and his mom laughing
over a scrapbook on the counter. Probably pictures of him from
when he was a kid. From before his father died. There weren't a lot
of pictures taken afterward.

Noah finished his beer. "I'm going to see if they need any help
inside."

At the sound of the door against the metal track, they turned
and stared. Zoe and his mom wore matching expressions of shock.

"She just told us about the kidney transplant," his mom said.

"So, how does that even work?" Zoe asked fifteen minutes later at
the dining table. She swallowed half a mushroom. "The transplant,
I mean."

Alexis, who sat to Noah's right, sipped her wine. "I'm still learning about it, but it looks like I would have to go through two rounds
of testing to make sure I'm compatible. And if I am, then I'd have to go
through a bunch of other tests before the surgery can be scheduled."

"How long does that take?" his mom asked.

"Normally, about six months, but we don't have that much time. Elliott probably needs the transplant by Christmas."

"Oh my gosh," his mom said. "That soon?"

"He had two other donors fall through."

"So if you're not a match . . . ," Zoe said, letting the unfinished part dangle like the fork in her hand.

Alexis glanced at Noah before answering. "I don't know."

The way she said it made Noah's heart ache, because Alexis *did* know. It was quite possible Elliott would die, and dammit, Noah hated that she had that kind of pressure on her shoulders. He knew her well enough to know that if she wasn't a match, she'd consider it a personal failing. Noah wanted to rest his hand on her neck, give it a reassuring squeeze, but Marsh was already watching them.

"This must be such a shock for you," his mom said. "And after everything else you've gone through the past few years."

Marsh made an indecipherable noise. Noah sent him a warning glare, which Marsh returned as he sawed off a chunk of meat.

"So what are you going to do?" Zoe asked.

"I'm not sure," she said.

Zoe snorted. "You're a way better person than I am. I'd tell all of them to fuck off and leave my internal organs alone."

"For God's sake, Zoe," their mom admonished.

"What?" Zoe shrugged. "I'm just saying that Alexis is basically a saint for even considering it. She's never even met him, and she's willing to—"

"Wait," Marsh said, cutting Zoe off. "You've never even *met* your father?"

"Marsh," his mother said quietly, firmly.

"It's okay," Alexis said, stiffening as she straightened. "It's not something I'm ashamed of. The truth is, no, I never knew my father. I still don't really know anything. How they met. When they met. Why he left." She swallowed hard at that last part. "But it looks like he's been living just two hours away for most of my life."

"Where's that?" Marsh asked.

"Huntsville."

Marsh lifted an eyebrow. "He work for the military?"

Alexis shook her head and started to answer, but Noah interjected. He knew where Marsh was going, and he wasn't going to let him do it. "He's an engineer," Noah said.

"For NASA?" Marsh asked casually. Too casually.

"No," Alexis said. "Some tech company."

Marsh leaned back in his chair and reached for his beer. "Most of the tech companies down there are defense contractors."

A heavy silence fell across the table. Alexis looked at Noah. Noah looked at Marsh. Marsh looked back. Zoe looked at her mushrooms.

His mom sat up straight. "Does anyone want more squash?"

Less than an hour later, after a hasty rendition of "Happy Birthday" and even hastier goodbyes, Alexis slid into the car and pinned Noah with a challenging stare. "So, what was that between you and Marsh?"

Noah adjusted the rearview mirror before backing out. "Did my mom torture you with her dumb pictures?"

"No. I liked seeing you in your Batman costume when you were seven, and I'm going to tease you forever about that unfortunate peach-fuzz phase from middle school. But stop avoiding my question."

Noah turned right out of the subdivision. "He doesn't trust me."

"I knew it," she seethed. "Because Elliott works for a defense contractor. He thinks you're going to do something."

"Yep."

"But that's not who you are anymore."

"I know." He hung another right.

"You haven't been that person in a long time."

He glanced at her sideways. "I appreciate the indignation on my behalf, but in Marsh's eyes, I'll always be that person."

That person, of course, being an angry teenager with a genius IQ and a misguided need for revenge for his father's death. A rebellious kid who ended up in FBI custody because of a reckless, failed attempt to hack into something way out of his league. A kid who never actually rose above the hacktivist version of coffee boy, who immediately agreed to consult for the FBI and testify against the big guys, but who in Marsh's eyes would never, ever live up to his father's sacrifice.

Alexis jutted her jaw to the side. "I don't understand why he's so hard on you. Haven't you proven yourself a hundred times over?"

Noah merged onto the freeway. "It's complicated."

She traded righteousness for sardonic deadpan. "A sister I never knew existed just showed up to tell me my long-lost father needs a kidney. I can handle complicated."

Noah peeled a hand off the wheel and massaged the back of his neck. "He promised my father he'd take care of us, and it made sense when Zoe and I were young and when Mom was having such a hard time. But now, it's like he's mad that we don't actually need him anymore." He let out a breath. "Sometimes I think he's actually pissed off that I'm *not* that kid anymore, you know? The world doesn't make sense to him if I don't need an ass-kicking."

"I doubt your father wanted you to be Marsh's emotional punching bag for the rest of your lives."

The insight—so precise and accurate and classically Alexis—was a sucker punch to his chest. He white-knuckled the steering wheel. "I'm more worried about my mom."

Alexis muscles went rigid next to him. "Is he mean to her?"

"No," he said quickly. "Trust me. I wouldn't put up with that. I just feel like he's the reason she's never really moved on."

Alexis relaxed in her seat. "You think they're more than just friends?"

"I think whatever they are to each other, it's not healthy."

"It's hard to judge people's relationships from the outside."

Her words managed to both scold and shame him, because he knew that better than anyone. He'd been fighting the outside judgments about his relationship with Alexis for months.

A quiet ding from her purse saved him from having to respond. She dug around until she found her phone. She stared at the notification longer than necessary.

"What is it?"

"Candi."

"How the hell does she have your cell phone number?"

Alexis pressed her fingertips to her temple. "I gave it to her before I knew who she really was."

"What does she want?"

"She has to go back to Huntsville tomorrow night. She wants to know if I would be willing to meet her at her hotel."

"*Tomorrow?*" The question came out more defensive than he intended.

Her answer was another one of those frustrating shrugs. "I don't see how I can say no."

"Easy," he said, loosening his grip on the steering wheel because he was about to pop a knuckle. "You just say no."

"She's desperate, Noah. How can I stand by and force her to watch her father die knowing I might have been able to stop it?"

Noah swiped his hand over his hair.

Alexis stared at him. "What's wrong?"

"I'm tired of you caring more about other people than yourself."

"We're talking life or death here."

"Exactly. And you seem to forget that he's not the only one whose life is at stake."

"These transplant surgeries are safe. They do thousands of them every year."

Noah wanted to argue but stopped himself. She didn't need him putting more pressure on her than she was already putting on herself.

Instead, he dragged a hand from the steering wheel and covered the tangle of hers on her lap. "How can I help?"

Her relief was a living, breathing thing in the car. "Will you come with me?"

"Of course."

Alexis didn't respond. With her free hand, she turned on their favorite satellite radio station, and they rode the rest of the way like that.

Music doing the talking. Saying the things he couldn't.

CHAPTER EIGHT

Beefcake was nowhere to be seen when they walked back into her house. Noah helped her carry leftovers to the kitchen.

A red leash on the counter caught his attention. He picked it up. "What's this?"

"A cat harness. For Beefcake."

"*A cat harness?*"

"The vet said he needs more exercise, but I don't think I should let him out anymore, so I got him this leash thing to take him for walks."

"You're going to take *Beefcake* for walks?"

"I think he'll like it."

She said it with the kind of innocence with which children swear they heard reindeer on the roof on Christmas Eve. Alexis had a mile-wide naive streak about Beefcake. If she only knew the number of dead things that cat had dropped at Noah's feet over the past year . . .

She didn't know, though, because Noah always got rid of the

evidence before she could find out. "Have you tried to put it on him yet?"

"Not yet. I need to figure it out. Want to help?"

He eyed it skeptically. He had no idea how the contraption was supposed to work, but he knew with one hundred percent certainty if it involved Beefcake, it was going to end badly.

Alexis called out to the cat in her singsongy way. "Here, kitty, kitty, kitty."

A yowling noise in the hallway behind him made the air catch in Noah's lungs. He swallowed and turned around. Beefcake stood a few feet away. "Here he is," he rasped.

Lexa brushed past him. Beefcake glared at Noah through slitted eyes as Lexa cradled him to her chest and walked back to the kitchen.

"How about if I hold him while you put the harness on him?" she said.

It was the worst idea he'd ever heard, but he wasn't going to disappoint Lexa. He picked up the harness from where she'd left it on the table and approached woman and beast slowly.

A low growly noise was coming from Beefcake's chest. It was the closest thing he ever got to purring.

"I think we're supposed to wrap it around him and snap it across his belly before we do the leg part," Alexis said, turning and turning the cat over in her arms.

Noah gulped and held out the harness. He met Beefcake's eyes and saw his own murder flash through them. Carefully, Noah draped the harness on Beefcake's back.

Nothing happened.

Alexis lifted Beefcake higher so Noah could reach under and— he froze as the cat stopped purring. Everyone knew a cat's belly was the danger zone. But this cat especially. Noah had made the mistake of trying to pet him there exactly once.

"He's okay," Alexis said. "Can you snap it closed?"

Noah winced instinctively as he reached beneath Beefcake and located both ends of the straps. Holding his breath again, Noah gingerly connected the two ends with a quiet but firm snap.

Beefcake barely moved.

"Awww, look! He likes it." Alexis scratched Beefcake's ears and made lovey-dovey noises at him. "You really are such a good boy."

A really good boy were words that had never, ever been spoken about Beefcake.

"Now what?" Noah asked.

"Now I think we loop the other part around each leg."

Noah did the engineering in his head and decided the plans were flawed from the design stage. Because there was no way Beefcake was going to willingly put his legs through the holes of that thing.

As if reading his mind, Beefcake bared his claws.

The rest happened in slow motion.

Beefcake made a noise like a rabid raccoon and went full Crouching Tiger. He lifted his back legs, planted them in the center of Noah's chest, and dug in. Before Noah could even register the fact that he'd just been impaled, Beefcake shoved off and flew from Lexa's hands.

Noah clutched his chest and fell backward as Alexis gasped. "Beefcake, no!"

Dear God, he'd been stabbed. Noah collapsed against the wall, hand covering his heart. Or what was left of it. He was afraid to pull his hand away because he'd likely find it covered in blood.

"Oh my God, did he hurt you?" Alexis asked, running toward him.

"I'm fine." Noah's voice registered high enough to summon bats.

"Move your hand," she ordered. And just in case he wasn't going to obey, she peeled his fingers away.

"Oh no," she breathed. "You're bleeding."

Noah was afraid to look down, so he squinted and slowly dipped his chin.

Twin red splotches had soaked through his white T-shirt.

"We need to look at it. Cat scratches can get infected."

"It's not that bad."

She nodded toward the hallway. "Go in the bathroom. I'll be right there. We need to clean it."

"Lexa—"

She pointed toward the door with a look that ended the argument. He trudged back to the bathroom, turned on the light, and shut the door halfway. Then he grabbed the collar of his shirt at the nape of his neck and pulled it over his head. Two inch-long cuts between his pecs oozed blood beneath the dark mat of hair.

He heard Alexis's footsteps in the hallway, and suddenly the door swung open all the way. "There's some washcloths under the sink— Oh."

She stopped.

Stared.

Blinked.

Looked away quickly.

Circles of pink rose high on her cheeks. "Sorry. I . . . should have knocked."

"It's okay." Noah stepped back to make room for her, his own face getting hot as he watched her open the cabinet beneath the sink. She grabbed a washcloth and a basket of first aid stuff. She turned around, looked at him and then away again.

Noah blinked and looked down at his naked chest.

Was she *checking him out*? No. That was ridiculous. The guys had planted too many fucking seeds in his head. It was just wishful thinking. But she'd stared so openly, so hotly, that his chest hair had damn near ignited.

She turned around and soaked the washcloth in hot water. Looking everywhere but at his eyes, she then pressed the fabric to the first scratch. He instinctively sucked in a breath. She yanked the towel back. "I'm sorry. Does it hurt?"

He cleared this throat. "It's fine."

"Maybe we should go to the ER."

"For a cat scratch?"

"Cat scratches can be bad."

"This one isn't."

"It's pretty deep."

"Lexa, I'm fine."

She returned to her cleaning, every swipe of the fabric a creeping torture he'd never experienced before. But then she set the washcloth down and dabbed antibiotic cream on her fingers, and the torture began anew.

Because this time, she was touching him directly. Hot fingertips against his hot skin.

She looked up. "Does it hurt?"

He shook his head, amazed he could talk at all. "It's fine."

Except he wasn't fine. He was nearly hyperventilating. Not from pain, at least not from the pain of the scratch. Her touch was like a branding iron against his naked skin.

God strike him down for the most inappropriate reaction of all time given everything she was going through, but the first thing he thought was how amazing it would be to feel her hands on other parts of him, and suddenly his groin got the misguided idea that now would be the perfect time to stand at attention. *Fuck.*

He jerked away from her. "That's good."

Alexis blinked up at him, cheeks growing pinker. "I'm sorry. I—I'll get you a new shirt."

Alexis escaped to her bedroom upstairs and sank to the edge of the bed. She pressed her hands to her eyes. Nope. Didn't work. She could still see him.

Shirtless.

As in naked from the waist up.

As in trim hips encased in faded denim rising to a wide V of shoulders, bulging triceps, and toned pecs that played peekaboo beneath a layer of dark hair that gathered in the valley between before descending in a straight line down taut abs toward . . .

No. She wouldn't think about the *toward* part.

Holy shit, how did she not know he looked like that under his comic book T-shirts? And double holy shit, she had just ogled her best friend, *and he knew it.*

"Lexa."

She shot to her feet and turned toward his voice. He hovered in the doorway as if afraid to cross the threshold. In the play of light and shadow from the single lamp, his face was angular and sharp.

"You have a tattoo on your back," she blurted.

"Yeah. Didn't . . . Didn't you know?"

"No."

He took a tentative step into the room. "It's the date of my dad's death."

Her eyes fell to the wide spread of his shoulders. And then farther down to the hard ridge of his collarbone, and farther still to the dark hair covering defined pecs and tight . . .

"Lexa . . ." His voice was strained. Maybe even embarrassed.

Crap. She'd just been busted *again*.

Alexis quickstepped to her closet, threw it open, and yanked a sweatshirt from a hanger. It was his. He'd given it to her last winter to wear when she spilled spaghetti sauce on herself. She'd never returned it, and he never asked for it back.

He took it from her. "Thanks."

She shrugged. "It's yours."

Alexis sidestepped him to return to the other side of the bed, a safer distance. She looked at the floor as he pulled the sweatshirt over his head.

"I'm decent," he said, trying and failing to make a joke out of the sexual tension that made the air sizzle and crack like a fire.

She glanced up through hooded lashes. "Are you . . . Does it hurt?"

"No."

"I'm sorry about Beefcake. He's just—"

"I'm fine, Lexa." The corner of his mouth quirked up in a half smile that sent her heart into a rapid flutter. "But I don't think he likes the harness."

She laughed all nervous-like and then cringed at how unnatural it sounded. "Right. No, I think maybe I won't be using it."

She met his eyes and then quickly looked away, but her gaze instead fell to the bed, but that suddenly seemed way too intimate, so she looked back at him, and then, oh shit, her cheeks blazed as hot as if she'd just pulled fresh muffins from the oven.

This was ridiculous. She was acting like a teenager with her first crush. "Are you staying?" she blurted.

His expression went blank. "I— Do you want me to?"

"I—I was just asking. I mean, it's late, so I wouldn't blame you if you decided to go home, but you can stay if you want. I just—"

Her words became a jumbled run-on sentence as he walked toward her. He stopped inches away, and her breath lodged in her chest.

"Alexis." His voice was strained again.

She gulped. "What?"

"Do you want me to stay again tonight?"

She noticed everything at once—the low register of his voice, the clean, manly scent of him, his muscled forearms, the overpowering size of him. And heat. It radiated off him in waves as if he generated his own solar power.

Yes. I want you to stay. The words were there, but she couldn't get them out. Something was wrong with her. She was itchy in her own skin, jumbled in her own thoughts, unsure of her own emotions.

She put a foot of distance between them. "I'm okay," she whispered. "You can go."

The drive from her house to his had never been so long, and Noah was pretty sure he'd left more than a chunk of his skin behind. He'd obviously left his common sense. Because it was a test of willpower in the entire twenty-minute drive to not turn around, return to her bedroom, drag her into his arms, and beg her to touch him again.

That was pathetic enough. But even worse was that the only thing stopping him was a sliver of uncertainty that he'd imagined the whole thing.

Noah pulled into his driveway and squinted as motion lights flooded the lawn and garage with a yellow glow. Noah turned off his car, dragged his hands down his face, and groaned out loud as he dropped his head against the seat.

No, he hadn't imagined it. He'd been naked in front of enough women—not a lot, but enough—that he recognized the look on Alexis's face. *Desire.* And he had no idea what to do about that, which is why part of him was grateful she'd told him to go home. The other part of him? Noah shook his head. The other part of him needed a cold shower.

He unlocked his front door, punched in the alarm code on the keypad inside, and dropped his keys on the entryway table his mother had insisted he buy. Marsh, of course, had scoffed and said a man should decorate his own damn house.

Noah bypassed the stairs because there was no point even trying to go to bed. So he grabbed a beer from the fridge and wandered to the living room to collapse on his couch. He surfed the channels on his TV for ten minutes before giving up and turning the whole thing off. He could text her, of course. They often did to say good night, but after writing and deleting ten different messages, he gave up and tossed his phone onto the coffee table. It landed next to a plastic bag.

The book.

Great. He should've thrown the damn thing away.

Noah flipped it off. He wasn't going to read that stupid thing. What the hell was it going to teach him that he didn't already know? Marsh's voice was a mocking whisper in the back of his mind. *What kind of man reads a romance novel to figure out how the fuck to tell his woman that he's in love with her?*

Noah downed the last warm swallow of beer, still glaring at the bag.

Fine. He couldn't sleep anyway. He grabbed the book, cracked it open, and started to read.

AJ Sutherland's first mistake was going two miles over the speed limit in a dinky town like Bay Springs, Michigan, where the cops had nothing better to do than hide in dark alcoves with radar guns.

His second mistake was thinking anything had changed in the eighteen years since he'd been back to the northern resort town where he spent his summers as a teenager.

He banged his hand against the metal bars of the jail cell. "You know you can't hold me indefinitely, right?"

The officer who pulled him over and arrested him regarded him with a mixture of boredom and outright hostility. "You have a right to remain silent. You might want to use it."

AJ uttered an "argh" and ran his hands through his hair. "Look, Mr. Alvarez—"

"Mister?"

"Chief Alvarez. I get that you don't like me and never have, but you can't just throw me in jail for it."

"Son, I didn't arrest you because I don't like you. I arrested you because you have an outstanding warrant."

"*Bullshit. For what?*"

"*Watch your language. You might be a big, bad NFL player to the rest of the world, but around here you're just a cocky punk who walked away from his responsibilities.*"

"*What the hell are you talking about?*"

"*Daddy, stop.*" The female voice that interrupted their conversation was straight out of AJ's memory bank, and he'd be lying if he wasn't terrified to hear it. Because there was only one person on Earth who hated him more than Chief Sandoval Alvarez, and that was the chief's daughter, Missy.

She walked down the hallway and stood next to her father in a long, dark trench coat and with a briefcase in her hand.

"*Missy?*" AJ croaked.

She sighed. "*No one has called me that in a long time.*"

"*Sorry. Melissa, then?*"

A single eyebrow arched. "*What brings you back after all these years?*"

"*I have some decisions to make. This seemed like a good place to make them.*"

Her expression remained unchanged and unimpressed. "*I heard about that. You're thinking of retiring.*"

"*Thirty-six is old for a quarterback.*"

She looked at her father. "*Let him go.*"

"*Can't do that, sweetie. He's under arrest.*"

"*On what charge?*" AJ barked.

"Eighteen years of unpaid child support."

AJ tipped his head back to laugh but it died on his lips at the look on Missy's face. He blinked rapidly as his vision blurred. "Wh-What is he talking about?"

Missy looked at the floor and pinched her nose.

"Missy, what the hell is he talking about?"

She looked up. "You have a daughter."

CHAPTER NINE

By the time he pulled into the parking lot behind Mack's building the next morning, Noah was more than twenty minutes late and looking for a fight. Because he'd slept like shit, and that book? What the fuck was that? What kind of romance novel was about a guy who abandoned his child? He should have listened to his first instinct and thrown the thing away.

He stormed in the back door just in time to hear a loud clap and a man's commanding voice. "Work those glutes, kids. Squeeze those cheeks."

Oh no. No way. He absolutely did not have the energy for this today. Noah spun on his heel and was just about to *nope* the fuck out of there when he heard Mack's voice.

"Where the hell have you been? We had to start without you."

A frustrated growl emerged from Noah's throat as he turned back around. Mack stood at the end of the long hallway that led to the bar area. He wore long track pants, a T-shirt bearing the logo for his bar, and a whiskered scowl.

"Damn," Mack said, reeling back. "You could knock a buzzard off a shit wagon. What happened to you?"

"Fuck you. I'm here, aren't I? And why the hell did you make us do this so early on a Saturday?"

"Because the Russian has a game tonight." Mack turned around and nodded for Noah to follow. "Come on. We're just warming up, so you didn't really miss anything."

Great.

The pulsating beat of a techno song greeted him as he walked into the main part of the bar. Sonia and the guys turned and looked in unison as Noah and Mack walked in. They formed two sloppy lines along the wooden dance floor where, come ten o'clock tonight, drunken douchebags would attempt to out-line-dance one another before stumbling into the street to throw up.

Standing in front was a man in a baggy pair of sweatpants and a black tank top that read *Music City Dance Factory*. Tattoos covered both of his arms all the way to the wrist.

"That's Clive, our choreographer," Mack explained. "He owns a dance academy in Midtown."

Noah shook the man's hand, apologized for being late, and then purposely walked to the far back of the dance floor.

Clive clapped his hands. "Are we ready, then? Let's get back to working those shoulders. We don't want to pull any muscles."

Noah did. He desperately wanted a pulled muscle. He'd break his own goddamned arm to get out of this.

Clive moved into some kind of hip gyration, and Noah knew without even trying that his body was not going to move like that. Not with any amount of practice. Dear God. This was going to be beyond humiliating. This was going to be cruel and unusual punishment. There was no way in hell he was going to do this in front of Alexis.

From his spot in the back, though, he could see that he wasn't the only one who was going to look ridiculous. Colton, Malcolm, and Gavin were surprisingly good dancers, but everyone else looked like those windup singing animals that people bought at holidays to scare their dogs. They were all stiff-armed and robotic. This was going to be a disaster.

"Noah, like this." The Russian turned around in front of him in way-too-short shorts and a ribbed white tank top. Black hair poked from every opening, and bulging muscles gave the overall effect of a bear in a human costume. The Russian planted his hands on his hips and swiveled from left to right and then back to front.

"From here," he explained, gesturing just short of his junk. He then began to pump his hips. Dear God, Noah would never be able to unsee that.

Noah looked at Mack. "You could just shoot me instead, you know."

The Russian grabbed Noah's hips and tugged. "Like this."

"I got it," he snapped, knocking the Russian's hands away. "I'm fully capable of thrusting my hips at the appropriate time."

He just hadn't done so in a while.

A long while. Just over eighteen months, to be exact.

"You are in bad mood," the Russian said. "You sleep bad?"

Yeah. Horrible. He'd been tormented all night with alternating dreams of Lexa on an operating table and Lexa caressing his chest. Thrusting his hips was not helping matters.

For the next hour, Clive led them through a dance workout that left Noah panting and sweaty. By the time they were done, he felt like he'd just biked uphill for an hour straight. But just when Noah was close to running into the traffic outside on Broadway, Clive stopped and killed the music.

"Great job," he said. "We'll learn the second half next weekend."

Second half? Noah groaned and wiped his forearm across his brow. Ahead of him, Sonia bent and braced her hands on her knees while Mack leaned against a table to catch his breath. Gavin, Del, and Malcolm collapsed on the floor. Clive had even killed the professional athletes.

Colton sauntered over. "You look like shit today. Worse than normal, even."

"Fuck off."

"What's wrong? You and Alexis get in a fight or something?"

Noah curbed the urge to flip him off and instead stomped to the bar. Sonia tossed him a bottle of water.

"What was that?" Mack asked, jogging to the bar. "You got in a fight with Alexis?"

Noah barely had time to swallow. "No—"

"What was the fight about?"

"We did not get in a fight. Jesus."

"Well, something obviously happened," Mack said. "You were late, you do look like shit, and you're stomping around like someone broke your favorite *Star Wars* collectible."

Colton leaned on the bar. "I'm sure it was nothing, Mack. They're just friends, remember?"

Noah dug in his pocket for his keys. "I'm out of here."

Mack grabbed the back of his shirt. "Wait. We're going for breakfast at Six Strings."

"I'm not."

"Yes, you are. I need your opinion on a couple of things, and you obviously need to talk."

Gavin and Del both hollered from the floor that they had to go home for family stuff. Sonia said she had to go walk her dog, and two other guys—Derek Wilson and Yan Feliciano—said they had other stuff to do too. Nothing specific. Just stuff.

Cowards. All of them.

That left Malcolm, the Russian, Mack, and Colton to stare at Noah with eyebrows arched.

"I'm not going," Noah repeated. "I have stuff too." Which was true. It was just that his stuff wasn't until later that afternoon, but they didn't need to know that.

Mack stuck out his bottom lip.

Fuuuck. "Fine. I'll meet you there."

Noah checked his phone as soon as he got back in his car. No message from Lexa. Which wasn't entirely unusual. Sure, they usually had texted each other by now, but Lexa did say that she was going to have breakfast with Liv today. Still, they normally would have at least said good morning or played a round of Word Nerd by now.

Noah tossed his phone onto the passenger seat with a curse. He should have texted her when he woke up like normal. Because by not texting, he was making last night into something when maybe it hadn't been.

He drove on autopilot to the restaurant and swung into a spot next to Mack's car. When he walked in and sat down at their normal table, he was the last to arrive. A cup of coffee waited for him next to a menu that he'd long since memorized. He met the guys here at least every other week. It was off the beaten path, so it didn't attract a lot of tourists, which was good because most of the guys were recognizable.

"What took you so long?" Mack whined.

Noah dumped creamer into his coffee. "Why the hell are you monitoring my time this morning?"

"Because we need to make a decision by noon."

"On what?"

Mack thumbed the screen of his phone. "I'm reconsidering the boutonnieres."

Noah dragged his hands down his face. The last time they talked flowers, it took several hours just to get Mack to choose between white and red. "What's wrong with the one you picked out before?"

"I discovered that flowers have meanings."

"Oh, Christ." Noah ground the heel of his hand into a suddenly throbbing temple.

"I discovered that the Christmas rose can symbolize anxiety," Mack said. "I can't wear that at my wedding."

"It has the word *Christmas* in it," Colton said. "What could be more perfect for a December wedding?"

Noah stirred his coffee. "Is there a flower that means giant douchebag? You should get that one."

Mack ignored Noah and turned his phone around to show off a picture of a small white flower that looked almost exactly like Noah remembered the first one he'd chosen.

"I'm thinking of the white ivy flower," Mack said. "It stands for fidelity."

"Perfect," Noah said. "Go with that."

"Definitely that one," Malcolm said, sending Noah a silent thank-you with his eyes.

"Absolutely," Colton added.

"It's ugly," the Russian said.

Noah elbowed him to shut up. Mack's eyebrows pulled together as he studied the picture again. "You think it's ugly?"

"It's not ugly," Noah said. "The Russian doesn't know what he's talking about."

Colton got a look in his eyes that said he was about to start some shit. He propped his elbows on the table and leaned toward the Russian. "What kind of flowers did you have in your wedding?"

"I don't remember," the Russian answered, cheeks suddenly red.

Noah glared at Colton, who responded with an *I told you so* smirk.

The waitress interrupted to take their orders. While the guys took turns, Mack suddenly became engrossed in something on his phone. The waitress walked away, and Mack looked directly at Noah.

"So, Liv just texted me."

A cold shiver ran across Noah's skin. "And?"

"And when were you going to tell us that you spent the night at Alexis's house and she saw you without a shirt?"

Ah, fuck. Heat raced up his neck and blazed a path clear to his hairline. But embarrassment quickly became hope, because if she told Liv about it, then it must have meant something. Right?

Colton snorted. "I guess we know why you're off your game this morning."

"What happened?" Mack asked.

"Nothing," Noah gulped.

"Bullshit," Colton coughed.

"And you were shirtless *why*?" Mack asked.

"It's a long story," Noah mumbled.

Malcolm stroked his beard. "Why don't you start at the beginning?"

Noah blew out a frustrated breath, swiped his hands over his hair, and launched into the whole story—Candi, the kidney transplant, the story of Beefcake and his fucking claws. By the time he got to the part about Lexa walking into the bathroom and stopping dead in her tracks, his nipples had started to tingle.

He crossed his arms. "Any questions?"

The Russian raised his hand. Noah called on him.

"Did she sniff you?"

"What the fuck, man? No."

Another hand shot into the air.

Noah sighed. "Yes, Malcolm?"

"You said she acted weird when she saw you. Can you be more descriptive?"

"What more do you need?"

Mack piped in. "*Where* did she stare?"

The Russian pouted. "He did not raise his hand."

Mack raised his hand and repeated the question.

"She stared, you know . . ." Noah let his voice trail off. But when all the guys leaned forward, he gestured toward his pecs. "Here."

His face got hot again as he lowered his hand and waved it below the belly button. "And here."

One by one, the guys met one another's eyes and then in unison, busted into loud, table-shaking laughter. Noah looked around the restaurant and then hissed at them to be quiet.

Mack wiped his eyes. "Dude, she was *staring*. The real kind of staring."

"Sure sign," Colton said. "The happy trail is like catnip for women."

Noah gaped at him. "The happy what?"

The Russian lifted his shirt and pointed to his stomach. "The line of hair from your belly button to your pork and beans."

Mack leaned left to whisper, "*Frank* and beans."

The Russian looked baffled. "Who is Frank?"

Colton raised his hand. Noah shook his head. "Next."

"You don't even know what I'm going to ask!"

"Doesn't matter. It'll be inappropriate. Next question."

"Who is Frank?" the Russian asked again.

"Someone fucking tell him," Noah growled.

Malcolm leaned over and whispered in the Russian's ear. He giggled and covered his mouth.

Their food arrived, but Noah barely had time to take a single bite before the questions continued.

"So what are you going to do about it?" Mack asked.

Noah poked his eggs with the corner of his toast and feigned ignorance. "Do about what?"

"The *staring*," Colton said.

Noah lifted a shoulder. "Nothing."

"You can't do nothing, man," Colton said. "She *stared*."

Noah snorted even as his pits began to sweat. "You guys have read too many romance novels. Which, by the way, the one you gave me? It's total bullshit. Do you even know what that book is about?"

Mack leaned back in his chair. "I do. What's wrong with it?"

"It's about a guy who abandoned his daughter! You seriously expect me to learn something from this guy?"

"The secret baby trope is a very popular plotline in the romance genre," Mack said.

Noah made a noise that was part snort, part laugh. "Secret. Baby. Trope?"

Mack shrugged. "Guy finds out he has a kid he never knew about."

"And people find this romantic?"

Mack sighed and looked to the ceiling as if praying for patience. "It's a plot device for a larger message, Noah."

"What larger message?"

"Forgiveness."

This time, Noah laughed outright. "Bullshit. Some things are unforgivable."

Mack sipped his coffee. "True. But that's not the point."

"Yeah, the point is that there's no freaking way I'm going to learn how to build a relationship with Alexis by reading about a guy who's as much of a bastard as her father."

"You can't judge the book based on one chapter," Malcolm said. "Give it a try."

"No." He sounded as stubborn as he felt.

The Russian patted his arm. "Noah, why are you so angry all the time?"

"He's not angry," Colton snorted over the rim of his coffee mug. "He's horny."

Noah pointed. "Fuck off."

"Dude, Alexis could not be making it any clearer that she wants more and is ready for more," Mack said. "What the hell are you waiting for?"

"Didn't you hear what I just told you about her father? She's going through a lot right now. She's emotional, and—"

"Alexis isn't exactly fragile," Mack said.

Noah bristled. "I know." Just the opposite. Lexa was the strongest person he'd ever known. "I'm just saying she is going through some deep stuff now, and I'm not going to add to her burden by asking her why the hell she was staring at my nipples!"

The restaurant got instantly quiet, and twenty heads turned toward their table.

"He's talking about his dog," Mack said loudly with a lift of his hand. "Nothing to see here."

Noah heard a growl rumble from his chest. "I'm going to hack into your phone and leak all your nudes on Facebook."

Mack spread his hands wide. "Naked is my best angle, man."

"Look," Malcolm said, wadding up his napkin. "I think what Mack was attempting to say is that there's a fine line between being sensitive to what Alexis is going through and treating her like she doesn't know her own mind."

"Doesn't change a goddamned thing."

"Of course it does." Malcolm leaned forward. "Your relationship with her is built on unrequited feelings. That's not fair to either of you. She deserves to know how you really feel about her, and you deserve to know if she feels the same."

"I can't risk our friendship like that."

"And you'll be happy to remain friends with her, only friends?"

"If that's what it takes to be in her life, then yes."

"And I suppose if she started dating someone else, you'd be fine with it?" Mack asked.

At his blistering silence, Mack snorted. "That's what I thought."

Noah gave in to a sudden burst of weariness. He set down his fork and ran his hands over his face. After a long, quiet moment, he looked up to find the guys watching him in matching expressions of patience and amusement.

"I don't know what to do," he admitted.

"Luckily, we do," Mack said. "Be at my bar at three o'clock tomorrow."

Noah's stomach dropped. "What for?"

Mack grinned. "Initiation."

Fuuuck.

CHAPTER TEN

A few hours later, Noah pulled into Alexis's driveway again to pick her up for their meeting with Candi. He hadn't been this nervous to pick up a woman since . . . ever. Something had changed last night, at least in his mind, and he was going to have a hard time keeping it cool today. Which is exactly what she needed from him.

She met him on the sidewalk wearing a long cardigan, a pair of leggings, and a small smile. "I saw you pull up," she explained.

He held open her door and waited while she slid into the car before returning to the driver's side. He exhaled the breath he'd been holding before sliding behind the wheel.

"Thanks for driving," she said, not quite looking at him as she buckled her seat belt.

"You sure you want to do this?"

"I'm sure."

She didn't look sure, though. Her hands were a tangled mess in her lap, and her lips were a thin line. A raw, red nick in the corner meant she'd been gnawing on it with her teeth.

"You don't have to—"

She cut him off with a look. He raised his hands in surrender.

The trip downtown was short and quiet. And when Noah parked in the ramp for the hotel where Candi was staying, they sat in the dark and the silence for a moment, just staring at the glowing red sign that read ELEVATOR. He finally looked over at her.

"Ready?" Noah got out and rounded the car to her side. He held out his hand as she slid out of the passenger seat and, as if they'd done it a hundred times before, she folded her fingers in his. His heart kicked the underside of his ribs with a painful thud as they walked hand in hand to the elevators. Only when they walked in did she pull her hand away to push the button for the lobby floor.

Noah shoved his hands deep in the pocket of his fleece. "Where are we meeting her?"

"The hotel bar."

"She alone?"

"I think so."

The elevator opened into a marble-floored hallway. Noah pressed his hand to the small of her back as they walked out. Her muscles twitched beneath his fingertips, but she didn't try to move from his touch. His heart kicked again.

"Over there," she said, pointing to a darkened corner where a hostess stood beneath a sign bearing the bar's name.

Noah looked down at Alexis. "The Bluegrass Grill?"

Her eyes turned sarcastic. "It's like they just gave up."

"Do you think there will be banjos on the walls?"

"And drinks named after Waylon Jennings songs."

Noah ushered her forward, hand still on her back. "First person to spot the Willie Nelson picture wins."

The brief banter seemed to relax her, because her muscles softened beneath his fingertips.

The lobby bustled with bleary-eyed travelers dragging heavy suitcases and the remnants of last night's bad decisions.

The hostess smiled as they approached. "How many?"

"We're meeting someone at the bar," Noah said.

The hostess directed them to the center of the restaurant, where a circular bar on a raised platform glowed a soft blue from the pendant lamps that hung from the ceiling. It was nearly deserted but for a handful of guys who were hunched quietly over beers, their eyes glued to a football game on the six televisions on the wall.

A woman sat alone several stools away, her face turned toward the entrance of the restaurant as if looking for someone.

"That's her," Alexis said, her feet slowing.

Noah slid his hand higher on her back until his fingers met the tight cords of her neck. He squeezed and lowered his mouth closer to her ear. "You okay?"

Her only response was to keep walking.

Candi spotted them, fumbled the glass of water in her hand, and then winced as it spilled on the counter. A bartender waved off her apologies and began to wipe it up as Candi slid from her barstool.

Alexis grew tense again beneath his hand.

"Hi," Candi said, her voice shy and breathless.

"Thanks for meeting us here," Alexis said.

Candi darted a nervous glance at Alexis but then turned to face Noah straight on, and—wham. He felt the impact of recognition like one of Del's head smacks. Alexis hadn't been lying. Their eyes were identical.

"This is my friend Noah," Alexis said to Candi in a voice heavy with reassurance.

Noah had heard her use it a hundred times on angry customers who were pissed off that ToeBeans had run out of cranberry scones or some other stupid complaint.

Candi swallowed. "Hi."

Alexis stared at him and lifted an eyebrow. He knew that look too. The one that said he'd forgotten his manners and was acting like a brute. Noah swallowed hard and stuck out his hand. Candi stared at it hesitantly before accepting his handshake.

"Nice to meet you," he mumbled.

Candi bit her lip as if she wanted to repeat the sentiment but hated lying. She looked back at Alexis. "Are you hungry? We can get a table or—"

"The bar is fine," Alexis said. "This won't take long."

"Oh, right. Um, we can just sit here, then. I saved some seats."

Candi rushed to clear two other barstools of a coat and a purse. Alexis said a quiet thank-you and claimed one of the stools. Noah took the one beside her, and Candi returned to her own on Alexis's right.

The bartender came back. "What can I get you?"

Noah looked down at Alexis. "You want a pale ale?"

"Sure."

Noah nodded at the bartender. "Make it two." He peered at Candi. "Anything for you?"

"Just—Just water for me."

The bartender wandered off, and Candi swallowed hard. "So have you . . . have you made a decision?"

Alexis lowered her purse to the floor. "Let's talk first."

Disappointment tugged Candi's youthful features into a small frown. "Oh, okay. Did—Did you have questions?"

Alexis pulled in a long breath and let it out quickly. "I found a copy of your parents' wedding announcement." Alexis's fingers absently rubbed the palm of her other hand. "Judging by the date of the wedding announcement, he and your mother were likely together when I was conceived."

Candi blanched but then recovered. Either that was the first time it had occurred to her that her dear old dad had cheated on her mom, or she already suspected and now had proof. Either way, Noah felt a little sorry for her. It sucked to discover someone you trusted wasn't the saint you always believed them to be.

Alexis's tone turned gentle. "I'm assuming that's why he didn't want you to contact me when you first learned I existed."

Candi looked away. "I don't know." Her jaw suddenly jutted sideways. "I shouldn't have listened to him. I wanted to meet you even before he got sick."

The bartender returned with their drinks, and Noah was grateful for the distraction. It stopped him from saying things he shouldn't.

Candi sipped her water, looking everywhere but at Alexis. "Things haven't been great between Dad and me since I found out about you."

Noah's fingers tightened on his bottle. If she was trying to make Alexis feel sorry for her, so help him—

Alexis glanced at him as if she sensed his growing anger. Noah sucked down a long drink and looked at the TV. His attention, however, was firmly on the conversation that picked back up next to him.

"I did some research online," Alexis said. "Everything I read said this process normally takes six months or longer, but you said Elliott doesn't have that long. How would this work?"

Candi's expression changed instantly. She sat up straighter, and her eyes widened. "Are you going to do it?"

"I'm just asking what I would have to do."

Candi opened the purse on her lap and pulled out a well-worn blue folder with the logo for the Huntsville Memorial Transplant Center embossed on the cover. "I brought this for you," she said excitedly, sounding every bit as young as she apparently was. "There's two rounds of testing, and it does normally take several months, but since Dad—" Candi stopped and cleared her throat. "Since we don't have that much time, they can do it faster."

She handed the folder to Alexis. "We have a transplant coordinator. Her card is in there. If you call her, she can arrange the first blood test."

Alexis opened the folder. Noah looked over her shoulder. His eyes skimmed what he could see, his muscles growing more rigid with every word.

Candi reached into the pocket of her coat. "I also brought this for you." She withdrew a folded piece of paper and set it on the bar between them.

Alexis stared at it as if she was afraid of it. "What is that?"

"A copy of the DNA test."

Moments ticked by as Alexis stared at the paper. They didn't really need to see it. Anyone who looked at the two of them next to each other could tell she and Candi were related. Still, she reached for the paper, slid it closer, and then unfolded it.

"Thank you," she said.

"The transplant center isn't very far from our house," Candi said.

Alexis looked up quickly.

"So I was thinking that maybe . . ." Candi's voice trailed off in an insecure whisper.

"Maybe what?" Noah said gruffly.

Candi tugged her hands into the cuffs of her sweatshirt. "Maybe after you do the blood test, you should come meet everyone. Dad. Cayden. The whole family."

Adrenaline soured Noah's stomach at the word *Dad*. Elliott Vanderpool was not *Dad* to her. He'd made sure of that.

"No way," he said, setting his beer down harder than was necessary.

Alexis gave him another one of those looks. He clenched his jaw.

She turned back to Candi. "I don't know if that's a good idea," she said softly.

"But then you could meet everyone."

"I just don't know if I'm ready for that yet, Candi."

"Then why did you—" Candi cut herself off again, this time with a frustrated shake of her head. Her bottom lip took the brunt of whatever emotion she'd bitten back.

"Why did I what?"

Candi turned and pinned Alexis with the most direct gaze since they'd walked in. "If you weren't interested in meeting us, why did you allow your DNA profile to be shared with potential family members?"

And there it was. The question even Noah had been wondering but had been reluctant to ask. Alexis could have requested that her DNA results be kept private. They could only be shared with potential blood relatives with permission.

Alexis seemed just as reluctant to answer the question as Noah had been to voice it. She avoided it completely. "I think we should just start with the blood test and go from there."

"Come to Huntsville," Candi said, her voice a blend of desperation and exasperation. "*Please.*"

Alexis puffed out her cheeks and let out a long breath. "Look, I know what you're hoping will happen here. That we'll have some kind of big reunion with tears and hugs and stuff, but I think you should lower your expectations."

"But don't you at least want to meet your family?"

"They're not my family."

Candi's eyes pinched at the corners, as if the words had struck a painful blow. Once again, Noah managed to feel a small twinge of pity for the girl.

Alexis let out a weary sigh, as if she regretted what she said. "We share a bloodline, Candi. That doesn't make us family. It just makes us related."

Candi's lower lip took a beating again. She looked pitiful enough that Noah knew Alexis wouldn't last much longer before agreeing to whatever Candi wanted. Noah stood and dug out his wallet. This needed to end. He dropped a twenty on the bar and rested his hand on Alexis's shoulder. "We should get going."

Noah handed Alexis her purse as she stood. Candi slid off her stool, hands clenched against her stomach. "I have to go back to Huntsville. I can't leave without knowing what you're planning to do."

Alexis offered an empathetic gaze. "You know there's no guarantee that I'm a match, right?"

"Does that mean you'll do it?"

Noah held his breath as deeply as Candi held hers.

Alexis finally nodded. "I'll schedule the blood test."

Candi's hand flew to her mouth, and her eyes got wet. "Thank you. Thank you so much."

"I'll let you know how it goes," Alexis said, backing up until she collided with Noah's chest. He gripped her hips to steady her.

They were silent all the way back to the elevator. When the doors closed, though, Alexis turned to him. "Thank you for coming with me."

"Stop thanking me for shit before I get insulted."

Before he could react, she stepped closer and wrapped her arms around his waist. Every cell in his body collided as she leaned into him and pressed her cheek to his chest. They'd shared hugs before. Many of them. But this one felt different. At least to him.

He encircled her torso with his arms. She was hot and soft in his embrace. The ground tilted beneath his feet as a rush of tenderness and desire made his limbs weak and his breathing catch. Noah forced the air to keep moving in and out of his lungs and prayed she couldn't hear the way his heart reached warp speed.

He gulped. "What's this for?"

"For being such a good friend."

He coughed. "You're a cross to bear, but I endure it."

She chuckled and pulled away, but not all the way. Her arms remained at his waist, her hands near his hips. He looked down just as she looked up. Her gaze drifted from his eyes to his mouth and lingered there. And there it was again. That look. *Desire.*

The ding of the elevator brought them apart. Silence was like a physical presence between them as they walked to the car. Neither spoke until Noah pulled out of the ramp.

"You hungry?" he asked.

"Are you?"

"I could eat."

"Okay. Do you . . . Do you want to go somewhere or . . . ?"

"What do you want to do?"

"I don't care. We could go somewhere or go back to my house or whatever you want."

Jesus. Their conversation couldn't be more stilted and painful if they'd been trying. Noah dragged a hand across his beard. It was never like this between them, and he fucking hated it.

"How about this?" he said, forcing an easiness into his voice that he didn't feel. "Let's swing by the taco truck, take tacos back to your house, and start working on that LEGO set."

She nodded, and her hands loosened their assault on each other. "Perfect."

"Put some music on," he said lightly.

Lexa plugged her iPhone into his car and swiped through her playlists until she found their favorite. Twenty minutes later, Noah pulled into a parking space in front of the taco truck.

"I can get this," she said, reaching for her purse at the floor.

"My turn," he said, opening his door. "You made me a cake for my birthday."

He jogged over the curb and approached the counter. The guy who worked there knew Noah's order by heart now and immediately started working on the vegetarian tacos and rice. Noah looked back over his shoulder just in time to see her bring her phone to her ear and start talking.

Five minutes later, he got back in the car.

"That smells awesome," she breathed. "I'm hungrier than I thought."

Noah waited until he pulled back onto the street. "Who was on the phone?"

"I called the transplant center."

"And?"

"I can drive down tomorrow to meet with the coordinator and get tested."

"On a Sunday?" His air vacated his lungs. "They're not wasting any time, are they?"

If she caught the sarcasm in his tone, she ignored it. "My appointment is at one."

"Then I guess you'd better get some food into you and some decent sleep tonight."

He peeled his hand from the steering wheel and offered his pinkie. This was what she needed from him. Friendship. Nothing else. No matter how she looked at him.

CHAPTER ELEVEN

Alexis left for Huntsville just before eleven the next day after stopping at the café to make sure everyone was settled and able to handle things without her. Before pulling out into traffic, she hammered out a quick text to Noah.

On my way.

Call me if you need me.

She plugged in her music, turned it up loud, and tried to focus on driving, not the destination. Because she had no idea what awaited her. The transplant coordinator said the blood test itself was simple and wouldn't take long. But she first wanted to meet Alexis to go over how the entire process worked.

Whenever anxiety gripped her, she used the calming technique her therapist had taught her. Focus only on what she needed to do now, not what she needed to do when she got there or tomorrow or the day after. She could only control this moment and her reaction to it.

Normally, it worked. But her mind wouldn't cooperate this time, and not just because of where she was going and why. She'd almost kissed Noah yesterday. Again. And as hard as they'd both worked to pretend things were normal between them, things definitely were not.

Finally, her GPS directed her to take the next exit to the hospital and transplant center. She parked in a visitor lot, paused to check her reflection in the rearview mirror, and then got out. From the outside, the hospital looked more like a college campus than a renowned medical center. Inside the lobby, she stopped at the information desk for a visitor pass, and the receptionist—a volunteer who called her *dear* several times—directed her to a bank of elevators that would take her to the transplant floor.

She emerged into another lobby, this one sterile and staffed by nurses. They pointed to a waiting room and said someone would come for her.

Ten minutes after she sat down, a woman in street clothes walked in and called Alexis's name. When Alexis stood, the woman approached and held out her hand. "I'm Jasmine Singh, your transplant counselor."

She spoke over her shoulder as Alexis followed her back through a set of large automatic doors. "This will take roughly an hour. We have some paperwork for you to fill out, and some documents to sign. But mostly we'll be talking. Sound good?"

Alexis nodded.

"No need to be nervous," Jasmine said with a reassuring smile. "This is simple stuff."

They reached a small office. Jasmine held open the door and

waited for Alexis to enter. Her desk dominated one half of the room. On the opposite side was a seating arrangement with a small couch and two upholstered chairs. A coffee table sat in the middle. The nameplate on the desk had the letters NCC after her name, which meant she was a certified counselor as well as a registered nurse.

"Make yourself comfortable," Jasmine said. "Can I get you anything to drink? I have water and coffee."

"Water would be great," Alexis said, sitting on the couch.

Jasmine opened the door of a mini fridge wedged between two file cabinets. She returned with two bottles of water, which she set on the coffee table before claiming a chair facing Alexis.

"How was your drive here? You find it okay?"

"Fine," Alexis said automatically. "It's a simple drive from Nashville."

Jasmine crossed her legs and smiled. "If you have any questions at any point, don't hesitate to ask them. There are no stupid questions, and it's my job to make sure you have everything you need to make this process as smooth as possible for you."

She had an easy way about her. Friendly without being fake. But there was also a rote efficiency to her, as if she'd held this meeting a thousand times before. Probably, she had.

Jasmine picked up a black binder from the coffee table. "The way I prefer to do this, if it's okay with you, is to cover some of the logistical things first. Get some paperwork out of the way, get the signatures we need, and go from there. Is that acceptable?"

"Of course."

The woman flipped open the binder, set it back on the coffee table, and turned it so Alexis could read it. "Most of this is yours to keep, but originals of some of the documents you sign will stay with me."

Alexis leaned forward as Jasmine flipped through the pages. Pre-surgery checklist. Post-surgery checklist. What to bring and not to bring. What to expect on the day of surgery.

"This seems a little premature," Alexis interrupted. "I haven't even taken the blood test yet."

Jasmine nodded. "Normally, yes, we would wait on these things. But as you know—"

"He doesn't have a lot of time."

Jasmine's smile this time was sympathetic. "I know this must be difficult."

Alexis didn't have a response to that, so she looked at the binder again. "What else is there?"

Jasmine flipped a few more pages. "This last section deals with the financials of the surgery. In most cases, the recipient's insurance will cover all costs associated with the transplant itself—the testing, the pre-surgery prep, and post-surgery care. However, any future health issues associated with the surgery would be covered by your own insurance. You indicated that you do have insurance, correct?"

Barely. Like most small-business owners, Alexis bought her own insurance through the federal marketplace, but the coverage wasn't great.

Jasmine misunderstood Alexis's nonanswer. "There are many programs available to provide financial assistance to donors. But that isn't something we can guarantee or have any authority over, so I do need a signature from you indicating that you understand your financial obligations associated with the transplant."

Alexis signed where Jasmine indicated.

The woman flipped the binder shut and slid it closer to Alexis. "We recommend that you keep that handy and have it with you during all prep work. There are pockets where you can add information as you get it. But I'm always available for questions or clarifications."

Alexis smiled, or something like it, and opened her water.

Jasmine scooted back in her chair. "You should also know that part of my job is to assess that you are doing this of your own free will without any financial or emotional coercion."

Alexis paused and lowered the bottle from her mouth. "What does that mean?"

Jasmine's face softened into the kind of expression that always spelled discomfort on the horizon. "You've had a lot going on in your life."

"You googled me?"

Jasmine did that calm smile again. "Tell me how you handle stress."

"Caffeine, therapy, and a relentless pursuit of justice."

Jasmine laughed. "Any therapy after the incident?"

"Of course. I also host a yoga class for survivors."

Jasmine nodded and made a note in her file. "I understand you weren't aware that Mr. Vanderpool was your father until recently."

Alexis set the bottle down on the table. "What does that have to do with the surgery?"

Jasmine adopted a calm, neutral expression. "It's my job to assess your emotional well-being. Finding a father you never knew would be a heavy emotional load."

"It was a shock," she finally said.

Jasmine waited for Alexis to continue, prodding with nothing more than encouraging silence.

And for some reason, Alexis acquiesced. "I mean, I knew I must have had a father somewhere at some point."

"But you never thought about finding him?"

Alexis shrugged. "It never seemed important. I had my mother, and we were a perfect family just the two of us."

"And now that he has found you, can you tell me how you'd feel if the surgery didn't work?"

Alexis started. "Didn't work? In what way?"

"His body could reject your kidney."

"But isn't that what all the tests are about? To make sure his body won't reject it?"

"Of course. But there are never any guarantees."

"But there are, aren't there? If he doesn't get a kidney, he will die. Right?"

The woman tilted her head. "He will need a kidney to live. Yes. But another donor might be found. He's on the transplant list."

"But the chances are better for survival, aren't they? If he gets a kidney from a relative instead of a stranger."

"Statistically, yes. Recipients have a longer life span post-surgery when they have a living donor who is a relative."

"Then it should be me."

Jasmine leaned forward. "Alexis, do you *want* to do this?"

"Yes." Her answer surprised even herself with its certainty, its forcefulness.

"Why?" Jasmine asked.

"What do you mean why? Because he could die if I don't."

"Wanting to protect someone from dying is different from wanting someone to live."

Alexis sat back against the couch. "That's a horrible thing to say."

"Alexis, what you say to me stays with me. Mr. Vanderpool will never know what is said here today, so you can be honest."

Annoyance prickled along her spine. "I am being honest. Are you trying to talk me out of this?"

"Absolutely not. I'm just trying to understand your reasons for being here."

So was Alexis. "I don't know what you want me to say to that."

"There are a lot of good, legitimate reasons to do this. But obligation should never be one of them."

"It's not obligation." Her voice sounded defensive to her own ears.

Jasmine crossed her legs again. "Then tell me what it is."

Alexis opened and closed her mouth. The answer was there, but she was afraid of it, just like when Candi asked her why she'd allowed her DNA results to be shared with relatives. She wanted to test it on her tongue, let it marinate until all her senses had time to experience it, accept it, before she said it out loud. So she hid her trembling hands under her thighs and gave half the truth. "I know what it's like to lose a parent. I can't let Candi go through that."

Jasmine uncrossed her legs and leaned forward, hands clasped on her knees. "So it's empathy?"

"Yes."

"Do you wish to have a relationship with Mr. Vanderpool after this?"

Once again, Alexis hedged her answer. "I've never even met him."

"And yet you're willing to give him a kidney?"

"People give kidneys to strangers all the time, don't they?"

Jasmine did that silent-studying thing again before nodding and leaning back in her chair. "Let's get that blood test taken care of."

* * *

An hour later, Alexis sat in her car with a small bandage over the crook of her elbow. The cookies they gave her sat untouched on the seat. Her phone was in her hand. All she had to do was dial the number.

Candi answered immediately with a breathless hopefulness to her voice. "Alexis?"

"Okay," Alexis said. "I'll meet the family."

CHAPTER TWELVE

Noah arrived ten minutes early for his initiation, and Mack—annoyed—told him to stay put in his office.

"Are you serious?"

Mack pointed. "Book club is very serious."

He walked out and shut the door behind him for good measure. Noah dropped into the chair in front of Mack's desk, dropped *Coming Home* onto the clean, sparse desktop, and stared at the book. He'd tried to do more reading last night but couldn't. Mostly because his mind was firmly focused on Alexis and her trip to Huntsville today. But also because he didn't care what Mack and the guys tried to tell him. No story about a man who was too selfish to know he'd left behind a pregnant girlfriend was going to help him figure things out with Alexis.

Noah had just taken up pacing and swearing when the door finally opened. The Russian filled the doorframe like a bouncer. "Follow me."

Noah hesitated, but he grabbed the book and obeyed. The Russian walked with the heavy-footed sobriety of a prison guard. And as soon as they entered the club, Noah understood why. The lights were dim but for a spotlight shining on a table in the middle of the dance floor where Mack, Gavin, Del, Colton, and Malcolm waited with equally somber expressions. A single seat was unoccupied.

Noah pulled the seat out, but Mack kicked it out of reach. "You haven't been invited to sit yet."

"You must first take the oath," Del said.

Noah laughed. "Are you serious?"

Mack's expression turned dark.

"Right. Sorry. Book club is very serious."

"Raise your right hand," Mack said.

Noah did as he was told.

"Repeat after me," Mack said. "I, Noah Logan, solemnly swear to uphold the principles of a Bromance Book Club man."

Noah mangled it but got most of it out.

Mack continued. "I vow to do the hard work on myself to overcome a lifetime of toxic masculinity."

Noah repeated it.

"And to use the lessons of the manuals to become a better man."

"Amen," the boys said.

"May I sit now?"

Mack nodded formally. Noah sat down just as Malcolm leaned forward. "We will now commence with the interrogation."

Noah's eyes darted among the men. "Interrogation?"

"We must decide if you're worthy," Colton said.

"This is ridiculous," he groaned.

"Rules are rules, ass face," Mack said.

The Russian giggled. "Ass face."

Noah spread his hands wide. "Fine, ask your questions."

"Why are you here?" Malcolm asked.

"Because Mack's been on my ass about it."

Colton slapped the table. "No. Wrong answer. Try again."

"Because I—" Noah stopped. He wasn't ready to say this out loud. He'd said it to himself a hundred times, but saying it to the guys was a whole other level of honesty.

"Say it, Noah. Admitting it is the first step," Gavin said.

Noah rolled his eyes, puffed out his cheeks, and spoke on the exhale. "I'm here because I'm pretty sure I'm in love with my best friend."

The guys nodded solemnly.

Del took over the questioning. "What scares you most about being here?"

"That you're going to hypnotize me and tell me to strip naked or something."

"Not good enough," Colton barked. "Try again."

"I'm scared about fucking it up."

"Fucking what up?" Del asked.

"My relationship with her."

"And why does that scare you?"

Noah made a *What the fuck?* expression. "Why do you think? Because I don't want to lose her."

The guys exchanged a look that either meant *acceptable* or *get a load of this bullshit.*

Malcolm took over the cross-examination. "When was the last time you had a real relationship?"

Noah shifted uncomfortably. "What does that have to do with anything?"

"You wanted our help. You have to work with us."

Noah adopted a petulant pose, arms crossed as he leaned back in his chair. "I don't know. Five years ago, I guess."

"You guess?" Malcolm lifted an eyebrow.

"She was a woman I knew from MIT. We dated for a year."

Mack jumped in. "And no one since then?"

Noah lifted his shoulder in a defensive shrug. If he'd known he was going to be quizzed about his entire love life—or lack thereof— he would've reconsidered this entire thing. "What is the point of this?"

"The point is to break the fucking cycle," Mack said. "Women aren't rehab centers for emotionally stunted man-babies who think the key to a serious relationship is to just wait for the right woman to come along. You have to be ready to be uncomfortable, to stretch yourself, to be vulnerable."

Noah snorted. "You should write greeting cards. That was good."

Malcolm sighed. "You're resorting to sarcasm because you're uncomfortable with a man expressing himself so openly. We get it. One of the most insidious ways that toxic masculinity destroys men is that it strips us of the ability to express our emotions and to connect, not just with women, but with other men. Because real men don't do that, right?"

Noah felt his head nod.

Malcolm continued. "How many times have you been told in your life to *be a man*?"

Unbidden, Noah's memory banks unleashed a torrent of unwelcome flashbacks, almost all involving Marsh.

Don't let your mother see you cry like that. You're the man of the house now.

You need to grow up and be a man.

Men don't act like this.

"Have you ever been told that real men don't cry?" Malcolm asked quietly.

Noah nodded again. Discomfort inched across Noah's skin like a bug crawling up his arm. He wanted to swat it away, to slap it and destroy it. The last thing he wanted was to talk about it.

"We all have," Malcolm said. "But there's a big fucking difference between what society teaches us what a real man does and what a good man does. And good men are willing to do the hard, emotional labor on themselves to be strong partners to the people we love."

"But we can't do that alone," Del said. "We need our friends to help us."

"And that is the point of all of this," Mack finished.

Gavin patted his shoulder. "We're here for you, man. Really here for you. All you have to do is talk. Tell us something personal."

"You know this is weird, right? All of it."

"Is it, though? Or are you just terrified of learning a new code for manhood?"

Was he? Was it really possible that the hipster radical he considered himself to be was actually just another *emotionally stunted man-baby*?

"Start with something easy," Mack said. "It takes practice learning to really talk to other men, so start with something that won't require a ton of work. Something you maybe have been embarrassed to tell us before. Something—"

"I like the *Moana* soundtrack," Noah blurted.

Gavin blinked. "As in the Disney movie?"

"I wouldn't have said it if I knew you were going to make fun of me!"

"I'm not making fun. I'm just clarifying," Gavin said.

"I like the fucking *Moana* soundtrack, okay? That song, the one about how far I'll go. I love that shit. I blast it in my house. It makes me feel good."

Malcolm spread his arms wide. "Sing it for us."

Heat blazed a path up his neck. "I'm not fucking singing for you."

"Fine," Mack said, standing up. "Then I will."

A nightmare broke out along with a sheen of sweat on Noah's brow. Because Mack began to sing.

Then Del joined in.

Then Malcolm.

Soon every man in the room except for Noah was singing, arms wide.

When they were done, a sniffle drew their attention to the Russian. He had tears running down his face. "That was beautiful."

"See?" Mack said. "Even the Russian gets it. He's not afraid to express his emotions."

The Russian held his arms wide. "I need hug."

"I got it," Mack said, walking over and squeezing the Russian's massive girth.

"I kind of hate you right now," Noah said.

"Because we're right?" Del asked.

"Because I'm feeling really obligated to hug the Russian."

"No, you hate us because this is hard work," Mack said, sitting down again.

Noah ground the heels of his hands into his eyes. "Just tell me what to do."

The group spoke in annoyed unison. "Read the book."

"Okay, but how the hell is this book supposed to help me? It's about a guy who abandoned his daughter, which is not someone I want to learn any fucking lessons from right now."

Malcolm got that *teacher about to drop some wisdom* look about him. "How do you think this book ends, Noah?"

"It's a romance. I would assume they end up together and live happily ever after."

Malcolm nodded. "Exactly. All romances end that way. Even though readers know the minute they pick up romances how they're going to end, they still read them loyally. Why do you suppose that is?"

"The sex?"

Colton slapped the table again. "No. Wrong answer."

"It's the journey," Malcolm said. "It's how they get to that happily ever after that matters and makes these books so special and instructive."

"The journey," Noah repeated.

"There is no more universal story than of two people working through their shit to overcome huge obstacles and find their way to happiness," Malcolm said. "But every journey is different, every obstacle unique. And it's in that unique journey that we find lessons for our own lives."

"Can't you just give me a cheat sheet?" He was only half joking.

"Not if you want this to really work," Mack said somberly.

"Just keep reading," Malcolm said. "Your journey starts now."

CHAPTER THIRTEEN

The drive from the hospital to the Vanderpool house took only twenty minutes, but Alexis felt every second of the drive like a nervous first-timer on a roller coaster. Every mile brought her closer and closer to the drop-off. And when she finally pulled into the driveway, her stomach plummeted in a free fall of fear, gravity, and the inevitable tug of *what have I done?*

Why hadn't she brought Noah for this? The thought of meeting these people, her father, alone seemed wise before, but now she wished he was next to her. Telling her she could do this. That everything would be okay.

The two-story Federal-style house sat an acre back from the road on a manicured lawn of lush green grass under a canopy of soaring oak trees. Meticulously maintained window boxes of geraniums in vibrant shades of red, pink, and orange popped against white shutters, and an American flag lifted and waved in the soft breeze from its anchor on a porch column. The only thing missing was a white picket fence, and it could have been a spread in a magazine.

All of the other things she was feeling—fear, regret, longing—were replaced with something that was becoming as familiar as it was unwelcome. *Resentment*. This house was straight out of her mother's dreams. Quiet. Statuesque. Safe. But she'd had to work two jobs just to save enough for the down payment on their tiny house in Nashville.

This was the kind of home that required money and job security and a support network. The things her mother never had.

This was a family home, the kind that boasted stability, prosperity, security. This was the kind of house where a mom never had to worry about how to feed her child, where you could get a puppy because you could afford it, where medications were never rationed, where birthday parties had clowns and big cakes and bouquets of balloons.

Alexis parked behind a shiny BMW sedan and a Range Rover SUV. A black Mercedes was parked in the garage alongside a bright red Lexus.

She quickly texted Candi that she was here. Candi responded to wait on the porch. Which was an odd request, but maybe because Elliott was sick they were trying to be quiet or something.

Didn't matter. Alexis just wanted to get this over with and go home. It wasn't until she climbed the porch steps that the sense of stomach-plummeting fear gripped her again. She was about to meet her father.

Her father.

The front door opened, and Candi stepped out, pulling the door behind her. She swallowed nervously. "Hey."

"Hi." Alexis looked beyond Candi's shoulder to the door. "Is something wrong?"

Candi did the nervous swallow again. "No. I just, I wanted to greet you by myself before we go in."

"Oh."

"Everyone is here. Mom and Dad; my brother, Cayden; and his wife and their kids." Candi bit her lip. "*Our* brother, I mean. I keep messing that up."

"It's okay." She gestured toward the front door. "Should we . . . ?"

Candi opened the door and waited for Alexis to walk in. The sound of muted laughter from somewhere in the back of the house greeted them as Alexis did a slow turn in an entryway that was bigger than her kitchen. The foyer stretched at least fourteen feet to the ceiling and boasted a massive crystal chandelier.

Candi pointed down a long hallway that ended in a kitchen. "They're in the sunroom."

Alexis followed Candi down the wide hallway lined with built-in bookshelves and bracketed on each end with elaborately molded archways. It led into a chef's kitchen with an eight-foot island down the middle and a view of a sloping backyard and in-ground pool.

Off to the side, partitioned from the kitchen by a wall of windows, was the sunroom.

Alexis stopped short, her hip colliding painfully with the edge of the island.

There were six of them. An elegantly dressed woman sat on one end of a couch gazing lovingly down at an infant and a toddler playing on the floor. A youngish man sat next to her. He had hair like Candi's and a big smile. On the floor, a woman fussed with the baby's clothes. And watching them all from a leather recliner, a proud glint in his eye, was Elliott.

His hair was grayer than not, and his skin had a dull, weathered look. Alexis would've thought it was from too much time in the sun, but she knew that particular look. It was the look of illness. But his smile was the same one from the wedding announcement—broad and full of life. He looked like a man who laughed a lot.

Alexis spun around, her chest tight. "I don't think I can do this."

But before she could escape, which was entirely her plan, the older woman called out from sunroom.

"Who was at the door, Candi?"

Alexis met Candi's eyes. A guilty shadow in hers brought a red filter of anger to Alexis's. "What is she talking about?"

Candi didn't answer. Not directly anyway. She smiled at something or someone over Alexis's shoulder. "I brought a friend to meet you, Mom."

"A *friend*?" Alexis whispered.

"Well, bring her on in," the woman said.

The snap of the recliner sent the air out of Alexis's lungs in a single, panicked exhale. How the hell was she going to get out of this now? She squeezed her eyes shut against the next sound—footsteps.

"Welcome," the man said in a gentle voice.

There was no way out of this. Alexis turned around—and found herself once again staring into eyes exactly like hers. He wore a gray sweater that was probably once a perfect fit, but illness had made the shoulders droop and the hem hang long. He extended his hand. "I'm Elliott."

Alexis looked disbelievingly at Candi. "Are you kidding me?" she hissed. "You didn't tell them I was coming?"

Elliott lowered his hand, confusion tugging his eyebrows together.

Candi finally found her voice. "Dad, this is . . . this is Alexis."

Elliott offered his hand again. "Nice to meet you, Alexis. Candi so rarely brings anyone over anymore now that she has moved—"

Alexis cut him off. "Alexis *Carlisle*. That's my name."

Elliott blinked several times, staring at her with a sudden intensity that made her squirm and want to laugh at the same time. Then his Adam's apple bobbed with a nervous swallow, and she decided to go all in.

"I believe you knew my mother, Sherry."

Elliott pulled his hand away and turned a hard eye toward Candi. "What did you do?" he asked in a fierce whisper.

"I had to, Dad." Candi's voice cracked.

The tension from the kitchen must have drifted into the sunroom, because the older woman stood up. "Is everything okay?"

Elliott turned around. "Everything's fine."

No one bought his reassurance. One by one, Lauren, Cayden, and his wife—whatever her name was—all turned their attention to Alexis and stared.

Candi started to answer in shaky word fragments. "She could be a match, Dad. For a kidney."

Lauren gasped and surged forward. "What? Oh my gosh. Candi, this is your friend? Why do you think she could be a match?" Her ballet flats made delicate tap-tap sounds on the hardwood floor as she walked into the kitchen.

Cayden and his wife picked up on the excitement. Each came rushing forward with a child on their arm and matching expressions of hope on their faces. Alexis groaned and looked at Candi, whose skin had gone unnaturally pale.

"I know you didn't want me to contact her, Dad, but—"

"Why wouldn't you want Candi to contact her?" Lauren asked, her joy from just moments ago now replaced with confusion. "What is going on?"

Tears formed in Candi's eyes. *Oh, brother.* Alexis held up her hands. "Okay, listen. Maybe we should save this for another time."

Elliott schooled his features into something reasonable, something deceptive, as he faced his wife. "Probably a good idea. We don't want to get too excited. I doubt some random friend of Candi's is a match."

Some random friend? His words ricocheted through Alexis like an errant pinball, bouncing off vital organs and shredding what was left of the wall around her heart. The crack became a chasm, and it quickly filled in with a feeling she thought she'd buried through therapy and time. A feeling she'd never hoped to feel again after she exposed Royce. It was a desire to hurt someone the way they'd hurt her.

"Oh, I don't know, Elliott," she breathed, regretting the words she hadn't even yet spoken but unable to do anything to hold them back. "From what I've heard, your children are often the best match."

"Excuse me?" Cayden said, his gaze darting back and forth between Alexis and his father.

"What is she talking about, Elliott?" Lauren asked.

"Dad, please, let me explain." That was Candi.

Cayden exploded this time. "What the hell is going on here?"

Alexis looked to Candi for help, but she was staring at Elliott, who was too busy looking guilty as fuck to be of any use.

"Seriously?" Alexis finally blurted at Candi. "You're going to make me do this?"

"I—" Candi could barely get a word out.

Oh, for God's sake. Alexis tossed her hands in the air. "Congratulations, it's a girl."

The sarcasm missed its mark. They stared in silence, except for Elliott, who was boring a hole in the floor with his averted eyes.

Alexis sighed and groaned at the same time. "I'm his daughter," she said. "Surprise."

She could have tossed a grenade in the middle of the room, and it wouldn't have done as much damage as her words. There were shouts and hands covering mouths and some swearing, and oops, some tears from Elliott's wife.

"What is she talking about?" Lauren screeched. "Your *daughter*?"

Cayden handed the crying baby to his wife but kept his glare firmly on Alexis. "This is bullshit. I don't know who you think you are—"

"She's our sister," Candi said. "I have the DNA to prove it."

Cayden turned his anger on Elliott. "Is this true? She's your *daughter*?"

Lauren let out another sob and whipped around, hands pressed to her mouth.

Elliott finally found his balls and stood up straight. "I didn't want you all to find out this way."

"Oh my God," Cayden breathed. "It's true?"

Another loud sob from Lauren sent Elliott racing to his wife's side. He circled to face her. "Honey, please. Let me explain. It was a long time ago."

"Thirty-one years, to be exact," Alexis quipped.

Lauren's eyes widened as her brain did the inevitable math. "We were together then, Elliott."

"No!" Elliott grabbed his wife's hands. She yanked them back.

"We were . . . It was that summer when we broke up. Lauren, please. Listen to me."

"It was that woman, wasn't it?" Lauren moaned.

The words were a slap across Alexis's face. "*That woman* was my mother, and her name was Sherry Carlisle, and if you don't believe I'm his daughter, just look at my eyes."

Lauren paid no attention to Alexis, her weepy eyes locked on her husband. "She's the one who called you when you came back from San Francisco."

Wait. What? Her mother had called him? Alexis stormed forward. "Did—Did she tell you she was pregnant? Did you fucking know about me?"

Apparently the f-word was too much for Cayden's wife, because she hightailed it from the room with the children.

Cayden brought his rage back to Alexis. "I think you'd better leave."

"No!" Candi cried. "She's a match, Dad. I know she is. She got the blood test today, and—"

"Stop this, Candi," Elliott growled. "It's not a guarantee. And you never should have brought her here without talking to me first."

Lauren covered her whole face with her hands and began to wail.

Elliott faced Alexis. "Cayden's right. I think you need to leave." He leveled his angry stare at Candi. "I'll deal with you later."

Alexis shook her head. "Look, if I'm not wanted here, I have no problem leaving."

She spun on her heel and retraced her steps on shaky legs to the door. Candi raced after her. "Wait. Please stay."

Alexis yanked open the front door and pounded down the porch steps. Candi jogged after her and grabbed her arm.

Alexis whipped around. "What the hell was that, Candi? Your mother didn't even know? How could you do that to me? How could you do that to *them*?"

"I—I was only thinking about—"

"My kidney. Yeah, I get it."

"No. I was only thinking about saving my father's life. Excuse me if I don't know the proper protocol for all this."

Alexis clenched her fists and stomped to her car, digging her keys from her pocket.

"Please don't go," Candi pleaded.

"He obviously doesn't want me . . ." Alexis stopped short in horror as emotion clogged her throat at the slip of the tongue. "He doesn't want my kidney."

"He doesn't know what he's thinking right now. He was just surprised."

Alexis snorted, pulling open her car door.

"Just wait here, okay? Let me go talk to them some more."

Alexis slid into the front seat, and just before she yanked the door shut, she said, "Don't call me again."

CHAPTER FOURTEEN

She drove in a fog. Until anger and resentment and the sting of rejection settled into a blessed numbness. Until oncoming cars on the freeway merged into a single blur. Until the nearly constant buzz of her phone on the floor of the passenger seat became a backdrop to the sound of recriminations in her head.

She should have known better.

She should have listened to Noah.

She pictured him in his house, standing in his kitchen with a bowl of whatever he'd heated up for dinner in his hand, shoveling it in as quickly as he could so he could get back to work. Or maybe he was reclined on his couch, legs stretched out and crossed at the ankles as he watched a documentary on TV. Or maybe he was at his computer, glasses on his face and his hair standing at wild angles because he'd dragged his hands through the strands too many times.

She'd seen him do all those things. His mannerisms were as familiar to her as her own.

And suddenly all she wanted was him.

It was six o'clock by the time she got off the freeway at the exit that would take her to his house, a two-story Craftsman that looked modest on the outside but was completely remodeled and modernized on the inside. Noah had installed solar panels along the roof, all new electricity and energy-efficiency stuff, and a bunch of other things he'd tried to explain to her once but she didn't and would never understand.

Floodlights illuminated the shadowed driveway when she pulled in. She'd barely turned the car off before the front door opened. Noah came out barefoot in a pair of jeans and a faded MIT sweatshirt. Every emotion she'd been smothering for the two-hour drive returned in a flood as she slid out of her car.

"Hey," he said, jogging down his porch steps. "I've been trying to reach you. Is your phone dead? What happened?"

Alexis shut her door, met him halfway on the sidewalk, and threw her arms around his waist. He immediately wrapped her tightly in his arms and held her against his chest. "What happened? What's wrong?"

Alexis pressed her cheek to his warm breastbone, the sound of his heartbeat a reassuring cadence.

"Talk to me," he said against her hair.

"He . . . He threw me out."

Noah's arms stiffened. "He what?"

Alexis pulled away from him and looked up. "He told me to leave. He doesn't want me or my kidney."

Noah's face hardened into something that should have been intimidating but was instead thrilling in its protectiveness. "I should have been with you."

"I'm glad you weren't. It was too humiliating."

Noah took her hand and pulled her up the sidewalk. "Come inside."

"What were you doing?" she asked, following him back up the porch steps. "Am I interrupting anything?"

"Just my panicked pacing because you weren't texting me back. I thought you'd gotten in a car accident."

She laughed quietly, but he turned around at the front door.

"I'm not kidding. I was about ten minutes away from calling hospitals along the freeway."

"I'm sorry. I . . . I was—"

"It's okay. I'm just glad you're here."

He held open the door for her to walk in first. His house was warm and smelled like pizza. Her stomach growled instinctively.

"When was the last time you ate something?"

"I don't know."

He nodded toward the kitchen as he shut the door. "There's some left. I didn't order any meat in case you wanted some."

The gesture brought a flurry of butterflies to her stomach and made her heart do the *thud-thud* thing again. "Thank you."

"What did I tell you about thanking me too much?"

"Would you rather I take you for granted?"

"I'd rather you get it through your head that I'm here for you, no matter what."

Alexis toed off her flats and left them by the front door. His house was a standard layout for a Craftsman style. The entryway opened into a long hallway with rooms on either side and a staircase off to the right. There were three bedrooms upstairs, one of which he used as a home office.

The hallway ended in the kitchen, which led to a small dining area where she'd shared countless dinners with him over the past year. The brown place mats she'd crocheted for him during a brief attempt at the craft were piled in the center of the table, unused and mostly unusable. But he'd kept them anyway.

"Sit," he said, nodding toward the table. "You want something to drink?"

"Whatever you're having."

He stuck a couple of slices of pizza in the microwave and then pulled two pumpkin ales from the fridge. The sleeves of his T-shirt stretched over the bulge of his biceps as he twisted the top off each bottle. Heat raced up her neck as her mind immediately returned to the image of him without a shirt.

She scarfed down the soggy reheated pizza as she filled him in on what had happened. With every new revelation, his expression alternated between rage and sympathy.

"I should have listened to you," she said.

Noah lowered his bottle to the table. "Don't do that."

"But you were right."

"I could have just as easily been wrong. You had to see it for yourself."

"You're a better judge of character than me."

"No, I'm not. I'm a cynical asshole who thinks everyone has an agenda, and you're a goddamned ray of sunshine who automatically assumes the best intentions."

Alexis laughed. "A goddamned ray of sunshine?"

He gave her a half-hearted smile. "All this wedding stuff is starting to rub off on me."

"Anyway," she breathed, leaning back in her chair. "I guess that's that. I get to keep my organs, after all."

Noah carried her plate to the sink, rinsed it off, and loaded it in the dishwasher.

"Thanks for feeding me."

"What are friends for?" He returned to the table and held out his hand. "Let's start a fire outside."

She folded her fingers in his and let him pull her to her feet. But as she followed him outside, the fire she was most concerned with was the one that had ignited inside her.

After lighting the fire in the firepit, Noah went back inside for two fresh beers and a blanket. He returned, handed her one of the beers, and then sat down next to her on the cushioned patio sectional that she'd helped him pick out last spring. It cut a ninety-degree angle around the corner of the covered patio where she'd helped him hang string lights and decorate with a row of hanging baskets. The flowers had long since died, but the baskets were still there.

How many nights had she sat here just like this with him? And why now, all of a sudden, did the space seem smaller, more intimate? Her hands shook as she spread the blanket over their laps, and when he slung an arm over the back of the couch, her lungs stopped working at the innocent brush of his fingertips against the nape of her neck.

If he was equally affected, it didn't show. He stared quietly into the flames, his face cutting a hard angle in the dancing, flickering shadows as he raised the bottle to his mouth. The strong, long lines of his throat worked against a swallow.

He looked over. "Talk to me."

He'd said those same words to her countless times, but tonight, she understood the simple gift of them. He never prodded, never pushed. He was just there, willing to listen, always. Expecting nothing in return.

"About what?" she asked, breathless.

"About whatever has you staring at me so hard."

Yeah, that wasn't going to happen. How was she supposed to tell her best friend that she was suddenly overcome with a need to kiss him?

Alexis tore her gaze to the fire. "He didn't . . . He didn't even ask about her."

His fingers brushed her neck again. "Your mom?"

"To not even . . . to not even *acknowledge* her as anything more than just some woman he'd had a summer fling with." A tear stung the corner of her eye. "She deserved better than that."

"You both deserved better."

"I'm not sure he even cared about her."

"Would it matter if he had?"

"I don't know. Maybe."

Noah set his beer on a table next to the couch and shifted in his seat so he could face her more directly. Under the blanket, Alexis curled one leg under her to make room for him.

"Why does it matter?"

The tear swelled and blurred her vision. "Because she deserved to be loved."

"*You* loved her."

"I know, but it's not the same. She deserved a true love."

"Tell me about her," he said, voice tight.

Alexis leaned her head against his arm. "She loved squirrels. Other people would try to keep squirrels off their bird feeders, but her bird feeders were for the squirrels."

"Sounds like someone else I know."

"She loved Fleetwood Mac. And Stephen King novels. She let me read *It* when I was in middle school, and I didn't sleep for a year."

Noah smiled. "Is that why you hate clowns?"

Pain struck her in the chest. "No."

He didn't prod. Just waited for her to explain.

"I wanted a clown for my birthday party one year. We couldn't . . . We couldn't afford it. So my mom dressed up like one for me."

"Why did that make you hate them?"

"I don't know. I think maybe because even as a kid, I knew it was wrong. That she felt bad about it. Like she had failed me somehow. And that wasn't fair to her. I wish I'd never asked for it."

The burn of resentment that she'd felt at Elliott's house once again scorched her throat. "I bet Candi had clowns at her birthday parties. I bet Lauren didn't have to pick up extra shifts to pay for it either."

"It's unfair. All of it."

Alexis sat up and took a drink of her beer. "You know what's really unfair? I remember that the doctor was wearing a red tie the day we found out my mom had cancer. But I can't remember what *she* wore that day. I don't want to remember his tie."

Noah let out a pained breath and leaned toward her. "Honey—"

"Memories are unfair, you know? They don't tell us until it's too late that this one, this detail, is the thing you need to hang on to. Why do we remember the weird little stuff but not the big things?"

Noah shook his head. "I don't know."

"My mom . . . she told me once that the hardest part about being a parent is that you never know when it's going to be the last time you do something for your child. The last time you will wash their hair. Fix their lunch for school. Help them tie their shoes. It's true as a child, too, though. When you watch your parent die. No one tells you this, warns you. That you need to hang on to every detail because it could be the last time you go to a movie together or go shopping together. I remember our last Christmas together but not what she said when she opened my presents to her. Why can't I remember those things? I want to remember so badly."

"Come here." Noah opened his arms to her, and she went into them willingly. It was an awkward embrace, hindered by the way they sat and the tangle of the blanket around their legs, but it was perfect. He was perfect.

"I learned to pretend when she was sick," Alexis said. "That it wasn't really happening. You know? Maybe if I just went on with life, just acted like everything was normal, that she wasn't dying, then maybe she wouldn't. But then she just got worse and worse, and then came this day and I knew it was over. And I just kept rubbing her hand and saying it was okay. She could go. I'd be okay. I'd be just fine when she was gone. But I'm not fine."

"I'm sorry," he said against her hair, one hand cupping the back of her head to hold her against his shoulder. "For all of it."

"I feel selfish. Making it all about me."

"Grief doesn't make you selfish, Lexa." His mouth was on her hair. "Does it make me selfish that I wanted to tear down the entire U.S. government to get back at them for taking my father away?"

"You were a child. I'm an adult."

"So am I, and I still hate them for it. So if you're selfish for being pissed off at Elliott fucking Vanderpool, then so am I. And so what? We both lost our parents when we were far too young."

"You know what I used to hate?"

He nuzzled her hair with his lips. "Hmmm?"

"Navigating other people's emotions about *my* mother's death. People either have no idea what to say, or they think they do and end up saying something entirely stupid and you feel sorry for them, so you say something to cover for them. It's exhausting."

He laughed, but there was no joy in it. Only understanding. "After my dad died, I got to a point where I thought I would punch the next person who tried to tell me how sorry they were."

"Or ask if there is anything they can do."

"Everything happens for a reason . . ."

She groaned. "They're *here for you*."

"You're so strong."

"As if there is any alternative but to just keep getting up every day and going about your life."

"Exactly."

She sucked in a shuddered breath and squeezed her eyes shut. "I don't think I could do this without you."

"I promise you won't have to find out." He lowered his mouth to her ear. "You don't have to be so strong all the time, Lexa. Not with me."

Alexis pressed her face into his neck and breathed in. He smelled like his laundry detergent, and it wasn't until this moment that she realized it was her favorite scent. It smelled like safety and security.

And desire. Hot, burning need. For him and him alone. And she was sick and tired of fighting it.

The first brush of her lips against Noah's throat felt like an accident. A mere coincidence as she moved in his arms to get more comfortable.

But then it happened again.

He stopped breathing as her lips touched the pounding pulse in his throat and lingered there, hot and soft. And even then, Noah might have convinced himself it wasn't intentional if she didn't splay her fingers wide across his chest. If she didn't nuzzle his jaw with her nose. And if she didn't lift her head and whisper his name in a voice laced with a tone he'd know anywhere but had never heard from her.

Desire.

Everything inside him burst into a flurry of frenzied activity—heart pounded, blood raced, stomach clenched—but then it all froze in the next breath. He wanted to move, to say something, but couldn't because he was afraid to break the spell. If he so much as blinked, she might disappear. Or he'd wake up and realize the past thirty minutes had been a dream, that he'd just fallen asleep on the couch after reading that damn book. He'd had dreams of her like this before and awakened disappointed many times.

But it couldn't be a dream, because his sleepy imagination had never captured the pure sweetness of the way she was touching him now.

"Lexa," he rasped.

The tip of her nose brushed his in response. And even though they were now so close that her features blurred in his vision, he didn't need to see clearly to understand what was happening. His senses chronicled the moment by touch, by sound, by smell.

Her trembling fingers as they slid down the front of his shirt.

Her labored breaths as their mouths inched closer.

Her heated cinnamon scent as he breathed her in.

Warnings sounded in the back of his mind. *Go slow. She's vulnerable. Once you cross this bridge, you can't go back.* But even the most noble man would struggle to listen when the woman who held his entire heart was finally opening her own.

There were so few times in life when a man was faced with a decision of such stark consequences, but this was one of them. This was the moment when Noah had to choose.

Desire or restraint.

Passion or friendship.

Lexa or loneliness.

His brain knew the right answers, but his brain wasn't in charge. His heart was. With Alexis, it always would be.

So it was his heart that pulled her to straddle his lap. His heart that wove his fingers in her hair. And when her lips nudged his—once, twice, not so much a kiss as a question—it was his heart that answered.

At long last, *yes*.

He molded his lips to hers, and every doubt evaporated into a certainty that this is what they had been moving toward all along.

Alexis sank into him and let him take the lead. His lips nibbled and massaged, cherished and explored. She kissed him like he'd known she would. Tenderly, passionately. One hot hand pressed against his back while the other clung to his bicep. When he changed the angle and went deeper, when his tongue swept inside her mouth, he heard a moan and realized belatedly it had come from him. Suddenly, she slipped her hand inside the front of his T-shirt. The next moan he heard was hers, and a thrill raced through him as she rasped his name, as if the mere acting of touching him was enough to drive her senseless. It was for him. Her fingers crept higher and higher until she spread them wide across his hardened nipple.

Oh, God. He shuddered, groaned, whispered urgently for her to do it again.

So she did.

In the next instant, he rolled her onto her back.

That's all it took. The touch of her fingers against his nipples, and suddenly he was a man possessed. He dove deeper into her mouth and settled between her thighs. She tangled with him, opened for him, wrapped one leg around him.

Alexis let out another one of those moans that sent a surge of lust to his groin, and his body acted of its own accord. He tilted his hips, ground into her, and she gasped in his mouth, so he did it again. And again. And again. She lifted both her legs and wrapped them around his waist. Scorching heat and sweet tenderness blended in his chest, filling his lungs with a dizzying cocktail as she arched against him, panting and moaning for him to touch her.

So he did.

He slid his hand along her side until his fingers brushed the swell of her breast.

"Noah," she breathed, tilting her head back. Then she tangled her fingers in his hair and dragged his mouth back to hers.

He could have kissed her forever. Languidly. Passionately. Any way she wanted. But when her fingers left his hair and began to fumble with the button of his jeans, the voice of reason began to walk around banging pots and pans in his brain, like a morning wake-up call that drowned out the urgent beat of his heart and the throbbing swell in his pants.

Forever screeched to a painful, remorseful halt.

What. The Fuck. Was he doing?

He couldn't . . . *They* couldn't. Not now. Not like this. Not yet.

With a strength he didn't know he possessed, Noah wrenched his mouth from hers, rose above her on all fours, and squeezed his eyes shut. "Honey, wait."

Suddenly, it was over.

One moment she was working the button of his jeans, desperate to touch him and feel him inside her. And in the next, he let out an agonized noise and told her to stop.

Her whole body went cold at the sight of his closed eyes. "Wh- What's wrong?"

Noah straightened and sat back on his haunches. He covered his face with his hands. "This . . . We can't."

"Why not? What's wrong?"

Noah turned and sank against the other arm of the couch. With a tortured noise, he dropped his head and breathed in and out through his nose as if trying not to puke.

The final, lingering hum of desire evaporated like the last puff of mist from her essential oils diffuser. He . . . *He was rejecting her.* Oh, God. What had she done? Alexis scooted to sit up and brushed her wild hair from her face. Noah opened his eyes and looked up with an expression that could only be described as abject horror. As if he'd just woken up from a blackout to find a stranger naked in bed with him.

She was the naked stranger.

Naked and exposed and totally, one hundred percent regretted.

Alexis tried to scramble off the couch but got caught in the blanket and only managed to roll onto the floor. She fell ungracefully on her knees.

Noah shot up straight. "Are you okay?"

Alexis scrambled to her feet. "I'm sorry."

"Lexa, what are you doing?"

"I'm sorry. I—I shouldn't have . . ." She turned away from him—from that look on his face—and walked as fast as she could without full-out running.

Behind her, Noah stood so quickly that a bottle fell over and began to *glub-glub-glub* its contents onto the floor. "Lexa, wait."

She felt sick. Alexis wrenched open the back door. "I'm sorry. I'm so sorry. I have to go."

Noah managed to grab her hand and tug her back. "Don't. Not like this. Alexis, please. Listen to me. This isn't—"

She yanked free and began to run through the house so she wouldn't have to hear the end of that sentence. *Isn't what you think. Isn't what you want. Isn't what I want.*

Noah chased after her. Through the hallway. Out the door. Down the porch steps. Pleading the entire way for her to stop. "Alexis, wait."

"I have to go. I'm sorry, Noah. I shouldn't have done this." She got in her car and started it without looking at him. Seconds later, she left him standing in the driveway, hands stacked on top of his head.

She made it all of two blocks before her phone rang on the passenger seat.

It was two a.m. before the ringing finally stopped.

CHAPTER FIFTEEN

"Wow. Are you okay?"

Alexis averted her gaze from Jessica's when she walked into the café the next morning a half hour late. She set down Beefcake's cat carrier, let him out, and then hung up her coat. "Fine."

"You look like you've been crying."

"Allergies," Alexis lied.

Because, yes, she'd been crying. She'd cried all night. Big, fat sobs into her pillow and sometimes her cat. It probably wasn't fair to ignore Noah's calls and texts, but fairness wasn't going to wash away the dark stain of shame and humiliation that colored every memory of last night in her mind. And did it even matter what he said? She'd thrown herself at him, and he'd rejected her. Just like she'd feared he would. She couldn't talk to him. Couldn't face him. No matter what he said, the truth had been written all over his face when he pulled away from her last night.

He'd been horrified. There was no other word for it.

Maybe that's what stung the worst. He'd looked suddenly like a stranger to *her*.

Jessica hovered nearby as Alexis grabbed her apron and looped it over her head. "Are you sure—"

"I'm fine, Jessica. Let's just go to work."

Jessica reacted as if Alexis had yelled at her.

"I'm sorry," Alexis said, reaching over to squeeze her arm. "I'm not fine, to be honest, but I can't talk about it right now. Okay?"

Jessica nodded, her features relaxing again. "I'm here if you need to, though."

"I appreciate it."

Alexis wished she'd thought to grab a ball cap to wear today. Maybe it would shade the worst of her dark circles and red eyes.

Jessica gave her one last look before nodding and heading out of the kitchen. Alexis tried to lose herself in the routine of opening the café, but just when she'd finally settled in, Jessica walked back in. "There's someone here to see you."

Alexis's head snapped up. "Noah?"

Her tone managed to convey both hope and dread, a combination that sent Jessica's eyebrows up.

"No. It's some old guy."

That could be anyone over the age of thirty. Jessica's gauge for what was old was a lot different than Alexis's.

"I lied and told him you wouldn't be in until ten," Jessica said. "He said he'd just wait."

Alexis pushed open the kitchen door and followed Jessica's point to the tables outside. Her breath lodged in her throat.

Elliott.

He sat on a bench in front of the café, leaning forward with his hands clasped between his knees, staring at the small fountain that decorated the middle of the sidewalk welcoming visitors to East Nashville. The sunrise glinted off the gold band on his left hand and turned the gray in his hair into white sprinkles.

"I'm sorry," Jessica said. "I tried to get rid of him. I know you're probably not up for talking to anyone."

"It's okay. I'll take care of it."

"It's not another reporter, is it?" Jessica worried her bottom lip.

"No," Alexis said. "It's my father."

"*What?*"

But Alexis had already started to walk away. Her footsteps echoed on the floor of the empty café. Taking a deep breath, she opened the door. The jingle of the bell drew his head up. His lips parted, but no words came out.

She stopped in front of him. "Hello, *Dad*."

"I—" He cleared his throat.

Alexis couldn't help herself. She cocked an eyebrow. "It's Alexis. Did you forget already?"

He let out a loud breath and ran his fingers through his hair. "I'm sorry. I just—you look so much like your mother. It . . . It catches me off guard."

"Wow, and to think the last time we met, you threw me out."

"I'm sorry. It was just such a surprise. Candi didn't give us any warning about you. I—"

Alexis waved her hands to ward off anymore of his bullshit. "What are you doing here?"

"I was hoping we could talk."

"Gee, hard to believe there's much left to be said after yesterday."

"There is. A lot." He stood. Slowly. "Can we . . . Can we go somewhere?"

"I'm pretty busy right now. I have a business to run."

"Please, Alexis."

The pleading tone of his voice reminded her too much of how Noah sounded last night as he chased her down the sidewalk. Noah's voice had broken a part of her. Elliott's was close to finishing her off.

"I don't owe you anything. Not my time. Not my kidney. Not my compassion." The harsh words felt like pure cayenne pepper on her tongue.

"I know that."

Alexis turned around to look through the café windows. Jessica wasn't even bothering to hide the fact that she was staring. She was surprised Jessica hadn't pulled out a bucket of popcorn. There was no way they'd get any privacy in there, but Alexis was too damn tired to even think of going somewhere else. And it was too damn cold to talk outside.

"We can talk in my office."

His features melted in relief. "Thank you."

The bell jingled again as Alexis opened the door. He reached over her head to hold it open for her, the kind of casually polite thing that older men did for women, and it made her skin crawl. Alexis darted inside, her footsteps clipped and frantic on the tiled floor. His were soft and resigned behind her. Avoiding Jessica's gaze, she pushed open the swinging door to the kitchen and office area.

Her office was the size of a closet, and she regretted inviting him in as soon as he sat down across from her desk. She would have preferred the lack of privacy in the dining area over the claustrophobic sensation of being in a room alone with the man who'd just yesterday acted like she was about as welcome in his life as a stomach bug.

He rubbed his hands on his jeans. "Your café is really nice."

"Thank you." Her tone was more like *Fuck you*, and she wished not for the first time in her life that she had more of the fire of Liv.

"You've been open a year?"

"Almost two."

"The cat thing . . ."

She raised his eyebrows at his pause.

"So you . . . you bring in rescue kittens for adoption?"

"I like finding homes for abandoned creatures."

He smiled in a sad sort of way. Like he caught her meaning and understood he deserved it. Sadly, it didn't give her the satisfaction she'd hoped for. Excessive empathy was her personal cross to bear.

"Look," she said, taking mercy on him because this was painful. "Let's just stop with this small-talk crap, okay? I assume you're here because you realized at some point last night that you'd just let a perfectly good kidney go walking out the door. Let's just focus on that."

That seemed to shake him out of his stupor. "That's not why I'm here."

"If you expect me to believe you drove two hours at the crack of dawn just to get to know me, then you're an idiot."

"I drove two hours to apologize."

"Yeah, don't believe that either."

"Either way, thank you for agreeing to talk to me."

"Can't have your death on my conscience. I have enough to feel guilty about in my life."

"If you're talking about that situation with Royce Preston, you have nothing to feel guilty about with that."

Alexis snorted. "Thanks, *Dad*."

Jessica suddenly knocked and poked her head in. "I, um,

brought you guys some water." Her eyes darted to Elliott with unmasked curiosity. "Can I get you anything else?"

Alexis was dying for her daily chai latte, but her stomach was already nearing a revolt from an overdose of suppressed rage and betrayal. Caffeine would simply send her darting for the bathroom. "The water is fine. Thank you."

Jessica set both bottles on the desk, took another quick glance at Elliott, and then backed out.

Elliott twisted off the top of his bottle and took a long drink with an aggressiveness that suggested he wished for something stronger.

His fingers tightened on his water bottle. "I think it's really great what you're doing here, opening up your café for other survivors."

Alexis crossed her arms over her chest. "The transplant team gave me a bunch of information yesterday about how this all works. I haven't had a chance to absorb it all yet, but we should find out soon if I'm an initial match."

He held up a hand. "Please. I really don't care about that right now."

"Well, I really don't want to talk to you about anything else." She stood. "So you just wasted a trip. Do I need to walk you out or—"

"Just wait. I have things I need to tell you. Things I need you to understand about what happened back then between your mother and me."

The words *your mother* sliced through her. "Is this the part where you feed me some bullshit story about how you cared about my mom and never forgot her and—"

"I did. And I didn't."

Alexis rolled her eyes. Yet she stood there. Silently begging him to say more. Wishing it could possibly be true. That her mom hadn't just been *that woman*, because dear God, what would that make *her*?

Elliott must have sensed her weakening because he surged forward. "I need you to know she wasn't just some summer fling back then."

"Really? Because it sounded like you were just on a brief break from your wife."

"It's true. When I met her, I—" He squirmed as if this was embarrassing to talk about. And it was. Alexis wanted him to shut up more than she'd ever wanted anything.

"When I met your mom," he started again, "I was in a weird place in my life. Lauren and I had been together for four years, but she broke up with me just before I moved to San Francisco for a summer internship. She was pressing to get married, and I wasn't ready yet."

Alexis almost felt sorry for Lauren. Almost.

"Your mom was . . ." He exhaled with a nostalgic smile that Alexis might have found endearing if it wasn't obvious bullshit.

"I fell hard for her," Elliott said. "I cared about her."

Alexis snorted. "Oh, please."

"It's true. She was vibrant and funny and—"

"I get it. She was the manic pixie dream girl to your stuffed suit, and your feelings for her caught you entirely by surprise and made you question everything you thought you wanted out of life."

"Yes," he breathed without a hint of irony.

"So why did you leave her?" The question was out before she could stop it. She didn't want him to think she cared, that his abandonment meant anything or mattered.

"I had to go back to Pasadena. The summer was over."

"Why did she call you? Was it to tell you that she was pregnant?"

"No. I swear."

"Then why?"

"She wanted to know if it was true that I . . . had a girlfriend. When I told her I did, she said she never wanted to talk to me again." He leaned forward, a beseeching look in his eyes. "Alexis, please, you have to believe me. If I'd known about you, I would have—"

"What? Married her instead of Lauren? Or maybe you would have married Lauren and just sent me money and birthday cards?"

"I don't know. I don't know what I would've done, but I would not have just abandoned you."

His words mattered more than they should have, which meant they hurt more than they should have. And *that* meant she was careening toward a dangerous waterfall, the kind where she would open her mouth and let words spill out until she slipped over the edge. But he wasn't worth the emotional risk. Not after yesterday. She'd tested the waters—first by agreeing to meet the Vanderpools and then when she threw herself at Noah—and look at how both of those turned out.

"It doesn't matter now," she finally said, forcing her voice into a calm, steady cadence, the one she used with Karen. "It was a long time ago. I survived without you then, and I will survive without you again. This is a transaction. Nothing more. And once it's over, you can go back to your life and I'll go back to mine. Deal?"

A pained expression tightened his features. "What do I have to do to prove how sorry I am, Alexis? Just tell me, and I'll do it."

Alexis shook her head, tried to say the safe thing, which was nothing at all. But when she opened her mouth, a question came out. "If you found out about me three years ago, why didn't you reach out then?"

A tall shadow darkened the doorway. "Because he didn't need your kidney then."

CHAPTER SIXTEEN

Noah couldn't believe it. What the hell was that asshole doing here?

Elliott maintained an expressionless calm and extended his hand. "Elliott Vanderpool. You are?"

"The man who is going to throw your ass out of here."

Alexis splayed her hand in the center of his chest. "Noah, don't."

He looked down at her and cataloged her appearance. Puffy red eyes. Dark circles. He wanted to believe the cause of her suffering was the man sitting in her office, but Noah wasn't stupid. He was equally responsible, and it gutted him.

Elliott slowly stood. "Is this—are you her boyfriend?"

At that, Alexis made an indecipherable noise that caused a small eruption in his heart.

"It doesn't matter who I am. Stay away from her."

Elliott looked at Alexis. "It's not true. I'm not here because I need a kidney. I'm here because I *am* your father—"

Noah's hands curled into fists. "You dare to call yourself that after you threw her out of your house?"

Elliott raised his hands in a truce. "I came to apologize for that."

There was a lot of that going around today. "You need to leave."

"Noah," Alexis sighed, hand pressing into his chest. "Can you wait outside?"

He locked eyes with her. Beneath the naked pain was a detachment that scared him even more than when she'd driven away from him yesterday. More than the agonizing hours while he waited for her to call him back or respond to a single text. Even with her fingers against his chest, she was removed from him. Yesterday, there'd been nothing but heat in her touch. Today, it was ice-cold.

"It's okay," Elliott said, maybe because he was catching on to the tension between them or maybe because he was a fucking coward. "I was just leaving. I-I've said what I need to say."

Alexis faced the bastard. "Wait." She looked back at Noah. "Can you please wait outside?" This time she pointed, and the dismissal felt like a warning as much as a punishment.

Noah forced his feet to move, and she shut the door behind him. He paused to listen but then felt guilty. She didn't want him in the conversation. He could at least respect her wishes that much. Noah trudged to a tall chair next to one of the stainless-steel counters and sat down. Behind him, the kitchen door swung open, and frantic steps approached. He turned around just in time to see Jessica.

"What's going on?" she whispered.

"Hell if I know," he grumbled.

"Is that really her father?"

"Looks that way."

"Is that why she was crying this morning? Because of him?"

His head snapped up. "She was crying?"

"She tried to tell me it was just allergies. I tried to get her to tell me what's going on, but she wouldn't."

Her office door opened. Noah shot to his feet, and Jessica squeaked and ran.

Alexis came out first, looked at him briefly, and then turned back as Elliott emerged. "I'll let you know as soon as I do," she said.

"Know what?" Noah asked.

She looked at the floor as she answered. "If I'm an initial match."

A blood vessel burst in his brain. "Are you kidding me? You're going through with this?"

Alexis pressed her fingers to her temple. "Stop, Noah."

A buzzing noise in his ears drowned out Elliott's response. Noah watched through hazy eyes as the man said goodbye to Alexis, nodded in Noah's direction, and then shuffled out of the kitchen.

"I'll be right back," Noah said.

Alexis pinched the bridge of her nose. "Noah—"

He followed Elliott out. "You've got some fucking nerve."

Elliott turned around in the center of the café with a blank expression, as if he'd been waiting for exactly this and had been practicing how he'd respond. "Would you like to go somewhere private and talk?"

"No. What I have to say won't take long."

"I can see that you care about Alexis a great deal. And it probably doesn't matter much, but I'm glad she has you to support her during this."

"You're right. It doesn't matter. I don't need your fucking approval."

"No, you don't. And you probably won't believe this, but I care about what happens to her."

Noah snorted.

"Just because I wasn't part of her life until now doesn't mean I don't already think of her as my daughter. I'm sure your father would tell you that . . ."

"He would, if he were alive."

Elliott swallowed. "I'm sorry to hear that."

"Why should you be sorry? You made money off his death."

Elliott shook his head, face paling. "I'm afraid I don't know what you mean."

"You work for a defense contractor. My father died in Iraq when his improperly equipped Humvee ran over an IED."

"I'm sorry. Truly. And not just for your father. For everything Alexis is going through too."

"Really? Then prove it. Stay the fuck away from her."

The kitchen door swung open. "Noah," Alexis said quietly behind him. Her tone turned his name into an admonishment.

"I'm done," he said, stepping back.

Elliott cast one last look at Alexis and then turned away. The bell above the café door was a melancholy soundtrack to his retreat, followed by the ominous return of the thwap of the kitchen door. Alexis had gone back inside. Noah found her waiting for him in her office, standing by her desk.

Noah walked toward her, arms reaching to hold her. "Are you okay?"

Unlike last night, when she'd fallen so willingly into his embrace, she backed away from him. Her arms came around her torso, a protective shield. Her coldness brought a chill to his entire body.

"Lexa—"

"I'm sorry I haven't called you back." She dragged two trembling hands across her weary face. He wanted to pull them away and kiss every worry line. She sucked in a breath and started again. "I needed some time to figure out what to say."

Her blunt honesty, so Alexis, caught him off guard this time. "Then maybe I should talk, because I know exactly what I need to say."

Her head shook in tiny little denials. "I can't do this right now. I'm already behind, and I have a lot to do right now—"

"It can wait."

"It can't."

"Dammit, Lexa, stop talking to me like I'm some random angry customer who needs placating."

She swallowed hard and briefly met his eyes. He'd gone long enough without touching her. Noah closed the distance between them and cradled her face in his hands. "*Talk to me.*"

"This is all my fault, and I'm so sorry."

"Nothing is your fault."

"I shouldn't have kissed you."

Alarm bells began to ring in his head. He let his hands fall away as he backed up.

She looked everywhere but at him. "You were right to put a stop to it. It was a mistake."

No. No, it was not a mistake. It was the most important moment of his life. But he couldn't get those words out, because she hit him with another punch.

"I—I was vulnerable and upset, and I took advantage of you."

"Took advantage of *me*?" He'd been reduced to useless parroting of her ridiculous words.

She nodded, biting her lip again.

LYSSA KAY ADAMS

He shook his head. "Alexis, all I wanted was for us to take a break and talk about what was happening."

"And I'm glad you did, because clearly, we were making a mistake," she said.

He swallowed a groan. "I would give away all my money for you to stop saying that."

"But you obviously regretted it, and—"

"I didn't regret it!"

"I need some space."

He blinked. His brain heard the word, but his heart refused to accept it. "What—What does that mean?"

"It means that I can't think straight right now, and I tend to make really bad decisions when I'm in that kind of headspace, obviously—"

He bristled at the word *obviously*.

"—and I think it would be best if we just—"

"No. Whatever you're about to say, you're wrong. It would not be best."

"I need some time to get centered and figure a few things out."

He wanted to argue because, Christ, he could already feel her drifting away from him like a boat pulling away from the dock. He had to clear his throat to find his voice. "How—How much time?"

"Maybe we can talk this weekend at the bachelorette party."

"This weekend." His voice had gone flat and lifeless, just like he felt. They hadn't gone more than a single night without talking in almost a year. He lost feeling in his knees and sank against the counter behind him. "Alexis, I need you to be clear with me about what's happening here."

The sight of a tear dripping down her cheek made his stomach pitch. "I just need time."

She hugged herself and, with a last glance at him, walked away. He couldn't move as she crossed the kitchen, pushed open the swinging door, and disappeared into the café. Beefcake peeked around the corner from the back room and hissed.

"Yeah, well, fuck you too," Noah grumbled.

He peeled away from the counter, dragged his hands down his face, started toward the back door, and then stopped to turn around. He did it three more times before pounding his fist with an *argh*, throwing open the door, and stomping into the alley. It was another five minutes of indecision before he started his car and pulled out. He wanted to hit something.

Wait. Not something.

Someone.

CHAPTER SEVENTEEN

Noah whipped his car into the lot behind Temple. He grabbed the book from the floor, where it had fallen off the seat during one of his more aggressive turns on the way there. He folded it into one furious hand, slid from the front seat, and slammed his door because he wanted to and it felt good and he needed to warm up for the big show.

The back door was locked, as he knew it would be, so he resorted to pounding with the side of his fist until it finally opened. A kitchen worker he didn't recognize stuck her head out.

Noah shoved his hands in the door and pushed it open.

"Hey!" she yelled, racing after him.

Noah stalked up the dark hallway that led to the back offices. Sonia was just walking in from the other direction. She stopped short. "Whoa, what is wrong with you?"

"Where is he?" Noah growled.

"What?"

"Mack. Where is he?"

"In his office? Why?"

Noah stormed around her and continued until he reached the small cluster of administrative offices on the right. He rounded the corner toward Mack's office just as Mack himself emerged.

He stopped at the sight of Noah and flashed one of his goddamned grins. "Hey, man. I thought you couldn't come with us today."

"I'm not here for the fucking food tasting." Noah hurled the book at him. It struck Mack in the center of his chest and fell to the floor in a pathetic flutter of pages.

Mack looked down slowly and then back up, eyebrow raised. "You didn't like that one?"

His sarcasm turned Noah's rage into something frightening. "Fuck you. Fuck your books. And fuck your crazy, stupid Bromance Book Club bullshit."

Mack bent and picked up the book. "You broke the spine, man."

"Yeah? Well you broke me and Alexis!"

Mack's eyebrows tugged together. "What are you talking about?"

"What the fuck do you think I'm talking about?"

Mack stalked forward. "What did you do?"

Noah spun around. He needed to get out of there.

"Wait, Noah. Hang on a second."

"Fuck off."

Mack ducked around and blocked his path, arms spread wide. Noah backed up, hands clenched, ready to fight. "Get out of my way."

"Just wait, okay?" Mack said. "You came here, so you obviously want help, even if you're not willing to admit it."

And because Mack was right, or maybe because Noah was just a glutton for punishment, Noah actually obeyed.

Which is how, twenty minutes later, he found himself uncomfortably wedged between Colton and the Russian in the back seat of Mack's SUV as it sped down the freeway. From the passenger seat, Malcolm stared back at him with a disappointed expression. Ten minutes later—and really, any longer than that, and Noah would have thrown up in the Russian's lap, because Mack drove like shit—the SUV whipped into the parking lot of a plain brown building with a striped awning and a sign that read PRICKLY PEAR CATERING.

The Russian opened the back door and nearly fell out. "Come, Noah. We have good food and you tell us why you screw up so much."

Noah let out the longest sigh in history and trudged behind the group. A woman in a black apron was waiting for them and led them to a table near an open kitchen.

"You know I don't actually care about any of this, right?" Noah said, dropping like a grumpy teenager into a chair.

"That hurts my feelings," Mack said. "We're making memories."

The woman in the apron returned with a tray of mimosas. Noah ordered water instead.

Mack sighed and waited until the woman walked away before turning his attention to Noah. "We have about ten minutes before they bring the food out. So let's hear it. What the hell did you do?"

"You assume this is all my fault?" Which, of course, it was.

The guys exchanged one of their annoying looks and then burst into laughter. "Of course it's your fault, dumbass," Colton said.

"We need all the details," Malcolm said, "so we can fully understand the situation."

"The details are little fucking personal."

"We understand—"

Noah interrupted Malcolm. "And we're talking about Alexis here, okay? I'm not exactly comfortable talking about her like this."

Mack sighed. "You're part of book club, Noah. Being uncomfortable is part of book club."

"Just get it all out fast, like ripping off a Band-Aid," Malcolm offered.

So, with a deep sigh, Noah rattled off as few specifics as possible. When he was done, silence greeted him.

"Let me make sure I have this straight," Malcolm said after a moment. "She initiated it? As in, she kissed *you* first?"

Noah's chest got warm and tight all at once. "Yes, she kissed me first."

"Did she, like, throw herself at you with, like, arms and legs?" Colton asked.

"Or was it more tender, like a nudging of the mouth?" That was from the Russian, who didn't look like he could possibly even understand the word *tender* much less display it.

Noah looked away. "Tender, I guess. At first." Christ, this was embarrassing. He thought explaining the whole *she looked at my nipple*s thing was humiliating, but this was going to kill him.

Malcolm stroked his beard. "And you stopped her?"

"Not right away. It got kind of . . ." Noah's cheeks ignited.

"Kind of what?" Mack asked, doing his best and failing to keep the *yeah, baby* from his expression. Noah was going to enjoy hitting him soon. Hard.

"It became more than kissing?" Malcolm prodded.

"Jesus, yes."

Colton leaned forward. "Was there nudity involved?"

"*What?*"

"Nudity," the Russian explained. "It means naked."

"I fucking know what nudity means! And no, there was no nakedness."

Malcolm gave the Russian and Colton disapproving looks. "How long did it last?" he asked, returning his attention to Noah.

Forever and not long enough. "A few minutes."

Colton grinned. "So, was it just kissing or did you get some grinding action too?"

Noah flipped him off.

Mack jumped back in. "Just tell us what happened next."

Noah scrubbed a hand over his hair. "She started unbuttoning my jeans. And I panicked, and so I told her we should stop, and the next thing I know, she's running out of the house."

Colton gaped. "Why did you stop kissing her? Isn't that what you wanted? To take the relationship deeper?"

"Yeah, but I wanted to make sure she wanted the same thing!"

"How many more signs do you need?" Mack blurted.

"You guys don't understand. She's going through a lot right now. She had just come from her father's house and was upset. I didn't want to take advantage of that." Not to mention the fact that all of his brain cells were lodged in the largest, most painful erection he'd ever experienced.

"So instead you just made her feel rejected?" Colton snarked. "Nice going, whistle dick. No wonder she told you she needs space. You embarrassed her."

"I wasn't rejecting her!"

"She came to you after being rejected by her father," Malcolm said. "She worked up the courage to act on her feelings for you, and you put a stop to it. What else was she supposed to think?"

Indignation merged with shame. "It's your fault. If you guys hadn't given me that stupid book and—"

Mack grinned. "So you *did* keep reading."

"For fuck's sake." Noah dragged a hand over his beard. "Yes, I kept reading. But only because you guys filled my head with these crazy ideas. You screwed up my relationship with her!"

"Dude, you're the one who kissed her and freaked out," Mack said.

"And flashed your happy trail at her," Colton added.

The Russian giggled. "Frank and beans."

Malcolm waved his hands. "We're missing a step. At which point in all of this did you tell her how you feel about her?"

The table got quiet. Noah winced and looked at his lap.

"Noah, you *did* tell her how you feel about her, right?" Malcolm said.

"I—not exactly."

The reaction that followed could not have been more violent if he'd been caught cosplaying Kylo Ren with a white lightsaber. The group exploded in a burst of swear words and pounding fists.

"You idiot!" Mack finally sputtered.

Colton snorted and shook his head. "You realize you're a giant fucking moron, right?"

A sour taste stung the back of his throat. "I tried to talk to her," Noah protested. "She won't listen to me."

Mack snorted and looked at Malcolm. "What would you say is your pet peeve about poorly crafted romance novels?"

Malcolm crossed his arms. "That would be when two adult

characters avoid having a grown-up conversation that could change the course of the story."

Two waiters emerged from the kitchen then, balancing heavy trays of what looked like twenty different plates. The Russian clapped and tucked a napkin in his shirt. Noah didn't share his enthusiasm. His appetite was nonexistent. He picked listlessly at various options but barely tasted the food and ignored the conversation about which items Mack should pick for the wedding.

Malcolm nudged him with his knee. "You know what I love most about the books?" he asked quietly.

Noah bit back a mean retort. He didn't want to talk about the fucking books, but he also desperately wanted Malcolm's wisdom. So he said nothing.

"I love how they can make us cheer for pretty much any character if we just understand why they're doing something. We'll let them get away with pretty much anything—including pushing away the woman they desperately want—if they have a strong motivation. The *why* behind their actions."

The entire table went quiet, every man eager to hear what Malcolm had to say, like children sitting at the feet of their favorite teacher.

"The crucial question we have to ask, both in the books *and* in life, is why. Why does a character do the things he does? What is the underlying cause of his fears, his mistakes?"

Noah didn't like where Malcolm was going.

"You keep saying that you were afraid to make a move with her because she's vulnerable," Malcolm said. "But maybe you're the one who's vulnerable. Maybe you stopped kissing her not to protect her, but to protect yourself."

The silence that followed his words this time was reverent, somber, and made Noah's skin itch. He felt suddenly exposed, and not because he'd just admitted to making out with his best friend.

"Noah, why did you stop her from taking things further last night?"

"I told you. I wanted to make sure it was what she really wanted, that she wasn't just upset."

Malcolm shook his head. "You know Alexis. Would she do that?"

The sting of bile turned his mouth sour. Noah shook his head. No, she wouldn't do that. Self-loathing bled into regret and panic as the full weight of what he'd done settled in the dark, churning pit of his stomach. After more than a year of being accused by strangers of using her body for everything from revenge to furthering her career, Noah had all but acted as if she'd done the same—of using her body to satisfy some kind of temporary emotional need.

Holy fucking shit. What had he done? He shoved his plate away and propped his elbows on the table so he could bury his face in his hands.

"I think you stopped her because you weren't sure if it was what *you* wanted," Malcolm said.

Noah looked up at that. "Of course it's what I want!"

"Maybe all this stuff about not wanting to burden her when she's already upset is all just one big excuse. Maybe you're just afraid of what's on the other end of this change in your relationship."

Noah didn't like the truth in that accusation. Noah ground his hands into his eyes. "This is why I never wanted to act on my feelings. Because I knew it could ruin our friendship."

"It won't if you tell her how you really feel." Malcolm gently pounded a fist on Noah's back. "And more importantly, *show* her how *you* feel. Let her see it. Let her see you."

"Just tell me what to do," Noah said, desperation turning his voice into a whine.

"You gotta give her some space like she asked," Mack said. "But use the time to your advantage."

"What does that even mean?"

"Do some hard work on yourself," Malcolm said. "Figure out the why behind your own actions."

Which is why, an hour later, Noah found himself carrying the book once again to his couch.

Missy found AJ red-eyed and snotty, a half-empty bottle of Jameson on the coffee table in front of him and a neglected glass in his hand. On the TV, he'd paused the video of Tara's third-grade dance recital.

He looked up when she walked into the room. "I missed it all . . ."

"Yes, you did."

He wiped his nose with the back of his hand. "Why did you give me these videos?"

Missy sighed heavily and sank down on the couch next to him. "You wanted to see them."

"Well if your goal was to torture me, then you succeeded."

"Why? Because you weren't part of it? You're romanticizing a past you wanted no part of when it was happening. You would have missed it all anyway. The

178

dance recital? It was the same weekend that you played in your first Super Bowl. The Halloween talent show? Middle of October. That Christmas pageant? You would have missed it for a game."

"I would have fucking found a way to attend my own daughter's Christmas pageant."

Missy shrugged. "Maybe. Maybe not. I'm leaning heavily toward not."

She stood. "These things you're so upset about? That's the good stuff. You're sitting here crying over your whiskey because you missed the holidays and the birthday parties, but you don't see the other stuff. There are no videos of the weeks of sleepless nights where I had to walk up and down a hallway with a colicky newborn. There are no videos to show you of the homework fights and the eye-rolling years or the long hours of potty training or the embarrassing time she threw a full-on tantrum at Target and I had to carry her out like a football under my arm. Can you honestly sit here and tell me you wanted all of that? That you would have been there for all of that?"

His eyes darkened. "We'll never know, will we? Because you fucking kept her from me."

"You should have answered your phone."

"You should have fucking tried harder!"

She studied him quietly. "Maybe you're right."

His eyes widened in surprise at her admission.

"Maybe I should have called relentlessly every day for six months instead of one. Maybe I should have mailed ultrasound photos to your apartment. Hell,

maybe I should have flown cross-country with a new-born baby to show up unannounced at the NFL Draft. The thing is, I'm willing to stand here and admit to you that I could have tried harder, but only if you are willing to admit that it wouldn't have made a difference."

He blinked, face stony once again.

"And until you're willing to do that, there's nothing more for you and me to talk about."

Missy stormed to her bedroom and slammed the door. Several minutes later, she heard her bedroom door creak open. She rolled over in bed and saw AJ silhouetted in the doorway.

He leaned drunkenly against the doorframe. *"I want to hear about the tantrum at Target."*

Missy stared into space. She should tell him to fuck off but didn't. Instead, she scooted up in bed and leaned against the headboard.

"She was three, way too precocious, and long overdue for a nap. I needed to run in to grab a birthday present for one of her friends at day care. The minute we got in the toy aisle she saw something she wanted but my budget for the week only allowed for a toy for the little boy. She had a meltdown like kids do. Except I finally had to carry her out, and the minute we hit the parking lot she started yelling "HELP." She damn near got me arrested."

AJ's bark of a laugh caught her by surprise. *"What did people do?"*

"They looked at me like I was kidnapping a child! I was like, she's mine, she's just mad."

He laughed quietly again, but sober silence once again followed. "What was it she wanted?"

"I don't even remember. Probably a Disney Princess toy. She was really into those at that age."

He turned away from her, and then she watched as his shoulders dropped. And then his hands came to his face and . . . oh shit. He was crying. Openly weeping.

Missy threw back the covers and slid out of bed.

"AJ . . ."

He whipped around and yanked her against his hard body. His face dropped to her shoulder. "I'm sorry, Missy. I'm sorry that you ever had to make those kinds of choices, that my own fucking daughter had to go without a goddamned toy at Target because her mom couldn't afford it while her father was off making fucking millions of dollars."

She held him while he cried, until his strength gave way and he leaned against the wall behind them. He slid down to the floor and sat with one knee raised.

"You were right," he said.

"About?"

"It wouldn't have made a difference."

Missy took pity on him and joined him on the floor. "Thank you for admitting that."

He rolled his head against the wall to look at her. "I was terrified of being a father. Of what it would mean, not just for me, but for her. All I am, all I know, is football. *She was better off without me, and we both know it."*

"Is that your justification or your apology?"

"It's my regret." AJ reached up and pushed her hair off her forehead. "But it's not just Tara I regret. I missed out on other things too."

The weight and meaning of his gaze made her cheeks blaze.

"I missed out on you. On watching you be a mom and grow into the woman you are. I think I would have liked being part of that."

Her heart caught. He didn't know what he was saying. He was just full of remorse and whiskey sentiments. "You're still romanticizing things. You didn't love me. We wouldn't have gotten married, and even if we had, it would have been miserable. You know that."

"It wouldn't be miserable now."

She laughed out loud and let her head fall back against the wall. He really was drunk.

"We could try, Missy. Couldn't we?"

"No."

"Why not?"

She rolled her head to look at him. "Because you don't really want to."

"Yes, I do. I want to sweep you off your feet the way I should have back then. I want to buy you your dream house and pay for Tara's college and take you on trips. I want to give you jewelry and—"

Disappointment brought her back to her feet. "Is

*that what you think I want or need? What Tara needs?"
She shook her head before he could respond. "We don't
need you to show off for us. We just need you to be here.
There's no grander gesture than that. And it's the one
thing you have never been able to give us."*

CHAPTER EIGHTEEN

Alexis had never considered herself a coward.

Naive, maybe. Misguided for sure. But everything she'd ever done, every horrible mistake she'd ever made, had been rooted in *reasons*.

Not necessarily good reasons. Sometimes really bad reasons. Sometimes the reason was that she had no other choice. But not once did she ever feel like she'd done something purely out of fear.

Not until she told Noah she needed space and then walked away from him on Monday. It seemed like the right thing to do at the time, but as the days passed, doubt and regret followed by a punishing dose of loneliness made clear what had really been driving her decision: cowardice. She'd been humiliated by his reaction to their kiss, and so she'd simply gone into hiding. She'd spent all week avoiding everyone and their questions—Liv, Jessica, Sonia. She threw herself into work and dodged all attempts to get her to talk.

Even when the call came in from the transplant center with the news that she had passed the initial blood test, making her a possible match for the transplant, she had the transplant team tell Elliott and Candi rather than calling them herself.

So it really shouldn't have been a surprise on Thursday night when a vicious pounding at her front door brought her reluctantly downstairs. She opened the door and found Liv, Jessica, Thea—Liv's sister—and Sonia there. They held bottles of wine, cartons of ice cream, and determined expressions that left her no choice but to step back and let them in.

"Sit," Liv said, pushing Alexis toward the couch in her living room. "We'll take care of everything else. And then you're going to tell us what the hell is going on."

Alexis feigned ignorance. "What do you mean?"

Jessica and Sonia plopped down on opposite ends of the couch and tugged her down into the middle. "Don't play dumb," Jessica said. "You've been weird all week, and Noah hasn't been in the café since Monday morning."

"We've both been busy."

"Is that why he looks like a puppy who got his favorite toy taken away?" Thea asked, returning from the kitchen with spoons and ice cream. She shoved a pint of dark chocolate cherry into Alexis's hands and then lowered herself to the floor. Liv followed with wine and glasses.

"Did you guys have a fight or something?" Jessica asked.

Alexis poked her spoon into the ice cream. "No."

Jessica accepted a glass of wine from Liv. "Does it have something to do with him yelling at Elliott?"

"Yes, and no. I don't know where to start." She handed the ice cream to Sonia, who dug in without hesitation.

Liv suddenly gasped. "Holy shit. Something happened between you two."

Alexis's ears got hot.

"Did you sleep together?" Liv blurted.

"*No!*" Alexis sat up straight, but either her face or her tone of voice gave her away. She was holding out on them.

"Then what's going on?" Liv asked.

Alexis tossed her hands in the air. "For God's sake, we kissed, okay?"

Her friends gasped in unison so hard that Alexis's ears popped.

"Oh my God," Alexis moaned, falling back against the cushions.

Liv grabbed her hands and dragged her back up. "Details."

"Details?" Alexis snapped. "Fine. The details are that I kissed him and he told me to stop, so I told him I needed some space, and now things are totally awkward between us, and I'm freaking out about seeing him this weekend for the bachelor and bachelorette weekend. There. You're caught up."

Liv's face tightened in confusion. "Wait. He told you to stop kissing him? That doesn't make any sense."

"It makes perfect sense. I was wrong about what he wanted, and now I've ruined our friendship."

Liv sat back, shaking her head and biting her lip. "No, you don't understand. He—" She cut herself off with a wince.

"He what?" Alexis asked.

"I'm probably not supposed to tell you this, because Mack is super serious about book club, but this seems like an emergency."

Alexis shook her head. "What are you talking about?"

"Noah. He asked to join the book club. For you."

Alexis's heart skidded sideways. "He did?"

"He wants you, Alexis," Liv said.

The roar of her heart nearly drowned out her own voice. "Then why did he push me away?"

Sonia made an unattractive noise. "Because he's a man, and men are stupid shits."

Thea gave Sonia a *hush* look. "Because sometimes the scariest thing in the world for a man is to admit how he feels," she said. "Gavin and I nearly divorced because of that fear."

Liv shrugged. "And you know how I almost screwed things up with Mack because of the same thing."

"This is different. I kissed him, and he stopped and—" Shame turned her stomach to rot.

"And what?" Thea prodded. "Did he say anything?"

I didn't regret it! Alexis looked at her lap. "He tried to talk about it on Monday. He came to the café, but Elliott was there, and I was so upset about everything that was going on, and I told him I needed space."

Liv and the rest of the girls exchanged a heavy look. "So you actually pushed *him* away too," Liv finally said.

Alexis squeezed her eyes shut and pressed the heels of her hands into them. "I was confused and humiliated. And now I feel like I've destroyed the healthiest relationship I've ever had with a man."

Liv faced Alexis with an expression that said shit was about to get real. Alexis hated that expression. "This is why you've been avoiding me this week," she said.

"I'm sorry. I needed to hide for a while."

Liv softened her features and her tone. "I understand. I know that's one of the ways you cope with anxiety. That's why I didn't do this two nights ago, but I wish I'd known the reason you were stressed."

"Alexis," Thea said, quietly interjecting. "What kind of relationship do you want with Noah?"

"I kissed him, didn't I?" She was aiming for humor, but it fell flat when her voice wobbled. "I feel safe with him. And it's been so long since I've felt safe with a man."

Liv squeezed her knee.

"It's just hard to trust my own instincts sometimes. And when Noah pulled away from me, it just kind of destroyed that sense of trust in myself all over again."

Jessica slung an arm around her back. "You deserve to feel safe and happy. And if that's with Noah, then you need to be honest with him."

"I'm scared."

"Of course you are. But you're also the bravest person I've ever known. You're telling me you have the courage to take on someone like Royce Preston but not to tell Noah that you want more than friendship?"

Alexis managed a small laugh. "I told him maybe we could talk this weekend, but I don't want to make things awkward."

Liv snorted. "For who?"

Alexis motioned to all her friends. "You guys. Everyone else. This weekend is supposed to be about you and Mack, not Noah and me."

Liv pointed. "Stop. That's ridiculous. We're your friends."

"But this is your bachelorette weekend. I don't want to ruin it."

"The only thing that could ruin this weekend is if you weren't there."

"Trust me. The thought crossed my mind."

Liv pursed her lips, as if a decision had been made. "Well,

here's a better thought. You're going to use this weekend to your advantage. And we're going to help you."

Alexis gulped. "I've seen that look on your face before, Liv, and it's terrifying."

"Just leave it to us," Liv said. "By the end of this weekend, you and Noah will be naked."

CHAPTER NINETEEN

By Friday, Noah felt like the dirty floor of a public bathroom.

He'd known it would be torture to go a week without talking to Alexis, but he hadn't been prepared for the crushing loneliness of it. Waking up without texting her. Going to bed without calling to say good night. For someone who apparently hadn't been in a relationship, he sure as shit felt like he'd been dumped.

And worse than all of it was the memory of kissing her. Of holding her in his arms, finally. Of feeling her hands on him, hearing her little gasps and moans. His dreams had been downright pornographic all week, and that made him feel even more like shit, like a betrayal or something.

He couldn't sleep at all Thursday night in anticipation of finally seeing her again, so even though their plane to Memphis wasn't supposed to take off until ten o'clock Friday morning, he headed to the airport early. Just in case he could get Alexis alone.

Noah followed the signs to the area where private planes and chartered flights checked in. Colton had arranged for them to use some private jet for the weekend, and the lefty radical part of him cringed at the carbon footprint this one-night getaway was leaving on the Earth. Memphis was a three-hour drive, tops. They didn't need a damn plane.

He wished he and Alexis were driving together. It would give them time to talk, because there wouldn't be much time today and tomorrow. The plan was for the guys to head straight from the airport to a day spa for massages while Liv and her bridesmaids got pedicures. The entire group would then meet back up for dinner and barhopping at night.

Noah parked in the private lot outside the hangar where they were supposed to meet and swallowed away the disappointment when he didn't see Lexa's car. His disappointment soared when he realized the Russian was already there too.

Noah found him standing alone next to a massive suitcase and an inflatable inner tube. He was laughing at something on his phone. He held it out for Noah to see as he approached. "Raccoon eating grapes."

Noah nodded at the inner tube. "What's up with that?"

"They have pool at hotel. I cannot swim." He cracked up and turned his phone around again. "Raccoon eating banana."

"What the hell are you bringing?" Noah grumbled with a nod at the suitcase.

"I have special diet needs."

"That's all *food*?"

The Russian held out his arms. "You are having a bad day. Do you need a hug?"

"I'm good, thanks—*mrph*." He was suddenly smoochy faced against the Russian's massive chest. A beefy hand pounded him on the back and nearly knocked his ribs out of place.

"Yes, you need a hug."

"Can I interrupt or is this, like, a special moment?" Colton had snuck up on them, his voice laced with amusement.

Noah backed up, and Colton let out a shocked noise. "Holy shit, you look horrible."

The Russian pounded his back again. "He is having bad day."

He was saved from answering when the Russian turned his phone around again. "Raccoon eating marshmallow."

Colton tugged Noah away several feet and lowered his voice. "Since you're rooming with him, see if you can find out anything."

"About what—wait. I'm rooming with the Russian?"

"Yeah, didn't you know?"

"No, I didn't fucking know. Who decided that?"

Colton shrugged. "Mack, I guess. Nearly everyone else is bringing a wife or girlfriend, and I'm rooming with Mack's brother. So that leaves you and the Russian."

"Why can't I room with Liam?" His voice took on the quality of a whiny teenager.

"Because you have investigative skills." Colton nodded back toward the Russian's massive suitcase and lowered his voice. "Snoop through his luggage and see if you find any evidence of his wife."

"You seriously need to go on tour again."

"I'm working on my next album."

"Then find a hobby."

The Russian walked over, laughing behind hand. He turned his phone around. "Raccoon eating popcorn."

Noah glared at Colton, who winked and walked away. Noah wandered to the front of the hangar to watch for Alexis. But as the minutes ticked by, everyone else arrived except her. At a few minutes before ten, Mack announced that they could start boarding.

"What about Alexis?" Noah asked.

Liv and Mack shared a pitying glance.

"What?" Noah growled.

"She's driving herself," Mack said.

"You gonna be grumpy like this all weekend?"

Mack had the audacity to sound annoyed when he asked Noah the question two hours later. Once again, Noah found himself stuffed uncomfortably in the middle seat of a back seat as a chauffeur who picked them up from the airport drove them to the spa.

"Probably," Noah admitted. "You could have warned me that Alexis wasn't taking the plane with the rest of us."

Mack shrugged. "I assumed you knew."

The car slowed and pulled into the parking lot of a brick building. A sign near the driveway read OASIS DAY SPA. The woman at the reception desk blinked and swallowed hard when they walked in.

"Can I help you?"

Mack greeted her with one of his signature grins. "We have reservations under the name Mack. Bachelor party."

The woman blinked again. "When I saw on the schedule that we had a bachelor party coming in today, I figured it was a mistake and someone just left off the *-ette* part."

"Men need pampering too."

She winked. "Saving the strip clubs for later, huh?"

Mack stiffened. "No strip clubs. I don't like the idea of using my impending wedding as an excuse to sexually objectify women as if this is my last gasp of freedom."

The woman cleared her throat. "Of course. My apologies." She looked back down at her computer. "It says here you are each scheduled for a massage and a facial. Would anyone like to add a third treatment for a small upcharge?"

The Russian nodded. "I would like pedicure."

Noah slapped his hand over the Russian's mouth. "Nope. We're all good."

The Russian pouted. "My feet take beating in ice skates."

"No one gets paid enough to touch your feet, dude."

The woman stared unblinkingly for a moment before finding her voice again. "Right. Okay. Well, you gentlemen are all set. If you'll follow me, I'll show you to our changing room and lounge, where you can wait for your massage therapists."

They followed her down a dark hallway covered in deep red wallpaper and lined with potted palms. Plush carpet absorbed their footfalls. The hallway formed a T at the end, where a table displayed a single orchid next to a bubbling tabletop fountain. The woman turned left, and they once again followed in a single-file line.

She paused outside a door on the left and spoke in a soft voice. "You can use any open locker," she explained. "Clean towels and robes are folded on the bench in front of the lockers. When you're ready, you can exit through the opposite door to the lounge. Help yourself to refreshments. Your therapist will meet you there."

With one last skeptical look at the Russian, she turned and disappeared. Probably to warn whoever was unlucky enough to draw the short stick.

The locker room was only slightly more lit than the hallway and boasted the same dark red wallpaper. Incense burned on a sink-lined counter, and Noah's nose immediately began to drip. Great.

The guys all jostled for a locker, and then, at the same time, grew quiet.

"Wait," Colton said. "Are we supposed to shower first?"

"I don't think so," Mack said, but he sounded unsure.

"Haven't you ever gotten a massage before?" Noah asked him.

"No." He stared at the towel and robe in front of his locker.

"I feel like we should shower first," his brother, Liam, said.

Noah shook his head. "Didn't you guys shower this morning?"

"Yeah, but that was hours ago, and . . ." Mack gnawed his lip. "They're going to be touching us."

"Maybe someone should go ask that woman if we're supposed to shower," Del offered.

"No," Mack hissed. "We'll look like idiots."

"We already look like idiots," Noah said.

Mack looked around. "Seriously? None of us have ever done this before?"

Malcolm shrugged. "My massages have all been by athletic trainers."

Del and Gavin nodded in agreement. "Same," Gavin said.

Noah sat down on the bench in front of his locker. "Look, she didn't say anything about showering, so I'm not showering." He whipped his shirt over his head.

"Wait," Colton breathed. "Shit. Are we supposed to be naked?"

"I . . . I don't know," Noah said. "I think so."

"Like, bare-ass naked?"

"Wait," Gavin said. "Thea gets massages a lot. Let me text her."

The guys all waited as Gavin hammered out a text to his wife. A moment passed before he looked up. "She sent a laughing face emoji."

"Does that mean of course you're supposed to shower, dumbass, or . . ."

"I don't know." Gavin texted again, and, again, they waited

for a response. He looked up. "She said no to a shower, unless you're stinky."

The Russian stuck out his bottom lip and grabbed a towel. "I will shower."

"What about the naked part?"

Gavin texted the question. Then, "She said you can leave your underwear on if you want but most people get naked."

Colton winced. "I sort of feel like the Russian shouldn't be naked."

Del looked panicked. "So we, like, just lie there with our balls in the wind?"

"I think they'll put a blanket over us," Noah said.

Now Gavin looked panicked. "What if we fart?"

Noah swallowed hard. "Does that happen?"

"She's gonna be pushing on things," Gavin said. "It could shake something loose."

Del snorted. "That's stupid. Do you accidentally fart during sex?"

There was a mixed chorus of nos and at least two yeses.

"Who the fuck said yes?" Mack demanded.

No one owned up to it.

"Oh shit," Colton breathed.

They swiveled to look at him. He'd paled three shades.

"What?" Noah demanded.

He gulped. "What if we get wood?"

The silence in the room was tense and heavy.

"Does—" Noah swallowed. "Does *that* happen?"

Colton made an *Are you kidding?* face. "We're going to be naked, and a woman is going to be touching us."

"But it's not that kind of touching."

"Tell that to your dick," Colton said.

Gavin hugged his torso. "I'd rather fart."

"This is a mistake," Del said. "Maybe we should be getting pedicures."

"It's too late now!" Mack said.

The Russian emerged from the shower with a towel twined atop his head. His robe was at least three sizes too small and barely covered him in front. One misstep, and they'd all be getting an eyeful of his balls.

He sniffed his arm. "I smell like flowers."

"We're going to be late," Mack groaned. "Just get changed."

Everyone began to shed their clothes and stuff them in their lockers. Noah debated a full five seconds before pulling his boxer briefs off. Fuck it. He was going full Monty. He donned the robe, tied it around his waist, and followed the guys into the lounge. The Russian made a beeline for the refreshments table. He grabbed two cucumbers from a tray, trudged to a recliner, kicked back, and set the cucumbers on his closed eyes.

Noah looked at Colton. "Are we supposed to do that?"

Colton shrugged. "If we were supposed to eat them, wouldn't there be dip or something? Who just eats a slice of cucumber without, like, ranch dressing or something?"

"There are carrots, too, though," Del said. "Where the hell are we supposed to put those?"

Noah dropped into a chair by the fireplace. A moment passed, and then Malcolm joined him.

"You okay?"

Noah stared into the flames. "Great."

Malcolm clasped his hands between his knees and stared into the fire. "You figure anything out this week?"

"Yeah," Noah laughed with no amount of joy. "I can't live without her."

"Is that all?"

"Isn't that enough?"

Malcolm paused before answering. "I guess you'll find out, won't you?"

For once, Noah was not reassured.

CHAPTER TWENTY

"You look *amazing*."

Alexis turned one more time to look in the full-length mirror in her hotel room as Liv peered around the corner. This dress was the reason she'd driven herself. Because she needed to do some shopping, and even though Alexis had to admit that she looked pretty damn good in her new dress, she hesitated about actually wearing it.

"You're sure it's not too much?" She smoothed the red form-fitting skirt and turned to stare at her butt. A deep V-neck exposed most of her back. She paired it with some new leopard-print pumps. It was so outside of her ordinary style that she was afraid Noah wouldn't even recognize her.

Alexis puffed out her cheeks and let the air seep out. Nerves turned her stomach to a turnstile.

"It's perfect." Liv squeezed her shoulders from behind. "And hopefully you won't be wearing it very long."

Alexis elbowed Liv, who jumped back with a laugh.

Liv's phone buzzed, and Alexis held her breath as she watched her friend check the screen. Liv looked up with a coy smile. "Showtime."

Adrenaline made Alexis's knees weak. "This plan seems sort of childish in hindsight."

Liv shrugged. "A girl's gotta do what a girl's gotta do."

"But stealing his shoes just to keep him in the room?"

"We're all fools in love."

"You're sure you don't mind us missing dinner?" *Us*, assuming Noah was receptive to her groveling.

"If either one of you show up at dinner, I'll kill you both."

"But this is your big weekend and—"

Liv slapped a hand over Alexis's mouth. "This big weekend is about celebrating with our friends, and I can't think of a better way to celebrate than you and Noah finally getting together."

"What if he says no?"

Liv snorted. "He won't."

"What if he turns me away?"

"In that dress?"

"What if—"

"What if an hour from now you're collapsing naked on his chest?"

Heat shot up Alexis's cheeks. Liv laughed. "That's what I'm talking about."

Alexis bit her lip. "You're sure Mack didn't tell anyone about our plan?"

"I'm sure. As far as anyone will know, you have food poisoning from some bad sushi, and Noah lost his shoes."

"I can't believe I'm resorting to lies and subterfuge."

Liv laughed and kissed Alexis's cheek. "Good luck. Text me all the deets."

Liv walked out with a giggle, leaving a trail of perfume behind her. As soon as the door clicked shut, Alexis walked to her bed and sat down on the edge of the mattress. She pressed a hand to her stomach. She could do this. All she had to do was go knock on Noah's door and tell him—

A quick, efficient knock brought her back to her feet. Liv must have forgotten something. "I'm coming. Hang on."

Alexis opened the door. "Did you forget something?"

Her voice died on the last note. It wasn't Liv. It was a man. "I'm sorry. You must have the wrong room."

But then her brain caught up with the details. He wore a dark suit with no tie. He was looking at the floor. His hair was pulled back in a bun, and his feet were bare.

Noah lifted his face. "I can't find my shoes, but I was afraid you'd head down to dinner before I could talk to you. And I can't go one more second without talking to you."

She had an entire speech planned for when she saw him, but now that he stood before her, she forgot every word. "This wasn't the plan. I was supposed to come to *your* room."

"Lexa," he rasped.

She took a single step forward, and in an instant, Noah did the rest. He wove his fingers into her hair and tugged her into the hallway. She went willingly, eagerly. And when his mouth found hers, she wrapped her arms around his neck where his hair tickled the hot, exposed skin of her wrists.

He lifted his lips just enough to moan, "God, Lexa. I've missed you so much."

Then he kissed her again, hands in her hair, mouth wide over hers. Their kiss before had been a mere flirtation compared to this. With one strong arm, he hauled her firmly against his chest and then backed her against the hallway wall. He devoured her mouth like he could get drunk from her, and she gave as good as she got, tangling her fingers in his hair, slanting her head so he could go deeper. It was a no-holds-barred kiss. Openmouthed and soul-searching.

His hands suddenly cradled her face, forcing her to step back and look up at him. His gaze scorched her from the inside out. "I need you to listen to me. Don't talk. Just listen."

"O-Okay."

"I should have said this that night, and I've done a shitty job of trying to say it ever since then."

"Say what?" Her voice was as breathless as a Taylor Swift ballad.

"Do not ever think I regret what happened between us that night." His thumbs caressed her cheeks as he swallowed. "There are a million things in my life I regret, but kissing you will never be one of them."

Alexis leaned into him, pressed her lips against his. But then a quiet click made her suck in a breath.

His mouth hovered an inch above hers. "Your door just shut."

"My key is in there."

He didn't miss a beat. "Then come to my room."

She held his gaze. "And do what?"

"Whatever you're ready for."

She dug her fingers into his arms. "I made the first move before and look what happened. Tell me what you want. *Please.*"

His brow rested on hers. "Then let me spell it out for you like I should have done a long time ago." Noah palmed the back of her head. With gentle pressure, he urged her face up toward his. They traded breaths, lips hovering over lips. "I want you. All of you."

A thousand words hung in the space between them. A shared, unspoken recognition that this would change everything once again, but that this was always where they'd been heading, before either of them had even been willing to admit it. That this was the turning point from which they could never return. A bridge connecting two worlds—the world of friendship and the world of lovers.

"Let's go to your room."

He kissed her. Hard. Fast. But then he slipped his hand into hers and began to pull her down the hallway. His free hand dug into the pocket of his pants to withdraw the key card to his room. His fingers trembled as he pressed it against the key reader. When it flashed green, he yanked the handle and pushed open the door.

They barely made it inside before Noah turned to her.

"Come here," he rasped. He opened his arms to her. She fell into them, and it felt like coming home after a long trip. Home to a place she belonged, where she was safe and desired and cared about.

It felt like the first time, this kiss. It was slow and deep and . . . decisive. The word was an abstract thought, drudged up from the haze of desire and longing, but that's what it was. It was as if Noah had made some crucial decision and was communicating it the only way he could. Deeper and deeper, he feasted on her mouth as if kissing alone could satisfy his hunger. But every thrust of his tongue sent her closer and closer to the edge of an almost painful precipice. She wanted to fall. Fast. Fully. Without fear.

She settled a hand in the middle of his chest. He pulled back enough to peer down at her. "Are you okay?"

Alexis leaned against the wall behind her and held his gaze. "I have a confession."

He raised an eyebrow, the gesture both amused and uncertain.

"I know where your shoes are."

His mouth curled up in a smile. "You do?"

"Liv asked Mack to steal them so you'd be stuck in the hotel looking for them."

He puffed out a laugh. "Is that what you meant by the plan?"

"So I could come to you and get you alone and tell you that I'm sorry."

His smile faded into anguish. "For what?"

"I didn't give you a chance to explain."

"I should have tried harder."

"I should have listened harder."

Noah made a noise low in his throat and lowered his brow to hers. She felt something burst in her chest. Something that felt like joy.

"I missed you so much," she whispered.

"I missed you too. You have no idea how much." And then he hugged her. *Hugged* her. Tightened his arms around her, buried his face in her neck, and held her. It was so simple but so achingly romantic that Alexis feared she would cry.

She let him plunder her mouth again, but she finally grasped his head and held him steady. "I don't want this to change anything."

He cocked a grin. "Really? I hope it changes everything."

"What do you mean?"

"I hope this means I get to spend the night instead of leaving you." He kissed her throat. "I hope it means we get to take long showers together." He nibbled her ear. "I hope it means lazy kissing in the car."

She began to pant. "Okay, fine. I guess those things can change."

He laughed, and his mouth found its way back to hers. Noah rubbed his lips back and forth across hers, more caress than kiss.

"So we're going to do this, right?" she whispered.

"I sure as shit hope so."

"Then take me to bed."

A growl emerged from his throat. Then he bent and slid his arm beneath her legs. She laughed as he scooped her up. "Wow," she breathed. "This is positively swoony."

"Swoony?"

"You make me light-headed."

Noah grinned as he carried her across the sitting area and into one of two bedrooms in the suite. He lowered her feet to the floor next to the bed and leaned in for a kiss, but she shook her head and pushed him back. "I want you to see me."

He stepped back as if knowing instinctively what she wanted. As he watched, she reached behind her back and unzipped her dress. She slid each strap over her arm and tugged until the dress slipped off her body, leaving her in nothing but her strapless bra and panties and her heels.

He made a noise, a cross between a whimper and a growl. "Don't stop," he begged.

Heat flushed her skin under his gaze. She reached around again to unlatch her bra and let it fall. Her nipples puckered from the shock of cold air and hot desire. She kicked off her shoes and then tugged her panties from her hips.

And then she stood before him. Naked. Exposed. Fully. She curled her toes and propped one foot on top of the other. A nervous habit, even when naked.

He took his time, letting his eyes travel the full length of her and then back up. "You're—" He cleared his throat. "You're so beautiful."

"Your turn," she whispered.

He nodded, and then holding her gaze, he unbuttoned his shirt. It fell to the floor and was quickly followed by his white undershirt. His chest rose and fell with the same trembling quakes as hers as his hands went to his pants. His fingers shook as he undid the button and then lowered the zipper. When he hooked his fingers in the waistband of his pants and briefs, she held her breath.

Never breaking eye contact, he slipped both garments from his hips and let them pool on the ground. He lifted one leg and then another to free himself from them. And then stood before her, naked.

His voice was low when he spoke. "I'm not going to touch you until you tell me it's okay."

"Can I . . . can I touch you first?"

He stood stock-still but for the nearly imperceptible lift of his chin. Even the air locked in his lungs beneath the thick, matted hair of his chest. And that's where she began her exploration. She reached between them until trembling fingers met the warm flesh of his pecs. His Adam's apple bobbed in his throat. Alexis splayed her hands wide, felt the rapid beat of his heart beneath her hand. So strong, so full of life and energy.

Alexis slid her hands wide across each nipple, and when he responded with a sharp intake of breath, she paused there to do it again. Rubbing her palm over the hard, pebbled flesh that poked through the hair. Would he like to be kissed there? Was it the same for men as women? With a sudden thirst for the taste of him, she dipped her head and pressed her lips to one nipple. Noah made a noise, soft but urgent. Emboldened by it, Alexis flicked her tongue across the hard pebble. Noah's arm shot out to brace himself against the bedpost, leaning into her, urging her on. So she sucked the nipple into her mouth, twirled her tongue around it, as her fingers traced a slow path downward.

Every inch of him was hot, toned, tight. As if every muscle was engaged in the sheer act of restraint. But when her fingers circled his belly button, he gave up the fight. He growled, slid his hand along her jaw, and tilted her face to his. His lips claimed hers as she slid her fingers lower. His erection bobbed between them, hard and hot.

"Can I touch you here?" she asked.

"God, yes," he rasped.

Alexis wrapped her fingers around his hard length. Noah went instantly still but for the squeeze of his fingers against her jaw. And when she moved her hand up and down, he groaned and dropped his forehead to hers. He was soft and hard at once. She moaned as she imagined him inside her, sliding in and out of her wet heat. Wetness pooled between her thighs.

He suddenly gripped her wrist.

She looked up. "You want me to stop?"

He gulped. "I want this to last. But if you keep doing that, I'm going to be done for in about five seconds."

A surge of pure carnal power filled her with courage, boldness. Alexis slanted her mouth fully against his and brought his hand to her breast. Could she orgasm from sheer anticipation? She was almost there. It was a sweet agony, waiting for his fingers to flick across her throbbing nipples. But he seemed hell-bent on torture, because instead of going to the spot that needed him most, he placed simple caresses atop each plump round of flesh.

"Touch me," she begged.

His fingers brushed the curls at the apex of her thighs. The reverent tenderness in his touch . . . Instinct brought her legs apart to let him in, and he answered with a tender caress down the seam of her, parting her to his gentle probing.

He teased with featherlight caresses. He taunted with the slightest pressure, slipping just the tip of a finger inside her before retreating.

"I've dreamed of this so many times," he whispered against her lips. "Dreamed of touching you like this. Dreamed of us together."

She would have admitted *me too*, if she could talk, but she couldn't. Every sense, every cell, was tuned to the magic he worked between her legs.

Noah hoisted one of her legs over his hip, never breaking the kiss. His fingers pumped in and out of her, and he pressed the heel of his hand to her swollen, throbbing nub.

"Oh, God." Alexis's head fell back. Her body shook, legs trembled. Noah wrapped one arm around her waist to hold her as she rocked against his hand.

"Noah . . ." His name wrenched from her throat as waves and waves of electric pleasure shot through her. Her fingers dug into his shoulder as she held on, rode it out, soared on a rainbow of emotions she couldn't identify.

"I've got you," he murmured, tenderness in his voice as he tightened his arm around her waist. "Just hold on to me."

Alexis weakly wrapped both arms around his neck and hung on as he scooped her in his arms again before dipping her backward onto the mattress. Alexis wrapped both legs around his waist and dragged his mouth to hers.

His erection was cradled between her legs. Their bodies acted together, hips tilting into each other, into the bliss of hard against soft. Noah laced their fingers together and pressed her hands into the mattress above her head. But then he paused and lifted his mouth just enough to speak.

"Is that okay?"

"Yes," she whispered.

It had been two years since she'd been with anyone, but she'd *never* been with someone like this. Open and honest and tender. Someone who cared to stop and check in with her to make sure what he was doing was still okay. Someone who took his time, treating every inch of her skin like a treasure to be cherished. Of all the ways she'd reclaimed herself, this was the one that mattered most. Everything about this moment, this act with Noah, was hers. Willing and honest. Raw and wanted.

"Do you like this position?" he asked quietly, skimming his lips across her jaw.

No man had ever asked her that during sex. "Yes. Do you?"

"Any position with you is perfect."

They kissed slowly, languidly, fingers flexing together, bodies molding and melding as if this were all they needed. But it wasn't. They needed more. *She* needed more.

Noah must have felt it the same time she did, because lazy became hurried. Languid became passionate.

Noah suddenly rose up with a groan and slipped from her embrace.

"What's wrong?" she panted, a twinge of alarm turning the fuzzy edges of her desire into sharp focus.

"I forgot," he grunted. She watched as he crossed the bedroom naked, unzipped his duffel bag, and dug around inside. Then he pulled out a long sheath of condoms.

She couldn't help it. She giggled.

He turned around. "What're you laughing at? My ego is at stake here."

She giggled again. "You whipped those condoms out like a magician pulling a scarf from a hat or something."

He gave her a sexy grin and jerked his eyebrows suggestively as he crawled back into bed. "Want to see my magic wand?"

Alexis laughed and groaned at the same time. "I walked right into that one."

Noah rose on his knees above her.

"Do you want me to do it?" she whispered.

He slipped a foil square into her hands. She opened the condom and rolled it on him, slowly, reveling in his groan of pleasure.

She laid back again, and he returned to her, covering her body with his.

Alexis lifted a leg and hooked it over his hip, and as if he couldn't wait any longer, Noah thrust inside her. Alexis cried out and arched her back. She wrapped her other leg around him and hooked her ankles, sending him farther inside.

But then they both stopped.

Stopped moving. Stopped breathing.

He shuddered on top of her, and she understood, because she felt it too. The power of being joined, finally. The joy of it. The surprise of it. It was too much to take in all at once.

The perfection of it brought their gazes to a passionate collision.

His eyes were black with desire but round with an almost stunned expression. "Lexa," he whispered, his voice laced with wonderment.

She traced her finger along his jaw. "Make love to me."

He closed his eyes and dropped his forehead to hers. Then he lowered to his elbows, cradled her head in his hands, and began to move with an aching slowness. Their mouths found each other, tangling in an intimate dance as old as time but brand-new to them.

Noah's hips lifted, and he withdrew to the tip. She gasped at the pleasure.

"Talk to me," he murmured against her ear.

"You feel so good."

He moved again, slowly withdrawing before thrusting back in. Alexis tilted her head into the mattress with a groan.

"Like that?" he whispered, voice tight with restraint.

"Yes," Alexis moaned.

Noah did it again, slowly pulling out only to thrust back into her, harder and faster. A cry of pleasure burst from her throat, unbidden and unprompted. She gripped the comforter.

She whispered hungrily for him to talk to her, to tell her what he was thinking.

"You," he groaned against her mouth. "All I ever fucking think about is you."

He caught her earlobe with his lips. "You're the first thing I think of when I wake up and the last thing I think of when I fall asleep. And even then I dream about you."

Alexis wove her fingers in his hair and moaned. "What do you dream about?"

"Holding you. Kissing you. Touching you. Driving you crazy."

With every word, he became more frantic. "I dream about making love to you, Lexa. Over and over again."

His forehead dropped to her shoulder, his biceps bulging as he poised above her.

LYSSA KAY ADAMS

"Lexa," he moaned. "God, Lexa." He was panting, hard. Desperate. Out of control. And so was she.

Hot, surging pleasure flooded her limbs. She was so close. So close. And he seemed to know it, because he ground against her pelvis, and she was gone. Her whole body shook and then stiffened as she cried his name over and over, fingers digging into the mattress, head thrown back, heart exploding.

In the next instant, Noah let out a shudder and a guttural groan. And followed her into the abyss.

CHAPTER TWENTY-ONE

Noah couldn't move.

If he could stay here like this forever, he would. Wrapped in her arms, tangled in her body, his energy spent and his skin slick. Buried inside her forever.

He was only vaguely aware of the skim of her fingertips up his spine, of her breath against his neck, of the tandem pounding of their hearts. Her body surrounded him, welcomed him, embraced him, enlightened him.

He pressed his forehead to her neck and choked back the swell of emotion that made his throat thick and his eyes burn. Great. Just what he needed. To fucking cry after making love to her. But he had never experienced this before. He had never *made love* before. Not until now. Not until her. It had never felt like that for him.

Giving a woman pleasure had never been so fucking good *for him*.

She turned her face and nuzzled him with her cheek. "Are you okay?"

"I don't know," he murmured.

"We just had sex."

He puffed out a laugh. "Is that what that was?"

"It's been a while for me, but I'm pretty sure."

"I enjoyed it," he said, slowly regaining control of senses.

She mmm'd and burrowed her face into his neck. "So did I."

He was probably crushing her beneath his weight, so he forced himself up on his elbows, every muscle protesting.

"Hey." She smiled up at him.

He responded with a kiss. "Don't move, okay?"

She nodded.

Noah padded naked to the bathroom to dispose of the condom. He paused at the sink and splashed several handfuls of cold water on his face. When he stared in the mirror he was shocked to see the same face staring back at him that had been there before. Something should be different, shouldn't it? When a man experienced the most important sexual experience of his life, shouldn't it reflect on his face?

Or maybe that was the point. Nothing had changed, because this was always supposed to happen between them. They didn't change each other. They were perfect together as they were.

When he returned to bed, he found her curled on her side, head resting on her arm. She smiled as he crawled in next to her and brushed a wayward curl off her cheek.

"Now what?" She smiled.

"We could always do it again."

Her laugh was light and airy, and it made his heart turn over in his chest.

"God, I love that sound," he breathed.

"You always make me laugh."

"I hope I always do."

Her smiled turned coy. "I wasn't laughing two minutes ago."

"I know. Give me twenty, and we can start making that noise again too."

She pressed her hand to his stomach. "The noise I'm most concerned about right now is the rumbling coming from here."

"I missed dinner. Someone stole my shoes."

Alexis barked out a laugh. "Should we order room service?"

"Either that, or we could go dig around in the Russian's suitcase."

She laughed again and sat up. "Want me to get the menu?"

Noah tugged her back down. "I'll do it. You've cooked enough meals for me. The least I can do is scrounge up some room service."

Alexis sank against her pillows and tucked her arms behind her head as he slid from bed. "I could get used to this," she called as he walked out of the room.

"Get used to what?" He found the room service binder on the coffee table in the sitting room. "Me feeding you?"

"You walking around naked."

He returned to the bedroom. "Let's add that to the list of things we hope change after this."

He plopped back down on the bed, and she snuggled against him as he flipped open the binder. "See anything that looks good?"

"Besides you?"

He chuckled. "I could get used to *that*."

"What?"

"You openly lusting after me."

Her giggle made his chest swell.

"Do you think everyone has figured out what we're doing yet?" she asked, resting her head against his shoulder.

"Yes. Are you okay with that?"

"Yeah, are you?"

He flipped a page in the menu. "Hell yes. I want everyone to know."

She laughed. "I guess they need to find out sooner or later. I mean, if we're going to keep doing, you know . . ."

He gaped down at her. "Please, God, tell me that's not even a question at this point."

"I didn't want to make assumptions."

He closed the binder and tossed it off the bed. Then he rolled on top of her, lacing their fingers together on either side of her pillow. "I've waited a long time for you. You can safely assume that I want to do it as often as possible."

They kissed once more. And before too long, she started making that noise again, and he forgot all about room service.

"I think you might have killed me that time."

Alexis laughed as Noah rolled onto his back, panting. A moment passed, and he awkwardly sat up. Just like before, he ordered her to stay put as he got up to deal with the less sexy part of sex. She watched him pad toward the bathroom, and as soon as the door swung shut, she disobeyed and got out of bed. His shirt was in a ball on the floor. She grabbed it and pulled it on and wandered to the window overlooking Beale Street.

The bathroom door swung open. "I told you to stay put," he joked, coming up behind her. His arms circled her waist and tugged her tightly against his chest. They stood like that for a quiet moment, content again to just feel each other. Finally.

She covered his arms with her own. "I wish we could stay here forever," she sighed.

His lips brushed her hair. "Not me. Because I can't wait to take you home and start doing all those naked things we talked about."

She managed a laugh, but it came out thick and watery. He squeezed her. "Hey," he soothed. "What's that?"

"I'm sorry. Emotional after sex and all that. I'll stop. Just give me a minute."

His lips came down on her shoulder. "You don't have to apologize for being emotional. We're kind of on a roller coaster right now. I've been one step away from losing it since the minute you opened your hotel room door."

Alexis twisted in his embrace and wrapped her arms around his chest. His heart pounded beneath her cheek. Strong. Solid. Reassuring. He held her and let her catch her breath, pressing gentle kisses to the top of her head and rubbing his hands up and down her back and being so fucking perfect that she wanted to melt.

She finally risked a look at his face. "Why did we wait so long?"

"Because we weren't ready."

"But you said you've wanted this for a long time."

"I have. Longer than you know."

"But I kissed *you*, Noah."

He sighed wearily and rested his brow on hers. "And if the adrenaline had worn off and you regretted it, it would have fucking gutted me."

"I shouldn't have just run out that night. I'm sorry—"

He kissed her and shook his head gently. "No more apologies."

"I need to get this out. I had a whole speech planned."

He acquiesced with a resigned sigh. He slid his hands around her waist and gripped her hips. "I'm listening."

"It was disrespectful of me to not give you a chance to explain

217

things," she said, heart pounding. "Our friendship deserved better than that."

He lifted a hand from her hip to her cheek. "Lexa—"

"You're the best friend I've ever had, and that's the thing that I don't want to change."

"It won't." He lowered his mouth to hers, his kiss gentle and sweet. "Just promise me you won't ever go a week without talking to me again, okay? This was the worst week of my life."

She managed a small smile. "I have a hard time believing that."

He understood what she meant. "I was numb after my father died. I felt nothing. But I felt every second of you needing space."

Her voice caught. "I don't want any more space."

"Neither do I."

And then he kissed her.

Another apology. Another promise.

And within minutes the shirt was gone.

Alexis woke up the next morning disoriented. Sore, but in the best way.

Then she heard the soft snore behind her, and everything fell into place.

Noah.

His arm was heavy across her waist, his breath warm against her back. Her body hummed with desire but also the burning need to use the bathroom. Alexis stretched and slid out from under his arm.

Noah made a tired sound and tugged her back. "Not yet."

"But I have to pee."

He finally released her but told her to hurry back. She did the bathroom thing, tried to twist her hair into something less Medusa-like, and then brushed her teeth. When she returned, she found him awake and splayed on top of the covers, gloriously and confidently naked, legs crossed at the ankles and one arm curled beneath his head as he scrolled through his phone.

He looked over with an eyebrow raised. "Remember last night when you wondered how long it would be until everyone figured it out?"

He handed over his phone. A series of photos had been texted during the night.

Mack and Liv with a thumbs-up.

Malcolm and Del posed together with stupid grins.

Colton sent a video of himself making a kissy face.

Gavin and Thea grinned adorably.

The Russian's was last. *I will stay with Colton.*

She set the phone on the table next to the bed. "Looks like we missed a good party."

"Our party was way better."

She crawled into bed, and he opened his arms to her. Noah rolled and pressed their clasped hands into the blanket next to her head, bringing their faces inches from each other.

"Good morning," he murmured.

"Hi," she whispered.

"I slept really well last night."

"So did I."

Things got interesting in the place where her body cradled his, and pretty soon, he was diving for another condom. He sheathed himself and then leaned over her with a sexy smile, his hands on either side of her shoulders to hold himself aloft. Alexis lifted her head to kiss him, but he pulled back just enough so she couldn't reach him.

His smile teased. "Say the magic word, babe."

Alexis laughed. "You have to be kidding me."

Noah nudged the tip of his erection against her, and she tipped her head back.

"Jesus, abracadabra."

With a loud laugh, he entered her in a single, powerful thrust.

Time stopped.

She gasped.

He groaned.

Alexis lifted her legs around his waist to draw him farther inside her. They moved, rocked, caressed, and kissed.

"Alexis . . . ," he suddenly groaned. "God, baby. Slow down. I can't hold . . . I can't hold back."

Wanton satisfaction surged through her. She lifted her head and brushed her lips against his ear. "I don't want you to hold back."

He tried to pull out of her, but she grabbed his ass and pulled him back in. She was rewarded with a groan and a shudder. But still he hesitated, and she felt him shake his head. "No . . . not until you . . ."

She cupped his perfect, hard-as-rock butt cheeks and squeezed. "I've dreamed about this, too, Noah. About making you fall apart in my arms. Driving you crazy. Let me."

He groaned again, his body moving as if he could no longer stop it. "You feel so good. So fucking good."

She lifted her right leg and hooked it around his arm, opening herself wide beneath him. The move drove him deep inside her, and they both groaned. The pleasure was so intense he couldn't help but groan out her name and move again.

"Is that good?" she whispered against his lips, their labored breaths mingling in a rapid pant.

"So fucking good," he groaned, thrusting harder, faster.

She shifted and arched into him.

He paused. "Wait . . . are you okay?"

"Oh my God. Can't you tell?" She tightened her legs around him and met his thrusts with her hips. "Let it happen, Noah."

That same animalistic growl that had erupted from him earlier emerged again. He braced higher onto his knee and pumped faster and faster until his skin broke out with a sheen of sweat and . . .

Oh, God. Alexis clutched his biceps. The position he was in. He was hitting her in all the right places. How could it happen this fast? Her orgasm hit with a sudden flood of sweet relief that made her stiffen and cry out as much in surprise as pleasure.

Noah let out a sound of guttural male satisfaction and thrust into her again with a final, hard shudder. His entire body quaked above her. Then he groaned her name and collapsed.

Alexis couldn't help it. Again. She laughed. Again.

Noah rose up to gaze down at her. "*Now* what are you laughing at? And trust me, my ego really is at stake now."

Alexis slid her arms up his wide back. "I'm laughing because you do have a magic wand."

Noah answered with another one of those sexy grins and a twist of his hips. Alexis pulled his head down for a kiss. A noise from the front door made them both still. It sounded like—

Oh shit. The Russian was back.

Noah leaped out of bed and threw the covers over her naked body just as the Russian tiptoed by the open doorway, hands over his eyes. "I am not looking."

"Christ, dude. Why didn't you call first?" Noah growled.

"I need to shower. We have brunch."

Noah slammed the bedroom door. "I forgot about brunch," he grumbled.

Alexis sat up, holding the sheet over her breasts. "What would you say about getting in my car and just going home together?"

Noah returned to bed. "I'd say those are the best words that have ever been spoken."

CHAPTER TWENTY-TWO

Beefcake greeted them with a pouty yowl. Noah gulped as Alexis bent to pick him up. She kissed his hair and turned toward Noah. "He missed us."

"He missed you," Noah said, pulling their suitcases to the bottom of the stairs. "He's going to kill me in my sleep tonight."

"Maybe he's jealous," she said, setting the cat down. Beefcake immediately lifted a leg and started licking his ass.

Noah closed the distance between them, laced their hands together, and backed her against the wall. He kissed her until they were both breathing hard.

"What's this?" She laughed.

"It's been too long since I kissed you."

"Liar. You're jealous of Beefcake."

"You're goddamned right I am. He's been sleeping next to you for years."

Her arms wound around his neck. "We'll just have to make room for you in bed."

"I'm a little worried about being naked around him. He'll castrate me while I'm sleeping."

She dropped a kiss on his chin. "I'll protect you."

Noah patted her butt. "Go relax. I'm gonna scrounge something up for dinner."

"There's not much," she sighed. "I haven't gotten groceries in over a week."

"I'll come up with something."

"You're a dream come true."

He kissed her nose. "What're friends for?"

She pointed to the kitchen. "Feed me."

He winked. "Yes, ma'am."

As she disappeared up the stairs, Noah opened the fridge and blinked as he chronicled its meager contents. Eggs. Milk. Water. Half-and-half. Butter. Wine. She wasn't lying about not having much. The crisper drawers held some carrots that had seen better days and an unopened wedge of Parmesan cheese. He could probably use that.

He opened the cupboards. Jesus. Had she been living on air and caffeine the past week?

He spotted a box of fettuccine noodles. Perfect.

Next, he located her pots and pans, filled a stockpot with water, and set it to boil for the pasta. The water had just started to bubble when he heard her padded footsteps coming down the hall.

"How does fettuccine sound—" His voice died in his throat. She wore one of his old sweatshirts and a pair of flimsy sleep shorts.

She looked down at herself. "I changed. Is that okay?"

"Yep," he croaked. He cleared his throat. "Is fettuccine alfredo okay?"

She folded her arms on the island and leaned. "I had all the ingredients for that?"

"That and little else," he said, turning back to the stove. "What the hell have you been eating?"

"Whatever I can grab at the café."

"Which means what?"

"A lot of coffee and stale scones."

"You're going to burn out, babe."

"Then I guess it's a good thing I have you to cook for me."

His heart pinged. He liked the sound of that way too much, and the image that came with it. He'd cook for her every night, if he could.

"Can I help?"

"Nope."

"How about if I set the table?"

His heart pounded again. The idea of sitting down with her for a simple meal at her homey dining table like a normal couple was almost more than his catapulting emotions could take. He'd wanted this for so long that it seemed impossible this was real.

"Sure," he finally answered.

She moved around him, her hand casually sliding across his back. When she reached for the plates, his eyes drifted down to where her sweatshirt pulled away from the soft skin of her stomach. His breath vacated his lungs. Her dark gaze met his, and the hunger in her eyes likely matched his own.

After she set the table, Alexis turned on some music in the living room. The twangy, bluesy strains of Mumford & Sons broke the nervous pressure in the room. She returned to his side and opened the cupboard where she stored her wine and glasses.

Alexis selected a bottle of white and two glasses and carried them to the table. Noah made quick work of tossing the drained pasta and cream sauce in the stockpot.

Alexis filled their glasses as he carried the pot to the table and set it in the center.

"I feel like we should toast to something," she said.

Noah leaned back in his chair, glass aloft. "You start."

Her eyes drifted right in thought. Then they came back to his with a glisten. "To coming home."

His heart officially relocated.

Several minutes later, Alexis collapsed against her chair with her hand over her stomach. "I was starving. Thank you."

The music switched to a romantic ballad by a band Noah didn't recognize. Alexis bit her lip and stood, hand outstretched. Noah folded his fingers into hers and let her pull him to his full height. Her smile was coy, her gaze shy.

"What're you doing?" he rasped.

She tugged his hand as she headed toward the living room. "I want you to dance with me."

"Honey, there are very few things I suck at, but dancing is one of them."

She turned to him, arms outstretched. "Then just hold me while I rub my body all over yours in time to the music."

"That is undeniably the best offer I've ever received."

Her laugh was a sexy combination of lustful and sweet as he walked into her embrace. He gathered her right hand into his left and tucked it against his chest. He settled his other hand low on her back and drew her just close enough for their hips to touch as he led her in a gentle sway.

A pink flush rose on her cheeks. "You're better than you think."

He dropped his cheek to hers. "Only with you."

Their lips found each other naturally, and their dance became more.

Wordlessly, they helped each other shed their shirts, bumping into each other with elbows and chins, laughing and apologizing in heated whispers, and then it was back to kissing, naked chest to naked chest, content for a moment to just enjoy the feel of skin on skin. The coarse hair that covered his taut muscles abraded the soft, tender flesh of her nipples with every labored breath, every shift of his body.

He angled her toward the couch. "Lie down."

She obeyed, reaching for him as she did. But instead of joining her on the couch, he knelt in front of her. She rose on her elbows.

"What are you—"

He lifted his eyebrows and pulled off her shorts, never losing eye contact with her. Then he hooked one leg over his shoulder, then the other. He saw the moment when she realized his intentions. Her eyes widened. Her hands fisted the couch cushions.

He lowered his mouth between her legs and whispered, "Can I kiss you here?"

"Yes," she breathed, tilting her head back in anticipation.

He grazed the sensitive skin between her legs, and she moaned. And then her groan became his, because fuck . . . her taste. Sweet. So Alexis. He loved her with his tongue, using the tip to find and circle and massage the swollen nub. She writhed beneath him, and he felt her hand grip the back of his head.

Her breaths came in little pants. Her legs tightened against his shoulders. He already could tell the signs of her coming orgasm, and he increased the pace and the pressure.

"Noah . . . oh my God . . ." She bucked and cried out. He continued to stroke her until her spasms subsided and she sank languidly against the couch.

"Come here," she whispered, reaching for him.

Noah rose on his knees. His hands shook as he stood and undid his jeans. She helped to free his erection and cover him in a condom, and then she wrapped her legs around his waist as he bent over her.

He could barely think because the tip of him was already pressed against her opening, and fuck, fuck, he was like a virgin again. He buried his face in her neck and thrust. And the entire fucking world shifted. "Alexis . . ."

She gasped, arching into him.

Nothing had ever felt like this. Nothing.

She held him there, her face pressed into his neck. And that's when he felt it. The shudder in her chest. He rose up immediately, afraid he was crushing her. But she rolled her face away from him. He watched a tear roll down her cheek.

Fuck. What did he do? "What's wrong?"

She sucked in another shaky breath, but when she let it out, it came out with a small sob.

He reached up and turned her face back to him. "Talk to me."

"I'm sorry. I'm just . . ." She caught her breath. "I'm just happy."

Alexis woke up alone the next morning.

She rose on her elbows and tried to get her bearings, but then she heard the clink of dishes in the kitchen.

She pulled on a long T-shirt, padded downstairs, and leaned in the doorway at the end of the hall to study him. He stood at the island with his back to her, a bowl of cereal in one hand and his phone in the other, scrolling absently with his thumb until he set it down to take a bite. He'd showered but hadn't dried his hair all the way.

"Good morning."

He turned around and smiled, and in that instant, she never ever wanted him to leave. She wanted to wake up to that smile every day of her life. He set his bowl down as she approached. His hands gripped her hips and tugged her close.

"Morning," he murmured, dipping his head.

They shared a sweet, brief kiss that sent her heart into overdrive. "You're awake early."

"Habit." He squeezed her hips. "I made you some tea."

She leaned against the counter and met his coy smile with one of her own as she sipped her tea. "You know last night, what you did, the oral thing?" Her face flamed as she said it.

He lifted a single eyebrow, a sexy smile tugging his lips up at the corners. "Yeah, I remember the oral thing."

"I've never, I mean. No one has ever . . ." She shut up and bit her lip.

His face lost all traces of amusement. "You've never had oral sex?"

She shrugged. "Not on me. I mean, not done *to me*."

The look on Noah's face couldn't have been more disgusted if she'd told him she'd switched alliances from Finn to Poe. "What the fuck is wrong with the men of this country?"

She barked out a laugh as he suddenly blocked her against the counter with his arms. Boom. Her nipples pebbled and her thighs began to sweat.

His mouth dipped to her ear. "Did you like it?"

"I thought that was obvious," she panted. The heat of his breath made her weak and wet.

"Want me to do it again?" His tongue dipped into the cave of her ear.

"Yep," she squeaked.

"Good," he breathed, lips now tickling her throat. "Because knowing that I'm the only man in this whole goddamned world who knows how good you taste makes me want to do it over and over again."

"You—You think I taste good?"

"You are a fucking delicacy," he growled, lips now hovering over hers. "And I plan to feast on you every chance I get."

He devoured her mouth and then released her with a swat on the butt.

Alexis laughed and pushed him away. "Who is this man in my kitchen, and what you have done with my mild-mannered Noah?"

He winked at her, and her entire body went up in flames.

"I wish I didn't have to work today," she yawned, carrying her tea to the table. She sat down and drew one leg up on her chair. "But since I was off Friday and Saturday, I can't justify another day off, even if it's Sunday."

Noah shoveled another bite of cereal into his mouth. "I have about a thousand things to catch up on too. I wish I could cancel every one of them."

"New clients?"

"Old ones who can't train their employees to stop opening phishing emails."

"I love it when you talk nerdy to me."

He tipped his cereal bowl and drank the rest of the milk. Even that was sexy. After putting the bowl in the dishwasher, he joined her at the table and slid his phone toward her. "I started a grocery list. Add whatever you need. I'll get it after I finish work today."

Her heart ping-ponged in her chest as she glanced down at the list. "Steel-cut oats?"

"Those are for me."

"Planning on eating breakfast here a lot?"

"Yep."

"That's awfully presumptuous of you. We haven't even been on a real date yet."

"What're you talking about? We've been on a million dates."

"Not as a couple. Not since we've started, you know . . ."

He jerked his eyebrows. "Doing the oral thing?"

Her cheeks got hot again.

Noah sighed dramatically and leaned back in his chair. "Fine. Will you go out with me?"

"Depends on where you take me."

"Your bedroom?"

"I can do that."

Noah grabbed the seat of her chair and dragged it close to his. He took her hands and tugged her forward until she willingly straddled his lap.

Things were just getting good when her cell phone rang.

Noah nipped her collarbone and then let her go with a groan. She jogged into the hallway where her phone was charging. The number was from Huntsville.

Her pulse skyrocketed as she answered. "Hello?"

"Alexis? This is Jasmine from the transplant center."

Her breath lodged in her throat. "Yes, hi."

"I'm calling to tell you that we got the second round of compatibility tests back."

Alexis looked up to find Noah hovering in the doorway, eyebrows furrowed.

"Okay," she said on a breath. "What's the verdict?"

"You're a genetic match."

The roaring in her ears made it hard to focus on what Jasmine said after that. Something about scheduling her for the final tests to make sure she was healthy enough for the surgery. Something about needing to do it in the next couple of weeks and it would take two days.

Alexis finally thanked her and hung up.

"What's wrong?" Noah asked, walking closer.

"That was the hospital."

He stopped short. "And?"

"I'm a genetic match."

Noah dragged his hand over his hair. "Now what?"

"She wants me to come down for two days of testing to make sure I'm healthy enough for the surgery."

Noah stared at the floor, jaw hard and clenched.

"I have to do this, Noah."

"I know." His breath shook as he lowered his forehead to her shoulder. "How can I help?"

"Can you come with me?"

"You even have to ask?"

She kissed him. In five seconds flat, her T-shirt was on the floor. Thirty seconds later, he backed her to the couch and his mouth was on her breast and she was moaning his name. Twenty seconds after that, Noah dropped to his knees in front of her splayed legs.

She lost track of time after that.

CHAPTER TWENTY-THREE

This was her favorite way to wake up.

In the ten days since they'd returned from Memphis, Noah had spent every night in her bed and awakened her the same way every morning. It started with a kiss on the shoulder as his arm snaked around her waist. Then a slow, exploratory caress followed until she was fully awake, and then it always ended like this—wrapped up in each other, spent and sweaty, and deliriously happy.

Noah kissed her deeply, still buried inside her. With a groan, he wrenched his mouth away and burrowed his face in her neck. "Don't make me get up."

Alexis ran her hands up his spine. "Sorry. But I have a lot to do to get ready for the tests." They were going to drive down to Huntsville tonight and stay in a hotel, because she had to be at the transplant center in the morning to start the physical evaluations. "And you have to help Mack with the seating chart."

His groan this time was of the disgusted kind. He rolled off her. "I can't wait for this wedding to be over."

A laugh bubbled from her chest as she curled against his warm side. Noah picked up her hand from where it was splayed between his pecs and brought her fingers to his lips. "Are you packed and ready to go, or do you need to come home again before we leave?"

"I'll take all my stuff to work so you can just pick me up there."

Noah yawned. "I think the guys are going to pick me up here for wedding shit. Then I'll run home to pack a few things before coming to get you."

Alexis kissed his jaw. "You're a good man, Noah Logan."

He turned his head to catch her lips with his. "You make me want to be a good man."

Alexis melted on the inside. Noah wrapped his arm around her shoulder to palm the back of her head as he kissed her again. Soon, he rolled her onto her back, and his hand began its exploration again, and—

"Shit." Noah froze, eyes wide, unblinking, and staring off to the side.

"What? What's wrong?" Alexis followed his stare. Beefcake was beside the bed, paws perched on the mattress as if he wanted someone to pick him up.

Noah's Adam's apple bobbed. "If I move slowly, maybe he won't hurt me."

"He's not going to hurt you." Alexis patted the mattress. "Come on, Beefcake. You can do it."

Noah rolled off her and managed to throw the comforter over his naked lap just in time. Beefcake leaped onto the bed, lumbered over Alexis, and went straight for Noah.

Noah held rigidly still, not even breathing, as Beefcake stepped gingerly onto his chest.

"Oh shit." Noah gulped.

Alexis scratched Beefcake behind the ears. "Good boy," she cooed. "Noah is our friend."

The gravel of a deep purr vibrated through his thick fur. Eyes closed, Beefcake began to knead his front paws into Noah's chest.

Alexis gasped. "Awwww . . . look at that."

Noah swallowed hard. "Wh-What's he doing?"

"It's called making kitty biscuits."

"It's called tenderizing the meat."

"It's a sign of affection."

Beefcake began to purr louder as he folded his legs under him and settled into a rectangle on Noah's chest.

"A full meat loaf," Alexis whispered, emotion choking her.

"What the hell does that mean?" Noah hissed back.

"That's what you call that cat position. A meat loaf. They only do it when they're truly relaxed and content."

Beefcake was the picture of relaxation—eyes closed, purring with a steady motor, head lowered. "Pet him," Alexis whispered.

Noah's hand rose slowly from the mattress and hovered above Beefcake's back. Then, inch by inch, he lowered it until his fingers brushed Beefcake's fur. The purr became a rumble.

Alexis lowered her cheek to Noah's shoulder and sighed. "My two favorite men. Friends, at last."

Alexis was still melty and deliriously happy an hour later when she sat down with Jessica at a bistro table with her laptop and her daily planner. Two of the part-time college students who worked there manned the counter. It was past nine, so the worst of the morning rush was over. Still, she wanted to keep the meeting as short as possible. Even taking two days off for the physical evaluations was going to be tough, and she had an intimidatingly long to-do list to get through today. She shuddered to think how much she was going to have to do if she actually went through with the surgery. She'd be off work for a minimum of ten days.

Jessica pushed a plate bearing a scone and a cup of cut-up fruit closer to Alexis. "I haven't seen you eat anything."

Alexis popped a grape into her mouth as she pulled out a copy of the schedule she'd put together that morning. "Let me know if this works for you. Liv and Mack are both available to help out anytime you need it."

"Beth and I can handle it," Jessica said. "Don't worry."

"If anything comes up, just call me. If I can't answer, call Noah. He can get messages to me."

"Seriously, Alexis. We got this. You just focus on what you need to do."

Alexis closed her planner and ate another grape. "Thank you for pet sitting." Jessica had agreed to stay at her house while Alexis was gone. Beefcake wasn't exactly kennel material. He had a tendency to pee on cats he didn't know. "He'll be mad that I didn't bring him to work today, but just give him a treat, and he'll get over it."

A ding from the café door interrupted. Alexis glanced over and then quickly back with a smile. Bob Brown, the head of the East Nashville district business council, shuffled forward with an apologetic gait.

"Hey, Bob. What's up?"

"Good to see you, Alexis. Wish I was here under better circumstances."

A tinge of alarm shot through her. "What's wrong?"

He handed over an envelope. "Didn't want you to see this in an email."

Alexis opened it and pulled out a single sheet of paper. Bob stood nervously by as she scanned the words.

"Oh, for God's sake," she breathed, looking up at Bob. "Is this for real?"

"'Fraid so."

Jessica reached for the paper. "What is it?"

Alexis tried to keep the venom from her voice. "Karen actually did it. She filed a complaint against me. I have to answer to the zoning board."

Noah took a shower at Alexis's house and did an hour of work while he waited for the guys to pick him up. He'd left his own car at home last night, so he'd have the guys drop him off there after they helped Mack, though he still had no idea why it was so difficult to assign people seats for a wedding.

There was a knock at the front door just as he was shutting down his computer. He crossed the room, opened the door, and found Colton and the Russian standing there. "You could've just texted that you were here," he said.

"The Russian has to pee," Colton said, brushing past Noah as he walked in. He paused in the entryway and looked around. "Cute place. It totally looks like her."

"Shut up."

"All I said was cute place."

"It was the way you said it," Noah scowled. "And how the hell would you know what looks like her?"

Colton raised his hands and his eyebrows. "Chill, dude. I know there's always the threat of me stealing your girl because I'm me, but she's all yours."

Noah stepped back to let the Russian in. "Bathroom's over there," he said with a nod around the corner. As the Russian wandered off, Noah glared at Colton. "If he has to do more than take a piss, I'm holding you personally responsible."

Colton shrugged and headed toward the kitchen.

Noah shut the door. "Where are you going?"

"I'm looking around."

"Just don't touch anything." Noah hung a left into the living room where he'd been working. He shoved his shit into his backpack and walked into the kitchen to find Colton peering in the fridge.

"What are you doing? Get out of there."

"I'm hungry."

"You can't just take shit from her fridge!"

Colton swung the door shut. "There's nothing good in there anyway. Just a bunch of weird shit."

"It's not weird. She's a vegetarian."

Colton's gaze landed on the red harness hanging from a hook by the door to the garage. He grabbed it and let it dangle suggestively from his fingers. "Kinky. What exactly do you and Alexis do?"

Noah yanked the harness away. "It's a cat leash, douchebag."

"A cat leash?" Colton laughed. "You're kidding."

"Beefcake needs regular exercise."

The toilet flushed, and a moment later, the Russian wandered into the kitchen. "Where is kitty?"

"Hiding. He doesn't like strangers."

Colton suddenly froze. "Wh-What is that?"

Noah followed Colton's terrified gaze. Beefcake had appeared out of nothingness, a furry, motionless apparition at the end of the hall. A dark silhouette with glowing eyes.

"That's Beefcake," Noah gulped. Morning truce aside, he was still sort of afraid.

"No," Colton breathed. "That can't be Beefcake. There's no way that's a cat."

"That is no cat," the Russian said, reverence in his tone. "That is a majestic animal. Like Siberian tiger."

Noah inched along the wall, feeling with his fingers until he found the hallway light switch. Golden light flooded the space, and Colton let out a scream. Because Beefcake had somehow teleported ten feet forward.

"Pretty kitty," the Russian cooed, dropping to one knee.

Noah held his breath as the Russian crouched low and held out his hand. Beefcake rolled at the Russian's feet and began kneading the air with his paws.

"What is that noise?" Colton asked.

"He's purring."

"That's a growl. He's going to kill us. You actually put a leash on that thing?"

"He can't be let out on his own anymore. He kills birds."

"I'd be more worried about him luring a small child into the sewer."

The Russian made an *awww* noise and dropped his hand to the exposed fur of Beefcake's belly.

"Don't!" Noah cried.

But it was too late. Beefcake sprang like a trap in the woods. He wrapped all four legs around the Russian's arm and bit his hand. The Russian shrieked and stood, the cat hanging from his forearm.

"Bad kitty! Bad kitty!" The Russian waved his hand in the air, but that just made Beefcake dig his claws in deeper.

Noah smacked Colton's arm. "Do something!"

"What the hell am I supposed to do?"

"I don't know! You're a cat owner! Get a treat or something!"

"Like what? A baby?"

The Russian bellowed like a man who'd been shot and dropped to one knee with a desperate plea. "Help me!"

Noah smacked Colton again. "Meat. Get meat."

"You said Alexis is a vegetarian. There is no meat!"

"*I am the meat*," the Russian cried.

Colton ran to the fridge and dug around. He returned with a piece of cheese. "Beefcake . . . here, kitty kitty." Colton waved the cheese and approached slowly.

Beefcake sniffed the air, finally releasing his teeth from the Russian's hand.

"That's it. Good boy," Noah crooned.

Colton held the cheese close to the animal's face and then threw it into the hallway. Beefcake dropped to the ground and lumbered after it.

The Russian held his injured arm against his torso and stuck out his lower lip. "Kitty is mean."

Noah ran his hand over his hair. "Kitty is hungry."

"Why the hell does she keep a cat like that," Colton grumbled, inspecting the Russian's wounds.

"That's just Alexis," Noah said. "She has a soft spot for ugly and lonely creatures."

"I guess that explains why she keeps you too."

Noah flipped him off.

Colton tugged the Russian toward the sink. "We need to clean these scratches."

"I'll get the first aid stuff." He went into the bathroom where Alexis had insisted he clean his own Beefcake wounds and grabbed the first aid kit under the sink. When he returned, the Russian was wincing as Colton dabbed a wet paper towel to the scratch on his hand.

"Almost done," Colton said softly.

"Here," Noah said, handing over the ointment that Alexis had used on him. "Rub this on it."

"That's what she said."

The Russian giggled but quickly returned to pouting.

"We done yet?" Noah asked, cleaning up the wet paper towel. "I don't have all day for this shit."

By the time they walked into Mack's club, he was waiting at a table with Sonia with an impatient scowl. "You're late."

"We had a little emergency," Colton said.

"He had a run-in with Beefcake," Noah explained, dropping into the open chair next to Sonia.

The Russian held up his arm. "Kitty is mean."

"That cat is a menace," Mack said.

For reasons he couldn't identify, Noah felt obligated to defend Beefcake. "You have to be patient with him. It takes him a while to trust people. He lashes out when he's scared."

Mack spread out a drawing of the reception hall, ready to get started. At each table, names had been written and erased and written over. Clearly, Mack had been at this awhile. "We have to get this finished today so we can get the place cards printed on time."

Noah shrugged. "Why not just let everyone pick their own seat?"

Mack and Colton looked at him like he'd just suggested serving baked chicken buffet-style for dinner. "Are you crazy?" Mack sputtered.

"What's the big deal?"

"The big deal is that if you put the wrong person next to the wrong person, you might piss someone off. Or if you put someone at a seat too far back, they might get offended because they think it means they're not very important. And don't even get me started on what to do about Liv's parents."

Noah didn't know a lot about Liv's history, but he knew enough to at least understand why her parents would, indeed, pose a problem.

"There are politics here, Noah," Mack continued. "This isn't easy."

Noah held up his hands in a truce, mainly because he didn't actually care enough to fight about it.

"So, here's what we have to figure out first," Mack said, handing each man a pencil. "Since we're not doing a head table, we need to divide the bridal party up among other tables."

"That should be easy," Noah said.

Sonia snorted.

"It's not easy," Mack said. "It's an uneven number because not everyone has a significant other."

This time Sonia rolled her eyes, she being among the unattached.

"I was going to put Colton and Sonia at a table together along with Del and his wife, Noah and Alexis, and the Russian and his wife, but—"

Colton turned toward the Russian so quickly that he nearly fell over in his chair. "Your wife is coming?"

The Russian stared at his hands, lower lip stuck out. "She can't."

Colton kicked Noah under the table. Noah kicked back.

"That's too bad, man," Noah said. "We were all looking forward to meeting her."

"And it leaves us in a bind for the tables," Mack whined. "Because now we'll either have an open seat at that table, or I'll have to move everyone around because the tables hold eight people. And I still have no idea where to put Gretchen."

Noah cocked his head. "Gretchen? As in the woman you were dating before Liv?"

"Yes."

"You're inviting an ex-girlfriend to your wedding?"

"She and Liv are friends now, remember?"

Yeah, Noah knew that. Gretchen was also a friend of Alexis's because Gretchen had offered pro bono legal services to Royce Preston's victims. But still, she and Mack had dated. "I'm just saying it's weird."

Mack threw down his pencil. "You have no idea how stressful this shit is! I've got Liv's mom up my ass about making sure she's nowhere near Liv's father and his new wife, which means they have to be at separate tables, but that means choosing which one gets to sit at the main table with Liv and me or booting them both to separate tables, which will be weird because I plan to have my mom and her boyfriend sit with us. How can I only have one set of parents at the main table with us? Oh, and then there's the little problem of where to put Rosie and Hop."

Rosie was the woman Liv had lived with for two years before moving in with Mack, and Hop was Rosie's boyfriend. They were like grandparents to Liv.

"And don't get me started on how pissed off people are that we're planning to have kids' tables in a separate room," Mack added, "as if we're banishing children to a deserted island or something."

Sonia slapped a hand over Mack's mouth as she glared at Noah. "Happy now? This is what I've been dealing with *for a week*. I just got him calmed down this morning."

Noah leaned over the paper again and studied it. After a moment, he scratched his head. "Who is the Russian walking down the aisle with?"

Sonia lifted her hand from Mack's mouth and raised it reluctantly in the air.

Noah went to work. "Put Sonia and the Russian together at this table," he said, writing their names down. "Move Colton over here with Liv's mom."

Colton breathed an agonized *noooo*. "Can't I sit with Gretchen?"

"She's not part of the bridal party," Mack snapped.

Noah scribbled some more names. "Put Liv's father and his new wife at this table. Move Thea and Gavin and your brother and his wife to the main table with you and Liv, your mom and her boyfriend. Move your cousin and her wife over here with Rosie and Hop. No more open seats, and people who need to be separated are separated."

Mack blinked rapidly. "How—How did you figure that out?"

Noah tapped the pencil against his temple. "I'm a genius, remember?"

"I've been staring at this damn drawing for a week," Mack said, voice tight.

Noah patted him on the shoulder. "Don't wait so long next time to ask for help, man."

"Please don't make me sit with Liv's mom," Colton begged. "I've heard stories. She's horrible."

"All you have to do is sit next to her during dinner," Mack scowled.

"Bullshit. She's going to be all over me. I know how this works. I'm the good-looking, rich celebrity, and she's the lonely, bitter divorcée—"

"You have a super inflated sense of your own attractiveness, dude," Noah said.

"I'm *rich*. Richer than all of you combined. I'll be the richest man in the room, which automatically makes me the best-looking man in the room."

"And you wonder why you don't have a girlfriend," Noah scoffed.

Colton crossed his arms and pouted. "Great. You've had a girl-friend for like two weeks, and suddenly you're an expert?"

"That reminds me," Noah said, dragging his backpack from the floor to his lap. He unzipped the front pocket, withdrew the book, and slid it to Mack. "Here."

Mack grinned. "You finished it?"

"No. I don't need it anymore."

Mack tugged his eyebrows together. "What makes you think that?"

"Alexis and I are together."

Mack snorted. "Rookie mistake, slapnuts. Your journey has only just begun."

Annoyance flared his nostrils. "What the fuck does that mean?"

Mack slid the book back. "It means now is not the time to get cocky. Your relationship is new. There's still a lot that could go wrong if you're not careful."

"Yes," the Russian said, looking up from his lap, a somber expression turning his angular features dark. "Together does not always mean happy ever after."

CHAPTER TWENTY-FOUR

"Well, this is the sexiest thing I've ever worn."

Twenty-four hours later, Alexis emerged from the bathroom in her hospital room and twirled for Noah. Her flimsy gown snapped in the front and hung on her like an old pillowcase.

He smiled from his seat by the window. "Everything you wear is sexy."

"It's the socks that really make the outfit." The hospital had given her some no-slip socks with rubber grooves along the bottom.

Noah stood and walked toward her, all sexy and slow. Her body started to tingle as he dropped a kiss on her upturned lips. "You sure you don't need me to stay here with you tonight?"

"I have to pee in a jug all night."

"I can handle it."

"I'll be fine," she said, rising on tiptoe to kiss him again. "Go back to the hotel room and get some decent sleep."

He'd been there all day, waiting and working in between her various tests. She'd had a chest X-ray, an echocardiogram, a radiology test, and a variety of cancer screenings. Now she had to spend the night for urine samples and a sleep study.

A discreet cough from the door brought them apart. Alexis turned around as Jasmine walked in. "Am I interrupting?"

"No," Alexis said, but her cheeks were hot. "Noah, this is Jasmine Singh, the transplant coordinator."

"Pleasure to meet you," Jasmine said, extending her hand. "Sorry I missed you this morning when you arrived."

"Noah Logan," he said, accepting the handshake.

"I just wanted to let you know that I'm heading home now but can be paged if you need me."

"I'm sure I'll be fine," Alexis said. "Mostly I'll be sleeping."

Jasmine gestured behind her toward the door. "You have a visitor waiting. I thought I should check with you first before letting her in, given the unusual nature of your relationship."

That could only mean one person, and they hadn't seen each other or spoken since the horrible scene at the Vanderpools' house.

Noah's hand settled on her back and rubbed a soothing circle. She looked up at him. "It's up to you," he said quietly.

"Would it be best if I told her to come back another time?" Jasmine asked.

Her throat suddenly dry, Alexis shook her head. "No, it's fine. Send her in."

She would have to see the family at some point if she was cleared for the surgery. Might as well get it over with now.

Jasmine walked out, and a moment later, Candi's soft footsteps approached from behind the half curtain that separated the entrance from the rest of the room. She stopped short when she saw Noah and glanced nervously between the two of them. "Hi, um . . . Am I interrupting?"

Noah looked down at Alexis, his expression deceptively blank. "I can stay."

"It's okay," Alexis said, lifting her face for a kiss. "I'll call you later."

"I—I'm sorry," Candi stammered. "I should have called, but I wasn't sure if you'd want to see me, and I just really wanted to see you. But I can come back or—"

"Candi, it's fine. Noah was heading back to the hotel soon anyway, right?" She met his gaze and silently encouraged him to agree. He nodded, reluctantly.

He pressed his lips lightly to hers and squeezed her elbow. "Call me if you need anything."

With a polite nod at Candi, he walked out.

Candi swallowed hard. "He really didn't have to go."

Alexis scooted up onto her bed and motioned toward the chair that Noah had vacated. "Do you want to sit down?"

Candi's gait was stiff and awkward as she crossed the small room and lowered to the chair. She perched on the edge of the cushion the same way as that first day in Alexis's office. She clutched a black backpack to her lap.

Her swallow was audible. "I'm sorry again about what happened at the house. I should have told them before you got there. I just didn't know how, and, God, Cayden was such a jerk. He's not normally like that. I swear."

"I guess there's no normal way to respond when you find out without warning that your father had another child out in the world."

"I know I should have told them you were coming, but I was just so mad at Dad. He was being so stubborn, to not even consider you as a donor?" She suddenly stopped, a stricken look on her face. "I mean, not that you're just a donor to him. To me."

Alexis took mercy on her and offered a soothing smile. "I know what you meant, Candi. You don't have to keep apologizing."

"But I keep sticking my foot in my mouth."

"No, you don't. You're nervous. *I'm* nervous."

Candi's relief was its own presence in the room—calming and quiet. "I, um, I brought something, some stuff to show you."

"What kind of stuff?"

Candi reached into her bag and withdrew a black photo album before setting the bag on the floor. "Family photos and stuff." A sheepish expression turned her cheeks pink. "I—I sort of made this for you. To keep."

Alexis's chest tightened. "Thank you. That was very kind."

Candi flipped open the cover. "It has pictures of, like, the whole family. I thought you might want to, you know, get to know everyone."

Alexis wasn't actually ready for anything like that, but she didn't want to hurt Candi's feelings. She'd obviously put a lot of time into the project. So instead, Alexis smiled and patted the edge of the mattress next to her. "Show me."

"So, I sort of organized it chronologically," Candi said, sliding up on the bed. "This is our grandparents."

Alexis studied the first photo, a black-and-white picture of a beaming couple standing in front of a church altar.

"They got married in 1960. Dad was born exactly eight months later, which was sort of a scandal, I guess, because they tried to tell everyone he was premature but . . ." Candi shrugged. "The truth is that Grandma was probably knocked up on her wedding day."

Alexis lifted an eyebrow. "Unplanned pregnancies do happen."

Candi blinked. "Right."

"You mentioned an aunt and uncle. Does Elliott have siblings?"

Candi nodded and turned the page. "A brother and a sister. They both still live in California."

Alexis looked down at another photo of three children in an unmistakable sepia-toned filter of 1960s color film.

"That's Dad," Candi said, pointing at the oldest child. "And that's Uncle Jack, and this is Aunt Caroline." Candi paused and then looked up at Alexis. "You kind of look like her."

Alexis didn't see it. She'd been told all her life that she looked like her mother, and she was struggling to accept that anyone else's DNA could have shaped her features.

"We have six cousins too," Candi said, turning to another page. "Aunt Caroline had four kids, and Uncle Jack had two. They're all pretty cool, but our cousin Jimmy is sort of messed up."

"In what way?"

"He dropped out of high school and got mixed up in drugs and stuff."

"That's too bad."

"He's in rehab right now, though."

"And the others?"

Candi beamed. Every tiny encouragement on Alexis's part seemed to cement in the young woman's mind that they were about to become BFFs. Alexis almost felt guilty. She was just being polite, but Candi seemed to take her interest as evidence of a blossoming relationship.

And maybe if Alexis was willing to be honest with herself, she'd admit that it was.

"So, our cousin Stephanie just got married last summer, and she works for some bank doing financial stuff. I'm not really sure what it is. That's her brother." Candi pointed at another picture. "He goes to UCLA. I think he's majoring in business. Something boring like that. And our cousin Nicole graduated a couple of years ago from UC Santa Barbara and does, like, environmental stuff. She works for the forestry service or something."

Alexis listened as Candi prattled on. She felt like an intruder, hearing family stories she had no business knowing. This was a family. She was part of this bloodline but knew none of them. She was the crooked branch on the family tree.

Alexis cleared her throat. "Are your, *our*, grandparents still alive?" The words tripped over themselves.

"Grandma is. She lives in a nursing home, though. She has Alzheimer's."

"I'm sorry to hear that."

"Grandpa died ten years ago. He had a heart attack."

It took a full half hour to get through all the pictures, and by the time they were done, Alexis felt like she'd just sat through a PowerPoint presentation on her own personal ancestry.

"So, there you go. Now you know everyone." Candi handed the photo album to Alexis.

Alexis smiled as she accepted the heavy leather-bound album on her lap. The silence stretched out just long enough to get awkward.

Alexis finally cleared her throat. "So, Caroline and Jack . . . They aren't a match for Elliott?"

Candi shook her head. "They got tested, but neither of them matched. And Grandma can't donate because she has Alzheimer's. She can't consent."

"So it's really just me, huh?"

"I'm sorry," Candi said in a rush. "I didn't tell you that to make you feel bad."

Alexis rose from the bed and set the photo album on the table there. "Don't be sorry. I asked. You answered."

"I know, but I feel like I keep saying stupid stuff around you."

Alexis turned around and crossed her arms. "Well, stop feeling that way. This whole thing is weird."

Candi burst out laughing. "Yes, it is."

They shared a look through matching eyes, and something peaceful passed between them. Candi hadn't asked for this situation any more than Alexis had. They'd both been tossed unwillingly into the game of parental mistakes and consequences, and they had both suffered in their own ways because of it.

A warm sensation took root in Alexis's chest. "Tell me about you," she said, returning to the bed.

Candi blinked in surprise. "Me?"

"You've told me about everyone else in the family, but the only thing I know about you is that you feel guilty a lot and you once took a DNA test."

Candi shrugged, but the simple motion carried the weight of a lot of unspoken things. "I'm the black sheep of the family."

"How do you figure?"

Candi started picking at her chipped nail polish. "I have no idea what I want to do with my life. I've switched majors four times."

"So."

"We're Vanderpools. We don't do that."

"Then do things your own way. Life is short."

To Alexis's horror, tears flooded Candi's eyes. "I know."

"I'm sorry." Alexis winced. "That was a thoughtless thing to say given your father's health."

Candi shrugged half-heartedly. "It was hard for me, too, when I found out about you."

"I can imagine."

Candi's face darkened. "He denied it at first, that you were his daughter."

Alexis held her emotions back, hoping the sting of that information didn't show on her face.

"But I told him there was no way the test was wrong," Candi said. "I could only share that much DNA with someone who was my sibling, and unless I came from a different mother, which, obviously, I didn't, then you had to be his."

"He must have been pretty shocked."

Candi nodded, eyes staring at the window. "He begged me not to tell Mom. I hated him for that, you know? I hated him for asking me to lie for him."

"But you did."

"For Mom's sake, not his." She gnawed her bottom lip. "I feel bad that I didn't at least warn her before you came to the house. She shouldn't have found out that way. She's still mad at me."

Alexis pulled her legs onto the bed crisscross style and turned to face Candi. "Listen to me. Don't let this, *me*, get in between you and your parents. It doesn't solve anything to hold on to grudges."

"It's not a grudge. I don't understand how he could just walk away from you and your mom."

"You might not be here if he hadn't. Besides, he didn't know about me back then. He didn't know my mom was pregnant. She's as much to blame as he is."

The admission was as sour as a shot of apple cider vinegar and burned just as badly. But it was true, wasn't it? Her mother could have told Elliott she was pregnant. She *should* have told him, and the most frustrating thing about all of this was that Alexis would never be able to ask her mother why.

Candi shook her head as if fighting off the emotions that had made her lips tremble just moments before. "Do you have any pictures of your mom?"

Wordlessly, Alexis slipped off the bed, retrieved her phone from her purse, and tapped the icon for her photos. After clicking on the album where she kept photos of her mom, she handed the phone to Candi.

Candi swiped slowly, studying each photo as if trying to build a connection with the woman who'd once been part of her father's life. "She was really pretty," she finally said.

Alexis peered closer at the photo Candi was looking at—a picture of Alexis and her mother at Alexis's graduation from culinary school.

"Dad was right," Candi said. "You look so much like her."

"But the eye color is definitely Elliott's."

"And mine."

"And Cayden's," Alexis added. She immediately regretted it when she saw Candi's face light up.

Candi handed back the phone. "Thank you for showing me those."

"I don't have many extended family photos like you," she said, curling the phone into her hand. "My mom was an only child, and so am I."

"That sounds kind of lonely." Candi sucked in a gasp and smacked her forehead. "Why do I keep saying stupid shit?"

"It's not stupid. It *was* lonely sometimes." Another sour admission. Another burn of resentment, this time toward her mother. Her eyes grew wet, so she looked away quickly.

"How come you never looked for him?"

Alexis shrugged and returned the phone to her purse. "I didn't see the point."

"But you weren't curious who your father was?"

"I went through phases, I guess. But I had my mom, and she was all I really needed. I figured any man who would abandon her wasn't worth my time."

Candi winced.

"Sorry," Alexis said. Though why she was apologizing, she didn't know. There was no point in sugarcoating things. "I obviously didn't know the truth."

"But does it matter, really? He *did* abandon you. He cheated on my mother and walked away like there would be no consequences. Whether he knew about you or not, it's still a shitty thing to do."

Alexis climbed back onto the bed. "What part of that actually makes you mad? That he lied? Or that he cheated?"

Candi shook her head and bit her lip, as if to hold in something profound and painful. "He kept you from *me*," she finally said. "We could have been sisters. I always wanted a sister."

"Candi," Alexis sighed, folding her legs under her again. "Even if things had been different, we have no way of knowing how our lives would have been. You can't regret a romanticized Hallmark version of a past that never existed. We know each other now. Let go of what might have been and let that be enough."

"But . . ."

"But what?"

"I just . . . The only bond we have now is because he's dying. What about after the surgery? Will we still see each other?" She blanched. "I swear I'm not trying to pressure you."

Alexis rested her hand on Candi's arm. "I know you're not. And I wish I could give you an answer that puts your mind at ease, but I can't. I have no idea what the future will hold."

"But can we at least try?"

"Try what?"

"Being sisters."

Something akin to a punch to the chest made her heart crack and bleed. Alexis had to swallow several times to loosen the tight ball of emotion that had become lodged in her throat. "I don't know how to be a sister."

"I do. It's just like being friends. It's a friend you're related to."

A silence descended on the room, but for the muted sounds of the comings and goings of the nursing staff in the hallway. Alexis had come to detest the noises of hospitals when her mother was sick. The incessant beeping of monitors and the squeak of wheels. That and the annoyingly calm, hushed tones with which people seemed to speak around her, as if softening a voice could lessen the blow of bad news. And it was always bad news.

But inside her room now, the only sound Alexis could hear was the beat of her own heart, because, for once, her own thoughts were peaceful. Maybe this would be another one of those before-and-after moments that she'd look back on someday and realize it was when things changed, once again.

She suddenly, desperately wanted it to be.

"I should go," Candi said, sliding off the bed.

"Thank you for coming by and for the photo album."

Candi did the nervous lip-bite thing and tugged her hands inside the cuffs of her sweatshirt. "So I guess I'll see you later?"

"How about if I call you tomorrow to let you know how things went?"

Candi's smile brightened the room. "That'd be awesome."

Alexis scooted back on her mattress as Candi turned to leave.

"Hey, Candi."

Candi turned around.

"I always wanted a sister too."

"Really?"

Alexis managed a shaky nod. "Thank you for finding me."

It felt wrong to leave the hospital. Noah tried going back up to their hotel room, but the silence and the empty spot next to him on the bed drove him to distraction. So he ended up in the lobby bar instead, incessantly checking his phone as he nursed a beer. He'd left the hospital an hour ago, and there was still nothing from Alexis.

Noah lifted his hand to the bartender to order another beer. He tried to focus on the college football game on TV but didn't actually give a shit. He hadn't gone to a football school and could never understand the obsession people had with the game. He wouldn't ever say that to Malcolm, of course.

Noah checked his phone again. Still nothing from Alexis. With a frustrated shake of his head, he turned the phone facedown on the bar and tipped the bottle back.

"May I join you?"

Noah looked to his right, and a blood vessel burst in his brain. Elliott stood next to him, hands shoved in the pockets of a windbreaker.

Noah made a noise that was half snort, half *Are you fucking kidding me?* "Is that why Candi went to the hospital? To occupy Alexis so you could ambush me separately?"

Elliott blinked and started. "Candi's at the hospital with Alexis?"

Either he was an incredible actor or he honestly didn't know. Noah clenched his jaw. "What are you doing here?"

"I thought maybe we could talk." Elliott extended his hand. "We didn't meet properly the first time."

Noah jutted his jaw sideways. After a moment, he accepted the handshake but immediately returned his attention to the TV. He didn't want Elliott there, didn't want to talk, and sure as shit wasn't going to make this easy on him.

Elliott pulled out the stool next to Noah and sat down. The bartender scooted over and placed a napkin in front of him. "What can I get you?"

"Just ice water, please." He swiveled to look at Noah. "Can I get you anything?"

"No."

"I didn't know Candi was going to visit Alexis tonight."

"Well, she did."

"I'm glad. This has been really difficult for Candi."

Noah made an ugly noise and tipped his bottle back. "Forgive me if I find it hard to generate much sympathy for any member of your family."

"I understand your anger, but Candi is innocent in all of this."

"So is Alexis, yet it seems they're the two people hurting most of all because of you."

The bartender set a glass of water in front of Elliott, and he immediately downed a long drink. "I deserve that," he said, turning the glass round and round on the bar.

"If you're expecting me to argue that point, you'll be waiting a long time."

"That's fair."

Noah's anger got the best of him. He whipped his gaze to Elliott's. "Let's make one thing absolutely clear. Alexis is only doing this because it would never occur to her to say no. Because that's who she is. She takes care of people often to her own detriment, and it would haunt her the rest of her life if she didn't do this for you. So you can play the contrite patriarch all you want, but I hope you spend every day knowing that you don't deserve this gift she's giving you."

Noah stood, dug out his wallet, and dropped a twenty-dollar bill on the counter. Without so much as a glance at Elliott, he stormed off.

But Elliott's voice quickly stopped him. "I looked into your father's death."

Noah froze. He barely remembered turning around much less walking back, but somehow he stood next to Elliott's stool again. "What did you say?"

"You were right. His death was entirely preventable and should not have happened."

Noah's hands balled into fists. "How do you have access to information about my father's death?"

Elliott smirked, but it was more sad than arrogant. "I have a pretty high security clearance." He paused, and the sad smirk became remorseful chagrin. "Your father was sent to war with insufficient protection, and even though it wasn't my company, it was a company like mine that failed. And it failed for the exact same reasons that my company was under federal investigation. Greed. Pure and simple."

"That would make an excellent opening statement to Congress, but I don't buy a word of it."

"I just want you to know that I understand why you would question my motives."

Noah braced a hand on the bar and leaned down, seething and shaking. "What do you want? A gold star for stating the obvious?"

Elliott stood. Slowly. Bracing a hand on the edge of the bar to steady himself. "Mortality has a way of bringing things into focus.

It makes you realize what really matters and what doesn't. I just want you to know how sorry I am for your loss."

For the first time, Noah saw him as he was—a man staring death in the face and desperately wanting to make up for his mistakes. The flare of empathy that would have softened Alexis simply hardened Noah's anger. "And you think sorry is enough? It's not. Where was this remorse when your company was under investigation? If you want redemption, don't just apologize. Do something."

Elliott's smile was sad as he stepped away from the stool. He lightly patted Noah's arm. "I'm trying." He paused as if wanting to say more, but then shook his head as if deciding against it. Instead, he squeezed Noah's arm. "You're braver than I could ever dream of being. Your father would be proud."

He shuffled away, leaving Noah standing with his mouth agape and a single question racing through his brain. What the fuck was that all about?

CHAPTER TWENY-FIVE

Alexis was done with all her tests by noon. Noah spent most of that time pacing in the hallway and trying to figure out how to tell her about his bizarre run-in with Elliott. Now he waited outside Jasmine's office, where she and Alexis had disappeared more than fifteen minutes ago. He'd killed a few minutes by running her overnight bag out to the car, but now he was back to pacing.

He finally gave up and leaned against the wall opposite Jasmine's office door so he could will it to open. A few minutes later, Alexis walked out, smiling, laughing, and clutching a black binder to her chest. Jasmine followed.

"We're all set," Jasmine said. Her eyes locked with Noah's. "Thank you for supporting her through this. This can be a very emotional process for everyone involved."

"Everything okay, then? That's it?"

Jasmine and Alexis exchanged a look.

"What's that mean?" Noah demanded.

Alexis used her *placate an angry customer* voice again. "We have a surgery date."

Noah tried to control his expression, schooling it into something less than *holy fucking shit*. "When?"

They did it again—shared a look. Alexis was even more cautious this time. "Soon."

"How soon?"

"Two weeks."

Gravity failed beneath his feet, and he swayed. He propped his hand against the wall.

Jasmine's face softened into the sort of practiced patience they probably taught in medical school. "The sooner the better. Since everyone is ready now, there's no reason to wait longer than necessary."

Alexis came to stand by his side. "It'll be okay," she said, resting her free hand on his stomach. "We have plenty of time to prepare, and once the surgery is over, I'll have more than enough time to recover before Liv and Mack's wedding."

Like he gave a shit about the wedding. Noah bent and brushed his lips across hers.

"Call me if you have any questions or concerns," Jasmine said. "Make sure you study all the pre-op information I gave you, because it's really important that you follow all the instructions prior to surgery."

Alexis thanked the woman and then slipped her hand in Noah's as they walked down the hallway. They stopped briefly at the nurse's station so Alexis could sign a few papers, and while they stood there, the elevator opposite the desk dinged. The doors opened, and out walked Elliott, Candi, and a woman who was an older version of the bride in the wedding announcement.

"Lexa," Noah said, his hand instinctively coming to rest on Alexis's back.

She looked up at him and then immediately followed the direction of his gaze.

"Oh," she said, and the word managed to sound both bewildered and pleased. "Hi."

"Good, we caught you," Elliott said, slightly out of breath as they closed the distance to the counter. "We tried to text you that we were here, but you didn't respond, so we were afraid you'd already left."

Alexis dug her phone from her pocket and let out a quiet *shoot*. "I'm sorry. I didn't hear my phone. I was in Jasmine's office."

Noah splayed his fingers across the width of Alexis's back. "What are you doing here?"

Elliott smiled. "Just checking on our patient."

The word *our* sent heat racing up Noah's neck.

Candi walked to Alexis and embraced her. And the only thing more surprising than that show of familiarity was that Alexis returned the hug with equal ease. There was a warmth between them that made him both suspicious and jealous, which also made him feel like a total shit. He should be happy that Alexis and Candi had apparently reached some kind of peace.

When Candi stepped back, Elliott set his hand on his wife's back. "This is my wife, Lauren."

The woman looked brittle, like a hostage in a proof-of-life photo. He couldn't really blame her. Talk about shitty. She had to stand here and be polite in front of the living, breathing reminder that her husband had cheated on her before they got married.

Noah decided to take the high road with her. He extended his hand. "Nice to meet you."

Her smile was as tight as her fingers were loose. "Likewise."

Candi nudged her father with an elbow.

Elliott nodded. "Right. I know it's last minute, but we were hoping that we could maybe take you out to lunch." Elliott's eyes darted to Noah. "Both of you, of course."

Noah flared his nostrils. Lunch? "We were planning to head back—"

"Of course," Alexis said, her hand once again gripping his.

"Great," Elliott breathed, relief lifting both his voice and his smile. "That's great. There's a restaurant off I-565 called Bilbo's. It's an Italian place. Want to meet us there? Cayden and his wife are going to join us too."

Noah felt the subtle squeeze of Alexis's fingers around his. It managed to feel both reassuring and scolding. "That sounds nice," she said. "We'll meet you there."

They followed the Vanderpools out to the parking lot and parted ways to their separate cars. Noah opened Alexis's door for her and then went around to the driver's side. When he got in, she was on her phone looking up directions to the restaurant.

"It's about a fifteen-minute drive," she said, plugging her phone into the car's radio. The friendly GPS lady told him to head east out of the parking lot.

"You sure about this?" he asked casually, backing out of the parking spot.

"It's just lunch."

"With Elliott and his wife. That's not just lunch."

"The surgery is in two weeks. We need to get used to spending time with them. I'd rather get this awkward stuff out of the way now, wouldn't you?"

Which seemed as good a segue as he was going to get to tell her about last night. He pulled onto the ramp for the freeway and tried to keep his voice casual. "Elliott came to see me at the hotel last night."

Alexis whipped her gaze to his. "Why?"

"He said he looked into my father's death."

Alexis twisted in her seat. "Why would he do that? His company wasn't involved, was it?"

"No. I think he . . . I think he's trying to make amends, just in case."

"In case of what?" She swallowed. "In case the surgery doesn't work?"

"I don't know." Noah reached over to grip her hand. Then he brought her fingertips to his lips. "I think maybe he just wants to get my approval or something."

"What did you say to him?"

What do you want? A gold star? "I told him all I care about is that you're okay."

The restaurant Elliott had suggested was a chain Italian place, the kind that served everything family-style. Noah saw no small amount of irony in that but kept it to himself. Judging by the parking lot, it was popular. Noah found a parking spot in the back between a Subaru and a rusty pickup truck with a bumper sticker informing other drivers that his other car was just as much of a piece of shit.

A hostess greeted them when they walked in. Alexis gave them her name, and after a quick check of her schedule, the hostess smiled and said their party was waiting for them. Noah caught sight of the family—Jesus, all seven of them—as the hostess led them to a room in the back. Candi spotted them first and immediately stood with an eager wave.

Heads turned, and soon everyone else stood too. Alexis paused inside the room, hands twisted at her stomach. "Hi," she breathed.

"So glad you could make it," Candi said, moving in for another easy embrace.

Candi pulled back with a deliberate expression. "You remember Cayden, right?"

The room quieted as Cayden stepped forward. His face was as tight as Lauren's. He was obviously being forced into this little display of family togetherness.

He extended a hand to Noah. "Cayden Vanderpool."

Noah squeezed tighter than was necessary. "Nice to meet you."

Elliott introduced Cayden's wife, Jenny, and their two children. Then the room held its breath as Cayden finally turned his attention to Alexis. "How did the tests go?"

Alexis blinked. "Good. Fine."

Cayden's wife whispered something in the toddler's ear, and the little girl crawled off her lap. "She made something for you," Jenny said.

The child walked around the table and handed Alexis a crumpled piece of paper.

Alexis smiled. "What's this?"

"She made you a picture," Jenny said. Cayden, meanwhile, looked like he was trying to crack open walnuts with his teeth.

Alexis crouched low so she was eye level with the child. "This is beautiful. Thank you."

Noah looked over her shoulder at the scribbles of blue and white.

"She told me it was a snowman," Jenny explained.

Alexis laughed. "I can definitely see that."

The tension deflated as if someone had stuck a pin in it. Shoulders relaxed and smiles loosened. Alexis stood again, and Noah led her to a pair of open chairs at the table.

"So," Candi said, sitting down. "You should all be warned that I'm starving, so I plan to eat off everyone's plates."

A collective of groans went up as everyone returned to their seats. "She's horrible about stealing food," Elliott said. "Protect yourself accordingly."

"Have you ever eaten here before?" Candi asked, opening the menu.

"No," Alexis said. "I rarely have time to eat out anymore."

Elliott beamed. "You have your own restaurant to worry about, right?"

"Right."

"She prefers restaurants that locally source their products," Noah said. Alexis shot him a look that he couldn't decipher.

"We've celebrated so many special family milestones here," Elliott said. "Candi's high school graduation, Cayden's rehearsal dinner. It's our special place."

Tense silence reigned again as everyone buried their faces in their menus. Candi alone seemed oblivious, because her next question made everyone squirm. "Did you and your mom have a favorite restaurant where you celebrated things?"

Across from him, Lauren stiffened. Once again, Noah couldn't blame her.

"We had quite a few favorite places that we liked," Alexis said, which was a total lie. She and her mom had rarely eaten out. They were too poor. She had every right to tell Elliott that, but she seemed intent on protecting everyone's feelings but her own.

"You guys have to try Alexis's food," Candi boasted. "She makes the most amazing scones." Candi suddenly sat up straight, as if the solution to world poverty had just come to her. "You should totally make them Christmas morning! We always do a big breakfast Christmas morning. Wouldn't that be fun? You guys could spend the night and. . ."

Candi's voice trailed off as the reality of what she was suggesting fell across the table. All eyes swept to Lauren, who was literally trembling. "That . . . would be . . . lovely," Lauren said. "We can certainly discuss it."

"I mean, if you don't have plans already," Candi said in a more hushed tone.

Once again, Alexis sacrificed herself to save everyone else from discomfort. "I can barely plan a week from now."

"Right?" Candi said on a relieved breath. "Life gets so busy."

Then the waitress saved everyone when she showed up to take drink orders.

"Well, I know I'm starving," Elliott said. "And the food here is amazing. The lasagna is my favorite, if you want to try that."

"Lexa's a vegetarian," Noah said.

"I'll probably have the eggplant Parmesan," Alexis said smoothly. "That's usually my favorite."

"That's really good too," Candi said. "I've had that before."

Things went like that for a while as they waited for their drinks. Stilted conversation pockmarked by nervous laughter and occasional oohs and aahs at how cute the kids were.

Then Cayden leaned forward. "So, Noah. What do you do for a living?"

Alexis tensed as soon as Cayden turned his attention to Noah. She knew evil intent when she saw it, and Cayden's question was far too casual. "He owns a computer security business," she answered quickly.

Noah's gaze fell to hers with a quizzical tug of his eyebrows. "I work with businesses and individuals to secure their systems," he said to Cayden.

"You *own* the company?"

Alexis bristled at Cayden's tone. She knew that Noah didn't give off the traditional businessman vibes with his long hair and casual clothes, but Cayden's comment was heavy with arrogance. "He's extremely successful," Alexis said. "A lot of his clients are celebrities."

"Really?" Elliott said. "Anyone we would know?"

Noah took his time answering again. "Colton Wheeler?"

Candi made a *no way* noise. "Holy crap, are you serious?"

"He's also a good friend of ours," Alexis said. "We're all in a wedding together next month."

"Next month?" Elliott said. "That's cutting it kind of close with the surgery. Will you be okay by then?"

"I talked to Jasmine about it, and she said I should be fine. I still won't be able to do any heavy lifting, and I probably won't have as much energy as I might normally have, but nothing that will keep me from being a bridesmaid."

Alexis hoped the shift into wedding talk would redirect Cayden, but no such luck. He was on a mission.

"How did you get into that line of work?" he asked Noah.

Alexis held her breath as she looked up at Noah. Some people were fascinated to find out what Noah had done in his rebellious teenage years. Others, not so much. Noah liked to shock people with it sometimes, so her mouth fell open in astonishment when he finally answered Cayden.

"I studied cybersecurity in college," he said simply.

Cayden sipped his water. "How'd you become interested in that?"

Alexis rested her hand on Noah's knee.

"I used to be a hacker as a teenager," Noah said calmly.

"A hacker," Cayden repeated, as if he hadn't already known the answer.

Alexis groaned inwardly at the victorious gleam in Cayden's eyes. She glanced up at Noah and expected to find a *bring it on* challenge in his eyes, but again, he surprised her. "We preferred the term *hacktivists*. But turns out I wasn't very good at it. I got caught, learned my lesson, and have been on the straight and narrow ever since."

The straight and narrow? Alexis gaped at him. He looked down at her with a half smile and winked. And that's when she knew. He'd done it for her. He'd passed up a chance to fight the good fight just to keep the peace. For her.

The waitress appeared with a tray of drinks. As she passed them around, Alexis tugged Noah close and whispered in his ear. "You are so getting lucky later."

He smothered a laugh behind his water.

After lunch, they had a weak argument over who would pay the bill. Elliott won, and then the entire group walked out together. This was the awkward part. The goodbye.

They paused on the sidewalk in front of the restaurant. Alexis hugged Candi again and offered a polite nod to Lauren, who practically deflated in relief that she wasn't going to have to fake an embrace. Noah did the handshake thing with Elliott first and then Cayden, who then quickly ushered his wife and children to their car.

Alexis stopped in front of Elliott. "So."

"You'll call me if you need anything, right?" he asked.

It was such a dad thing to say that Alexis almost laughed. She shoved her hands inside her coat pockets. "I guess I'll see you in two weeks?"

He quirked a smile. "I don't know if we're at the hugging stage yet, but I'm willing if you are."

Alexis laughed for real this time and stepped forward. His arms came around her for a brief squeeze. When he released her, she backed up and felt Noah's hand on her back.

"Drive safe," Elliott said.

"You too," Noah responded.

They watched silently as Lauren, Elliott, and Candi walked to their car.

"Ready?" Noah asked.

Alexis turned and hauled his mouth down to hers for a hard, fast kiss. "You're a good man, Noah Logan."

"Don't tell anyone. It'll ruin my reputation."

She kissed him again, lingering this time with meaning. "Drive fast."

"You in a hurry for something?"

"Yeah," she said. "We have two weeks until this surgery. Let's not waste a minute of it."

CHAPTER TWENTY-SIX

Alexis had been right. Getting ready for as many as two weeks away from the café was a full-time job all its own. Now, with just two days until the surgery, Alexis held another meeting with Jessica to go over the schedule, what to do in case of emergencies, and—because she absolutely needed another complication—how to handle the upcoming zoning board meeting tomorrow evening.

Alexis wouldn't be there, obviously, so she'd pulled together all the documentation the board would need to make a decision. Jessica had agreed to sit through the meeting just in case. But for now, Jessica was more concerned with Alexis's pre-op binder. "Wow, you can't lift anything heavier than a gallon of milk for six weeks?"

"Can we focus on the zoning board meeting for a second?"

Jessica closed the binder and folded her hands primly on the table. "Sorry. Of course."

"Karen will probably lie," Alexis said. "And she'll definitely say things that make you mad. But you have to just bite your tongue and ignore it, okay?"

Jessica pursed her lips. "Easier said than done. I hate that woman."

"She knows it, too, and the best gift we could give her would be to throw some kind of fit at the meeting. Just let her present her case and direct the zoning board to all our documentation if they have any questions." Alexis took Jessica's hand. "Remember, we've done nothing wrong."

"Exactly. Which is why I wish we could fight fire with fire. The Karens of the world—"

"Are not worth our time or energy," Alexis finished for her.

Jessica didn't look convinced, but nor did she argue the point. Maybe, like Noah, she'd given up on trying to convince her to Hulk out on people.

Alexis went through the rest of her agenda items, thanked Jessica profusely for agreeing to stay with Beefcake again while Alexis was gone, and then gathered up her stuff.

"I'll be in my office," she said over her shoulder as she walked through the kitchen door. She sank into her chair, propped her feet on the desk, and dropped her head against the back of the chair. Almost done. Just a few more things on her to-do list, and she would actually be ready to go.

"Hey, wait!"

Jessica's voice brought Alexis's head up, just in time to hear the kitchen door swing open with a violent crash.

Alexis jumped up, walked out of her office, and nearly collided with a seething, furious Cayden.

"I knew it," he spat.

"Cayden, what the hell? What are you doing here?"

Cayden shoved his phone at her. Confused, she took it from his hands and tried to skim what was on the screen.

Leaked documents from embattled defense contractor, BosTech, reveal that company executives lied to congressional investigators two years ago during a probe into the reliability of the guidance system on the Night Hawk, a long-range missile drone used by the U.S. military since 2014. Nearly three hundred civilian deaths have been attributed to faulty radar systems. The leaked documents reveal that executives overruled concerns by engineers . . .

She looked up, confused. "I don't understand. What is this?"

"Mr. Straight and Narrow? I knew it was bullshit."

His tone of voice and the rage in his eyes sent a surge of adrenaline through her that made her back up on instinct.

"How do you think the media got these documents?" Cayden barked.

She shook her head to chase away the nagging whisper in the back of her mind. "Noah had nothing to do with this."

Cayden snorted. "Right."

"He wouldn't do that." Bile rose in her throat.

"So I'm supposed to believe it's just a coincidence?"

"Yes! He wouldn't do it. He wouldn't. He knows . . ."

"Knows what?"

That I care about you all. She didn't say it, because she could tell he didn't want to hear it and wouldn't believe it anyway. She didn't say it, because the truth of it took her by as much surprise as it would Cayden. And what a fool she was, because Cayden was staring at her like something he'd stepped in on the lawn.

"Noah didn't do this. I know he didn't."

Cayden pointed his finger. "You are the worst fucking thing that ever happened to this family. Stay away from us. We'll find him another fucking kidney."

His words reverberated off the stainless-steel appliances in the kitchen, and their echo followed him as he stormed back through the swinging door. As soon as he left, Alexis deflated against the counter. This wasn't true. It . . . wasn't true. Was it?

Jessica ran in. "What the hell was that?"

Alexis looked at her but barely saw her. "I need to go."

"Are you okay?"

No. No, she wasn't. Alexis grabbed her purse from the hook on the back of her office door and removed her apron. Her hands trembled when she unlocked her car and when she fumbled with the radio to find a twenty-four-hour news station on her satellite radio. The first one she tried was talking about the upcoming election, so she tried another one.

Just in time to hear a commentator say, "This leak has all the markings of a Hatchet operation."

A sour taste filled her mouth.

She pulled into Noah's driveway and turned off the car. Wooden legs carried her to his front door. She knocked and realized belatedly how ridiculous that was. She normally would just walk in, but nothing made sense. A moment passed before the door opened. He grinned. "Why are you knocking?"

But then he froze. "What's wrong?"

Lexa walked past him, her movements robotic, her face devoid of emotion. "Jesus, Lexa. Talk to me." He turned her around to face him.

"Cayden—" She stopped and licked her lips.

"What about Cayden?" He gripped her shoulders. "Honey, you're scaring me. What is going on?"

"He was just at my café. Someone hacked into Elliott's company and leaked documents to the media."

He blinked. "*Today?*"

She handed him her phone. "It's all right there."

Noah skimmed the screen and absorbed just enough to know it wasn't good. BosTech was in some serious shit if this was true. He wasn't surprised, though. Everyone knew they'd lied their asses off before Congress. "I don't understand. Why did Cayden—"

Cold adrenaline washed through him. "Are you kidding me? He thinks I did it?"

She nodded.

"Does Elliott think I did it?" And Jesus, when the hell did he start to care what Elliott Vanderpool thought of him?

"I don't know." Lexa stepped back, putting just enough distance between them to be meaningful. A cold draft from the open door replaced all the warmth between them, but it could just have easily come from the icy detachment in her gaze.

Noah's arms fell like lead against his sides as another sickening realization knocked him senseless.

"Holy shit, Alexis. *You* think—" He stumbled over his own words because his heart, mind, and mouth were at war with one another. Alexis stared unblinkingly at him with one hand clenched into a fist against her stomach. He wished she'd use it. Just slam it into his chin and be done with it. It would hurt less than what he was about to say. "Do you think I had something to do with this?"

She blinked and let out a breath. Two actions, connected but not. One was a hesitation. The other a sign of relief. Both added up to one conclusion that turned his stomach.

"No," she said, shaking her head. "I don't think that."

She reached out, but Noah backed up. "But did you?"

"No."

Noah might have found some small comfort in the tremble of her voice, but the hint of guilt that seeped into her eyes destroyed it. Destroyed *him*.

"You did. For at least one second, you thought I did this, didn't you?"

"No—"

"Yet you drove straight here to ask me."

"Of course I drove straight here! Cayden accused you."

"And you wanted to make sure it wasn't true."

His footsteps on the hardwood floor sounded a defeated retreat to his kitchen. Hers were the frantic march of a battle not yet over.

"That's not fair. I know you didn't do it. How many times do I have to say it?"

"How about one more time," he said, gripping the edge of the kitchen counter. "Admit it. For one moment, you actually thought I was responsible for this."

"Fine!" She threw her hands in the air. "I admit it! I thought maybe you did it. Why does this matter?"

"Because it does." He barely recognized his own voice, but the emotion rising inside him, tightening his chest and heating his skin? He recognized that. And he hated it.

"That is so unfair," she said, crossing the kitchen to jab a finger in his chest. "Of course people would suspect you. Even me, for just a tiny, split second. You have the means. You have the access. And you hate people like Elliott."

"But I love *you*!"

Alexis jumped. He'd never raised his voice around her like that. And certainly not to declare that he loved her for the first time. But the words were out there now in the worst possible way, and instead of the beginning of something, they felt like the end of it.

"I would never hurt you like that, Lexa, because I love you more than I could ever hate him."

Lexa's eyes glistened with a sudden sheen as she raised trembling fingers to her lips. She reached for him, but for the first time since he'd met her, he didn't want to feel her touch on his skin. He stepped back and shook his head.

"Noah?"

The crack in her voice nearly broke him. Not nearly as much, though, as the devastating reality of what this all meant. A bullet ricocheted off his heart and hit all the important places inside of him where scars had healed over. New ones opened. And he started to bleed.

It became a hemorrhage at her next words. "The surgery is off. Cayden told me to stay away from them. That they want to find another donor."

That sonuvabitch. Rage on her behalf momentarily replaced his own self-pity. "Christ, Lexa. And you trusted people like that over me?"

Her silence gutted him. Turned him into something ugly, mean, bitter. And so were his next words. "I warned you, Alexis. I told you they were just humoring you, that they didn't really see you as part of their family."

"Candi does."

"They knew about you for *three years* and never once contacted you, not even when your name and your face were all over the news. He refused to let Candi find you. He denied your existence. Until he needed a kidney."

She tried to reach for him again. "Noah—"

He stepped away. "Why did you let your DNA results be shared with possible relatives?"

She blinked, face pinched in confusion. "What does that have to do with anything?"

"You wanted to find a family."

"No, it was a whim."

"You were hoping your father would find you."

"I have no idea why you're bringing this up right now."

"Because I want you to be honest about everything that is happening here."

"I have no idea what's happening here!"

Another tear slipped down her cheek. Noah had to curl his hands into tight fists to stop himself from wiping it away or, worse, holding her. As he watched, helplessly, she sucked in her bottom lip and began to worry it with her teeth, and like some kind of cruel, ironic joke, he was struck by how much she looked like Candi in that moment.

They really were sisters.

"I know what it's like to be lured in by a false family, Alexis. To feel a void so deep that you'll risk everything that matters to you to feel some kind of acceptance again. But it's all a charade. The minute things go wrong, they abandon you. All their promises, gone."

"I have no idea what you want from me right now."

"I want you to be mad at him!"

"Why? To justify *your* anger?" She advanced on him again. "Would it make you feel better if I descended into some kind of rage spiral? I've learned to pick my battles."

"You walk away from battles. There's a big difference."

"Wow," she breathed, backing up. Her hand fluttered to her chest and began to rub. "How long have you been holding that in?"

Fuck. Fuck! Noah dragged a hand over his hair. "I didn't mean that, Lexa. I'm sorry."

"I took on Royce Preston! I told the entire world their favorite chef was a serial sexual predator! Was that me walking away from a fight?"

"No. I didn't mean—"

"Why can't you just accept who I am? That I just want some peace in my life!"

"If you let people walk all over you, it's not peace. It's cowardice."

"I think . . . I think maybe I need to go," she whispered.

"Don't." He followed her retreat toward the front door. "Just wait."

He tried to grip her elbow to hold her back, but she yanked free from his fingers. "Let me go, Noah."

"Lexa, please. I'm sorry."

She turned around. "I can't believe I'm about to say this, but I think I need some space from you."

Alexis had made this drive before, and she'd done it feeling exactly like this. Numb. Detached. Only this time, she was running away from Noah and toward Elliott.

Because maybe Noah was right. Maybe what she'd been calling emotional control was nothing more than avoidance of a fight she was too scared to have. By the time she pulled into the long drive-way of Elliott's home, it was dark. But nearly every light was on inside the house. She parked next to cars she now recognized—Cayden's BMW and Candi's Range Rover.

Ironically, this time, she didn't knock before going in. She threw open the door and followed the sound of angry voices to the kitchen. Cayden spotted her first.

"What the hell are you doing here?" he growled.

Elliott and Candi whipped around. Candi raced toward her. "Cayden didn't mean it," she gushed. "About the surgery. He didn't mean it."

Alexis tried to walk around her, but Cayden grabbed her arm. "You're not welcome here. This is a family matter."

"She *is* family," Elliott snapped.

Cayden reacted as if his father had slapped him. "You can't be serious. After what they've done?"

"She hasn't done anything!"

"This is because of her," Cayden shouted, pointing. "She brought that man into our lives, and look what he's done."

"He didn't do it," Alexis said. "He says he didn't, and I believe him."

"Of course he says that. You expect him to be honest? A man like that?"

Even as sorrow broke her heart, she rose in his defense. "Noah is a good man. You don't know anything about him."

"He's a criminal!"

Alexis spun on Cayden. "And what about you? Do you care at all about the lives that were lost because of your father's company? Do you care that BosTech was responsible for the deaths of hundreds of civilians?"

"How dare you?"

"Did you even read the whole story?" She yanked out her phone and unlocked it with her thumbprint. The screen immediately returned to the story she'd googled. And for good measure, she began to read out loud. "'According to the documents, the CEO was warned on at least four occasions by two engineers that the radar system was faulty. In each case, the CEO kept the warnings out of reports to Pentagon officials overseeing the drone program.'"

Alexis looked at Elliott. "Did you know that your engineers tried to warn the company? How could you do that?"

"Don't you dare come in here and start accusing my father of crimes when your boyfriend is the one who—"

"It was me!"

A stunned hush fell over the group as Elliott's words rose above them all. He stood in the middle of the room, breathing hard and looking weak.

"What—What do you mean?" Cayden asked.

"I leaked the damn documents."

Lauren covered her mouth with her hand and sank to the couch. "Why, Elliott? Why would you do something like that?"

"Because I've had to live with the guilt of this for years. I warned them, but I sat by and did nothing when they lied to Congress. I am not going to die with that on my conscience."

"You did this?" Alexis whispered, swaying backward against the counter.

"Did he put you up to it?" Cayden demanded.

"No. But if you're wondering whether Noah had anything to do with it, yes. He did. I was inspired by him. He told me what happened to his father. I don't blame him for hating people like me, companies like mine. And he told me that if I wanted to really earn redemption, then I needed to do more than apologize. So I did. I leaked the damn documents. It's time these people paid for their crimes."

Alexis couldn't move. Noah was right. It hadn't been a whim when she checked that box on the DNA test, the one that allowed her results to be shared. She wanted to find family. She wanted to find her father. But all of this was a charade.

Elliott could have avoided all of this by being honest, but he let Cayden and who knew how many other people assume that Noah was behind the hack. To assuage his own guilt.

She forced her feet to move. "I have to go."

Candi raced after her. "Alexis, wait."

"Leave me alone." She held up her hands to ward off everyone's attempts to get her to stay. "I wish I'd never met you. I wish I'd never met any of you."

"No, wait." Lauren shot to her feet. "You can't go. What about the surgery?"

Alexis laughed joylessly. "Noah was right. That's all you care about, isn't it? My kidney."

"No. Alexis, please . . ."

She spun on her heel. "Go to hell. All of you."

CHAPTER TWENTY-SEVEN

Noah moved through the next day as if detached from his body. He tried to throw himself into work, but his brain and heart weren't in it. Anger was like sandpaper inside him, rubbing every nerve raw until he was blind with it. At four o'clock, he gave up. But instead of going home, he headed toward his mom's house. At least there, he wouldn't have to spend another night sitting alone on his back porch with a bottle of booze and his thoughts.

As he pulled onto his mom's street, he lifted a wave at his mom's neighbors, Mr. and Mrs. Foster, who were stringing Christmas lights around the trunk of a maple tree that took up most of their yard. They would turn the lights on for the first time on Thanksgiving night. Christmas came early in the Oaks subdivision.

He pulled into the driveway and had to wedge his car next to a familiar sedan. Marsh was there. Great.

The man himself appeared from the side of the house as Noah got out. He carried a ladder with both hands and balanced a tool belt over one arm. He wore a faded pair of jeans with a crease down the middle because the man still couldn't leave the house without ironing everything into military precision.

Marsh leaned the ladder against the side of porch as Noah walked up the sidewalk. "What're you doing here?" he asked, wiping a gloved hand across his brow.

Noah had to bite back what he really wanted to say. *Since when do I need to ask your permission to come over?* "Came to talk to my mom. Where is she?"

"Inside with Zoe. Help me put up these lights, will ya?"

"I really need to talk to Mom—"

Marsh ignored him. He gestured vaguely toward the top of the garage. "Put the ladder over there, and I'll hand you shit."

"I'm not sure I actually know what to do here."

"Hammer. Nail. It's pretty self-explanatory."

Noah resisted the natural urge to make an obscene gesture and instead did what Marsh told him to. He took the hammer and a bag of nails from Marsh's outstretched hand. Gripping both in one hand, he held tight to the ladder as he climbed to the highest possible rung. "Start here?"

"Yeah. That should be good."

Noah leaned just far enough to press the tip of the nail to the wood and damn near toppled off the ladder trying to bang it in.

Marsh snorted from below. "Jesus, who the hell taught you how to use a hammer?"

Noah answered with a hefty whack at the nail. "Well, as you know, my father died when I was young, so . . ."

"You're going to bend the nail doing it like that."

Noah hit the nail again, and as Fate would have it, it bent in half. The flat top became lodged in the wood.

"Fuck, I knew it," Marsh grumbled. "Get down from there."

Noah descended the ladder.

"Give me that," Marsh griped, grabbing the hammer. "Wouldn't have asked you to help if I'd known you didn't know what the hell you were doing."

"I'm not any good at this shit. I usually just hire a contractor."

"A man should know how to hang Christmas lights at his own goddamned house."

"This isn't my house. It's my mother's. When I need something done at my house, I call a contractor."

Marsh glared. "Can you at least hold the ladder and hand me shit?"

"All MIT graduates can do that."

Marsh's face turned the color of canned cranberry sauce. "You want to keep that attitude in check, boy?"

"I'm an adult, not a boy."

"Could've fooled me."

The front door swung open then, and his mom walked out wearing a surprised smile and carrying a weathered cardboard box with the words *Christmas Outdoors* scribbled in Sharpie on the side.

"Noah! What are you doing here? I thought you guys were heading down today for the surgery."

Noah jogged up the porch steps to take the box from her. He bent and kissed her head. "Hey, Mom." He peeked inside the box at the tangle of lights and garland inside. "This for the front porch?"

"I was bringing them out for Marsh. What's going on? Where's Alexis?"

"No, she's, uh . . ." Noah let out a pained breath and a lie. "The surgery's been delayed. Let us know when dinner is ready."

His mom went back inside with one last look over her shoulder. Noah set the box down and returned to the base of the ladder. They worked in silence for fifteen minutes, speaking only when Marsh grunted out an order.

Finally, they'd managed to attach nails to the entire length of the garage. Marsh backed down the ladder, and Noah stepped aside to make room for him.

"You need to learn how to do shit like this, Noah." He nodded toward the box on the porch. "Get me them lights."

Noah stomped toward the front porch, but his suppressed emotions got the best of him. He turned back around. "Is there anything I do that you approve of?"

Marsh looked over from the ladder, eyebrows tugged together in confusion. "What the hell are you talking about?"

"I don't invest my money the way you think I should. I don't have relationships with women the way you think I should. And hell, I can't even hammer nails the way you want me to. So I'm genuinely curious if there is anything I do that lives up to your standards."

Marsh reached for the box with the lights. "It's not my standards I'm trying to hold you to."

"I don't need this shit." Noah turned on his heel and stomped toward the door, but his hand paused over the handle at Marsh's next words.

"I saw the news. Did you do it?"

It shouldn't hurt after all this time to have Marsh doubt him, but it did. It hurt like a motherfucker. Almost as much as to have Alexis doubt him. Noah turned around, jaw clenched. "I came here to talk to my mom, not get interrogated."

Marsh came down from the ladder and walked toward him,

his steps weary and his face tired. He suddenly looked old. The porch light turned his grayish hair a dark silver and deepened the grooves in his forehead. Noah suddenly swayed with the realization that this is what his father would look like now.

Marsh nodded toward one of the two Adirondack chairs on the porch. "Sit down."

Noah trudged to one of the chairs like a kid who'd just been sent to his room. And the fact that Marsh could still make him feel like that only fueled the fire inside him. He dropped into a chair. Marsh stood at the bottom of the porch steps, stance wide and confident. His father used to stand like that. It was a military thing, a manly thing, an *I know how to take up as much space as possible* thing.

"I asked you a question, boy. Did you do it?"

"No, I didn't fucking do it!" Noah shot to his feet. "But you know what? I wish I had. Everyone assumes it was me anyway, so I might as well get the satisfaction of bringing down another company with blood on its hands."

Marsh shook his head. "You haven't learned a goddamned thing, have you?" He gave Noah a sad once-over. "Look at you. Hands clenched. Jaw clenched."

"Because you're annoying the shit out of me."

"No. Because you're still a pissed-off kid with a computer and a need for vengeance."

Noah's knuckles cracked under the strength of his curled fists. "What the hell do you want from me? I went to college, consulted for the fucking FBI, and make millions now. Isn't that good enough for you?"

Marsh raised his eyebrows. "You think you're successful? You're not. You may have turned your life around, but you're still just as mad and reckless as you were then. And until you get over that anger, everything else—the money, the company, your celebrity friends—it's all just window dressing."

Noah inched closer, compelled by a need to lash out at something, anything. "You're right. I never got over the anger. I hope I never do. Because the day I stop being furious that my father was killed while the crooks responsible for it got rich is the day I stop breathing."

"And that attitude is exactly why I should have let you rot in prison like I wanted to."

Oxygen escaped Noah's lungs in a giant *whoosh*.

"And I did want to," Marsh continued. "As far as I was concerned, you were an ungrateful brat. Trying to bring down the country your father died fighting for was a disgrace to his legacy. If I'd had my way, you would have gone to trial and let the chips fall where they may."

Betrayal burned Noah's throat. "What changed your mind?"

"I made your father a promise," Marsh said, voice thick. "He died in my lap and made me promise I would look after you, raise you to be a man." Marsh's lips thinned. "You have no idea what responsibility is, Noah. Not until you realize you're the one thing that stands between life and death for another human being. And not until you realize that someone made that choice for you, and you're all that's left behind."

Noah pounded down the steps until he was inches from Marsh's face. "Is that what we are to you? The shit that got left behind? The heavy burden of responsibility on your shoulders? This is not what my father wanted. He didn't want my mother to never move on with her life because she's trapped in yours, dragged down by your own guilt. He didn't want me to live my entire life trying to live up to some version of manhood that no person alive could emulate. The only disgrace to my father's legacy is you."

The punch came out of nowhere. Pain exploded in Noah's cheekbone and radiated across the planes of his face. The metallic taste of blood filled his mouth as he stumbled and dropped to the ground.

Marsh loomed over him, fists clenched and breathing labored.

"Oh my God! Noah!" The front screen door slammed open and shut, and his mother ran down the steps. She crouched next to him on the ground, her worried face hovered over his.

Noah held his hand to his nose and came away with bloody fingers. "I'm okay, Mom."

"What the hell is going on here?" His mother shot to her feet and glared at Marsh. "What is wrong with you?"

"That boy is a disrespectful liar."

"That boy is my son!"

Marsh's hand began to shake. "You're coddling him. You always have."

"And you've treated him like a no-good loser!"

"I've tried to treat him like a son."

To Noah's shock, his mom got in Marsh's face. "You're not his father!"

"Really? Because I've spent far more time raising him than anyone else. Including you."

"Hey!" Noah rose on woozy feet. "You can say whatever you want to me, but do not talk to her like that."

The door banged open again as Zoe ran out. "What the hell is going on?"

His mom's hands shook at her sides. "I need you to leave, Marsh."

"What? Are you kidding me?"

"No. I need you to go. Now."

"Sarah, please." Marsh's voice had lost its bite. He was a man suddenly faced with the loss of something that mattered to him, and Noah recognized the signs all too well. Noah almost empathized with him.

"You will not talk to my son like this anymore," his mom said. "I should have intervened long before now. Just go."

Marsh's face sagged. He backed up, hands digging into his pockets for his keys. Noah, Zoe, and their mom watched silently as he climbed into his car and backed out.

"What the hell was that?" Zoe demanded, trailing behind them. "Did he seriously hit you?"

"Come inside," his mom said, tugging on his elbow.

Noah gently shook her off. "I have to go."

"No. Not until I look at you and you tell me what the hell is going on."

Noah followed his mom inside and to the kitchen, where she told him to sit at one of the stools lining the island. A timer began to shriek, and Zoe jumped halfway to the ceiling.

"It's the lasagna," she said. "I'll get it."

His mom went to the sink and dampened a wad of paper towel before returning to him. She dabbed at the blood beneath his nose. "I'm okay, Mom."

"Let me fuss over you."

He relented and tilted his head back so she could gingerly wipe the blood.

"Have you ever been punched before?" Zoe asked from the stove.

"Not like this. No."

"I wonder if you should go to the emergency room," his mom said.

"I'm fine."

"I can't believe he hit you." Her voice shook. "What happened?"

"Just a lot of stuff that's been boiling for a while."

"What kind of stuff?"

He lifted a corner of his mouth. "The kind of stuff I shouldn't have let boil over."

She gave him a frustrated look before returning to the sink. She tossed the bloody paper towel into the trash can and then washed her hands. But instead of turning around, she gripped the edge of the sink. "Zoe, can you leave us alone for a minute?"

Zoe snuck a glance at Noah before quickstepping out of the kitchen. He had no doubt, however, that she was hovering nearby to eavesdrop.

His mom turned around. "He's in love with me."

Noah felt the words like another sucker punch to the face. "He told you that?"

"Years ago. I wasn't ready for another relationship. It felt like a betrayal of your father."

"Are you . . . with him?"

His mom shrugged with a heavy sigh. "It's too late for that now. It's been too long."

"But are you in love with him?"

"He's been here for me in so many ways. But the way he treats you, I . . . I think that has always been what held me back. But then you seemed okay with him, so I never wanted to intervene, especially after you turned your life around. I didn't know how much tension there really was between you."

"I didn't want to tell you."

"Why?"

"I didn't want to burden you."

"You're my son. Nothing about you is a burden."

Yeah, that was some bullshit. Noah had been nothing but a burden for a good five years after his father died. He rose from the stool and walked to her. Without prompting, their arms came around each other.

"I'm sorry," he said, voice thick.

"For what?"

"For everything."

She squeezed him around the waist. "There's nothing for you to apologize for."

"I put you through hell."

"You were going through hell." She pulled back and gazed up at him. "But it's all over now." She winced as she brushed her fingers over the spot where Marsh's fist had connected with his face. "We need to ice this."

"I'm fine, Mom." He set her back and leaned against the counter again. "Hungry, but fine."

"You should have brought Alexis. Why was the surgery rescheduled?"

Noah's breath caught in his lungs. He tried to hide his reaction, but it was too late. He couldn't hide much from his mother.

She tilted her head, concerned. "Is everything okay with Alexis?"

"Fine," he lied, dropping another kiss on her head.

He walked to the cupboard to take out some plates. "You can come back now, Zoe," he called.

Zoe stumbled in as if she'd been standing by the doorway the entire time. When Noah finally left two hours later, his cheek had stopped throbbing even if the bleeding in his chest hadn't.

He pulled into his driveway and stared at his dark house. He could back out again and drive straight to Alexis's house and beg her to forgive him.

But he didn't. Because she wanted space.

Noah walked inside, grabbed an unopened bottle of bourbon, and carried it to the couch.

CHAPTER TWENTY-EIGHT

"Oh my God, what are you doing here?"

Jessica stared at Alexis when she walked into the cavernous zoning board room as if she'd just flown in on fairy wings.

Alexis took the seat next to Jessica. "I'm here for the meeting."

"Right. But . . . why?" Jessica looked back to the entrance of the room. "Is Noah with you? Did you decide to stop here on the way to the surgery?"

"The surgery is off. Noah is . . . not here." Her voice caught on a swell of a goddamned emotion she wanted nothing to do with, so she swallowed it away. "So I figured I might as well come to the meeting and listen to Karen's bullshit myself."

Jessica gripped Alexis's arm. "Okay, what the hell is going on? What do you mean the surgery is off? Since when? And why does 'not here' make it sound like you and Noah broke up?"

"I think we did." Oh, God. The air seeped from her lungs. It still didn't seem real. She'd gone to bed last night hoping that she'd wake up to discover it was all a bad dream. But it was real.

"Alexis, you have to give me more than that."

"I can't. Not right now." Her voice shook.

Jessica squeezed her arm. "You don't have to be here."

"Yes, I do." Because she had nowhere else to go. Her entire life was suddenly a drifting boat in the middle of rough seas. Every anchor she'd relied on to hold her steady for the past year was gone. Severed.

All she had was her business. So she was here.

At the front of the room, a mahogany half-moon table where the commissioners would sit faced the rest of the room. The audience section was mostly empty except for a small cluster of people who looked like city staffers and a lone blond head in the front row.

Karen.

As if she sensed Alexis's gaze, Karen swiveled in her seat and looked back. Her eyes widened at first, obviously surprised that Alexis had decided to attend the meeting after all. But she recovered quickly with pursed lips and gave Alexis the back of her head again.

A door behind the commissioners' table opened, and members of the board filed out balancing overstuffed binders, coffee cups, and cell phones. Nameplates in front of each chair identified the board members as they settled into their seats.

Empty seats began to fill up as more people entered the room. Alexis watched the clock and bounced her knee in time with the second hand.

Jessica took her hand. "Remember," she said in a voice mature beyond her years. "We've done nothing wrong."

The chairwoman's voice interrupted as she called the meeting to order. The first ten minutes of the meeting were devoted to normal housekeeping matters and a single item of old business left over from the previous month. Alexis began to bounce her knee again as the chairwoman called for the start of new business and recited in a bland affect the details of the complaint against ToeBeans.

"We received Ms. Carlisle's written correspondence regarding the complaint," the chairwoman said. "But we will also allow time for her to make a statement and answer questions, if she wishes. We'll begin, however, with public comment. Is there anyone who wishes to address the commission on this item?"

Karen shot to her feet. "Thank you, commissioners," she said into the microphone at the podium. "My name is Karen Murray, and I'm the owner of the Long Time Gone antiques shop, which is across the street from the ToeBeans Cat Café."

Alexis met Jessica's gaze, and together they shared an eye roll. Karen was using her best *I'm just a concerned citizen* voice.

"I was, of course, thrilled when Ms. Carlisle purchased and restored the vacant storefront for her café. I thought it was such a charming addition to our unique business district."

Jessica nearly choked. Karen was definitely putting on an Oscar-worthy performance.

"So please understand that the concerns I address this afternoon and in my complaint are only because I wish to protect and maintain the culture we've worked so hard to establish in our district. Our zoning laws were adopted for a reason, and no matter how compelling the reasons, we can't allow someone to violate those rules. There are plenty of places within more appropriate zoning designations for where Ms. Carlisle could host her yoga class and her little support groups."

Little support groups. Alexis's blood pressure skyrocketed at the trivialization of the important connections and healing that occurred every day in her café.

"Ms. Carlisle already received a variance to allow for cat adoptions, which I did not oppose at the time even though I feared even then that the increase in traffic would create a parking problem for other businesses. But this is just a bridge too far, I'm afraid. All I ask is that the commission follow the zoning laws and instruct Ms. Carlisle to stop using her café to save the world and stick to what she's supposed to be doing—serving food. Thank you."

Karen refused to look at Alexis as she scurried back to her seat.

The chairwoman thanked Karen for her comments and then looked at Alexis. "Ms. Carlisle, we weren't expecting you today, but since you're here, do you wish to address the commission beyond your written correspondence?"

Alexis shook her head. Jessica squeezed her hand. "Are you sure?"

Alexis felt the burn of Karen's seething glare from the front row.

No. Not again. She was not walking away from this battle. She stood. "Wait. Yes, I do have some things to say."

Heart pounding, Alexis walked past Karen's stunned expression to the podium and adjusted the microphone to her height.

"Thank you." She swallowed and tried to hide her shaking hands on top of the lectern. "Ms. Murray is correct in most of what she said. It's true that my café has become a gathering spot for survivors of sexual violence and harassment. It's true that there have been days when customers have arrived in the morning and didn't leave until the afternoon, but that does not make my café any different from any other coffee shop in the city where students sit for hours to do their homework or where book clubs meet to discuss their latest reads."

Alexis licked her dry lips. "I addressed the specific items regarding the zoning classifications in my written correspondence. I do not believe I am in violation of my permit, nor do I believe that my café alone is responsible for the parking shortage that has always plagued our district. But I will publicly reiterate what I stated in my written response that I will seek an additional zoning variance to allow me to continue to host my yoga class if the commission finds that it does, indeed, violate the current zoning permit."

Karen huffed behind her.

Alexis stared at her hands. She could stop now. She'd addressed the primary issue in Karen's complaint. She could do what she usually did and just ignore the rest.

"Ms. Carlisle, does that complete your comments?" the chairwoman prompted.

Did it?

"Ms. Carlisle?"

No. It did not complete her comments. Because she hadn't really told her story yet, and if she didn't do it, people like Karen Murray would continue to tell it for her. If she didn't continue this fight, the battle would never end.

Alexis licked her lips again and looked up. "No, I have a few more things to say, if I may."

The chairwoman nodded. "Please continue."

"This isn't about a zoning violation." Her heart pounded so hard that her ribs shook. "We all know that. If it were, then Ms. Murray would have filed complaints against Mrs. Bashar's yarn shop for her weekly widows knitting club meeting. This complaint is about me, and more specifically, about Ms. Murray's disapproval of me."

"Now wait just a minute!" Karen shot to her feet.

"Ms. Murray," the chairwoman said. "Please return to your seat."

"But that is just a lie! She's lying about me!"

Alexis tried not to roll her eyes.

"Ms. Murray," the chairwoman snapped. "You are out of order. You had your chance to speak."

Alexis continued. "In the year since I came forward with my accusation against Royce Preston, Ms. Murray has found almost weekly reasons to complain about something at my café. The state of my landscaping out front. My cat. She even complained about how bright the string lights are around my front window. I have been patient. More patient than most people would be, because I didn't think it mattered what people like her thought of me. But I realize now that it does matter. It matters because attitudes like hers enable men like Royce Preston to get away with their crimes for so long. It matters because she is now trying to hurt people I care deeply about—women who have already been victimized. And if someone like Ms. Murray is allowed to use the zoning system to carry out some kind of vendetta, then the laws are meaningless."

A round of applause interrupted her, and Alexis looked over her shoulder. It wasn't just Jessica who was clapping, though. Strangers had joined in too.

"I didn't ask for any of this," Alexis said. "I didn't invite women to come to me to share their stories or to start gathering at my café to find support and strength in other survivors. But it happened, and I am so grateful for it. They have healed *me*, and I will make it my mission to ensure these women have a safe environment. And if that violates the zoning laws of this city, then the city needs to change its zoning laws. Because I am done hoping that I can change what is in Ms. Murray's heart."

The applause thundered as Alexis turned away from the podium. She met Karen's eyes and smiled. Not out of spite. Not out of forced politeness. But because she honestly no longer cared what Karen thought.

The chairwoman pounded the table with her gavel and asked the audience to please quiet down. Alexis's legs trembled as she walked back to Jessica, who yanked her in for a tight hug.

Tears threatened behind her eyes. "I need to go," she whispered.

"Don't you want to stay to see what the board decides?" Jessica asked.

Alexis shook her head. She'd done what she needed to do. She'd said what needed to be said.

Now there was someone else she needed to talk to.

The grass at the cemetery was soft beneath her shoes.

Damp and soggy. Every footfall sank heavier than the last.

The gas station bouquet in her clenched hand grew heavy, petals wilting and drooping upside down. It had been several weeks since she'd been to her mother's grave. The urn next to the gravestone bore the dried, brown remnants of last summer's geraniums. Neglected by her absence.

Alexis placed the bouquet on the ground, the vibrant colors a stark contrast against the darkened granite bearing her mother's name. Behind her, she sank onto the concrete bench that café patrons had donated so Alexis would have a place to sit when she visited. It used to warm her to sit here and talk with her mother. Today, though, the cold seeped through her clothes and chilled her entire body.

Alexis tugged her coat around her and stared at the ground.

She didn't even know what she was going to say until she opened her mouth.

"Why—Why didn't you tell Elliott about me?" she whispered. Her voice sounded weak. Pitiful. "All those years, you could have told me the truth. I could have handled it."

Her mind imagined her mother's answer. *Because it was for the best.*

"Best for who? Me? You? Don't you remember how hard things were?"

But we got through them together.

"But it could have been easier. He had money."

Which isn't everything. We had each other.

"You could still be alive. If we'd had more money, you wouldn't have had to work so hard, and maybe—"

You know that's not true. I had cancer. I would have died with or without his financial support.

"But—" Her voice cut off as her mother took control of the imaginary argument.

Say what you really want to say, Alexis. Tell me what's really bothering you.

"I'm mad at you, Mom." Her voice shook with the weight of betrayal and, yes, anger. Anger that had festered for too long, been ignored and avoided. Anger that had been unleashed last night at Elliott's house, anger that had burned all night and all morning, anger that erupted into hot flames at the zoning board meeting. Anger that threatened to consume her whole. "You left me alone, Mom. And maybe I didn't have to be. How could you do that?"

Headlights from an oncoming car behind her illuminated the headstone. She sniffled and wiped her face, hoping the car would slowly pass. It didn't. She heard the soft crunch of tires draw closer. The car stopped, and the headlights went out. Of course. *Of course* someone else would be here at this exact time to visit someone in the same section as her mother's grave. Because she couldn't even get a moment to herself in a cemetery.

Behind her, a car door opened and shut with a gentle thud.

"I thought I'd find you here."

Alexis turned on the bench, heart in her throat. Elliott stood twenty feet away, hands shoved in the pockets of a winter coat.

She turned her back on him. "What do you want?"

"I was worried about you. Candi and I have both been trying to call you."

"I didn't want to talk to you."

"I understand."

"Then you'll understand when I tell you to get back in the car and go away."

Elliott walked closer and gestured toward the bench. "May I?"

"No." But Alexis scooted sideways anyway to make room for him. She'd ask herself why later.

Elliott placed his hands on his knees and stared at the gravestone. "I came here once last year."

Alexis looked over at that. "Why?"

"I had some things I needed to say to her."

Alexis ground her teeth. "You should've said them when she was alive."

"I know." He focused his gaze on her. "Do you want to know what I told her?"

"Not really."

"I told her that I missed her."

Alexis stood up. "Jesus, not this bullshit again."

"I told her that she'd raised an amazing young woman, and I wished I had been part of it."

Alexis hugged her torso and stared at the gravestone. She felt her lip tremble and hated him for it. "You had three years to contact me. Why didn't you?"

"Because I was a coward, and I was ashamed."

Alexis snorted. "Points for honesty and self-awareness, I guess."

He didn't respond.

"It's not fair," she said, staring at her mother's name etched in stone.

"No, it's not."

"She was all I had."

"I know."

"I don't want to know the things I know now. I don't want to be sitting here like this, mad at her because of you. Do you understand that?" She turned back around to face him. "You made me mad at my own mother. You stole something from me. Something so fucking precious. You stole my *peace*." Her voice choked and cracked. Elliott's hands twitched as if he wanted to reach for her, comfort her, but he wisely kept his fingers curled around his knees. She sniffled again. "And now, because of you, I've lost Noah too. You made me doubt him, and I hurt him so badly."

"I'm sorry, Alexis."

"Stop saying that. Just fucking stop apologizing!" Alexis tightened her arms around her torso, a barrier against the crashing wave of emotions. Of anger. "What are you really doing here? What do you want?"

He stood. "A chance to make things right. A chance to be a father."

"I don't need you to be a father." She advanced on him with rage in her steps. Rage she had tried to bury for so, so long. "Do you hear me? I don't need you to be a father! I don't fucking need you! I've never fucking needed you!"

She punched his chest. Once. Twice. He took the assault without a flinch, which pissed her off even more. She wanted him to wince. To cringe. She wanted him on his fucking knees. She wanted him to hurt like she hurt, to know the emptiness that gutted her now.

"She was enough. You were a sperm donor who never existed. Do you hear me?" She pounded his chest again. "I was fine without you!"

"I'm sorry—"

"Stop. Saying. That." Every word was another punch against his chest. "I don't need your apologies and your regrets."

"Then tell me what you need, Alexis." He gripped her arms. "Tell me, and I'll do it."

"I need you to apologize to her!" She yanked from the hold of his fingers and pointed at the headstone. "I need you to stand here and tell her you're sorry for breaking her heart. For using her as a summer fling that meant nothing to you and then walking away. I want you to apologize to her for the dreams she had to give up. For making her work two and three jobs at a time to take care of me. I need you to apologize to her for letting her die without ever knowing that you actually fucking cared about her."

"I can't," he said, his voice thick. "I can't do that, because she's gone. She's dead, Alexis, and if you think that doesn't tear me up inside, knowing that I can never say those things to her, you're wrong. All I can do is make sure you never feel alone again."

"Then take my fucking kidney, you asshole. Because if you don't, you'll die. And I'll be left to stand in front of another goddamned gravestone, and if you think I'm angry now, just fucking wait until you die."

"Which is exactly why I can't go through with this. I want you to be part of my life of your own free will and because you want to be. But if you do this now, you'll always wonder if I'm a father to you out of a sense of obligation or gratitude, and not simply because I want you there." He tilted her chin up with his finger. "And I do want you there. I want you to be my daughter."

A dam burst inside her. Horrified, Alexis buried her face in her hands. Sobs became a torrent of ugly sounds and snotty breathing and angry, ragged gasps. He reacted instantly. His arms came around her, and he held her. For the first time, father held daughter, and it was as strange and awkward as it was healing and new. He was warm and smelled like a blanket fresh out of the dryer. Her hands fell away from her face, and she let her arms dangle at her sides. Not returning the embrace but not rejecting it either. Hugging him back would have felt wrong, like a betrayal of her mother, and she just wasn't ready to go that far.

Elliott must have felt her resistance, because he stepped back. Alexis became fascinated with the grass at her feet as she wiped her cheeks again.

"Can I ask you something?" he asked, shoving his hands back in his pockets.

She shrugged.

"What about Noah?"

Her battered heart took another beating. "What about him?"

"Where do things stand between you two?"

She looked up. "That subject is still a little above your pay grade, I'm afraid."

"I understand. But can I ask you something else?"

She shrugged again.

"Do you love him?"

Heat rose on her neck. This was officially on the high side of embarrassing.

"You don't have to answer that," he said quickly. "But if I can offer some unsolicited advice? From someone who has been married a long time?"

She rejected the urge to tell him to shove it, but only because she did want some advice, and that pissed her off.

Which actually felt kind of good. Being pissed off, that is. God, she was so messed up.

"People screw up. A lot. The key to a lasting relationship is the ability to forgive over and over again."

A lump became lodged in her throat.

Alexis kicked the wet grass with the toe of her boots. "I don't . . . I don't think I know what forgiveness actually is. I thought I did. I thought it meant being at peace and never feeling anger. But I . . . I think maybe that's not really forgiveness. I think I've just been avoiding feeling anything bad for a long time. And it's not the same thing, is it?"

A smile decorated his voice. "Are you *asking* for advice this time?"

"Not if you're going to make a thing out of it."

He chuckled. "No, it's not the same. You have to let yourself feel all the bad things. Anger has its place. It protects us from being taken advantage of. But eventually, you have to let yourself stop hating whoever hurt you. Forgiveness means recognizing that you are a different person because of the pain but realizing that so are they because of the pain they caused. I think it's deciding that the new people you are are better people and that together you're worth something."

A low rumble of thunder in the distance was followed by a shift in the wind. A storm was coming. Alexis faced the headstone again. "I'm sorry I worried you and Candi."

"I'm sorry I stole your peace."

"Does that make us even now?"

He came to stand at her side. "Not even close. I have a lifetime to make up for."

"Then take my kidney and prove it to me."

"Well played." There was affection in his voice, a warm undertone that snuck beneath her skin and wrapped around the cold place in her chest.

She dared to look at him. "I think I forgive you."

His eyes shimmered with a sheen of tears. "I'll try to be worthy of it."

"I'll see you tomorrow morning at the hospital?"

He smiled softly. "See you tomorrow."

She watched him walk back to his car. He turned just before getting in. "What about after tomorrow?"

"Maybe," she whispered.

He winked. "I can live with maybe."

CHAPTER TWENTY-NINE

Noah knew he was in trouble when he was jolted awake at—fuck, he had no idea what time it was—and found four pairs of angry eyes staring down at him.

Mack, Colton, Malcolm, and the Russian crowded around his couch like an offensive line. Mack cracked a knuckle. "Wake up, donkey dick."

Ah, shit. Noah closed his eyes and threw an arm over them. It didn't help the throbbing. "What day is it?"

"Christ," Colton said, disgust dripping from his tone. "Are you serious? How long have you been drinking like a loser?"

"Not long enough."

"It's Thursday night," Malcolm said, grabbing Noah's arm and hauling him up against his will. "And you have a lot of explaining to do."

"Leave me alone." Noah tugged his arm free and flopped back down.

"Not until you tell me why Liv got a panicked message from

Jessica saying that Alexis told her the surgery is off and you guys broke up."

You guys broke up. So it was real. Not some horrible dream. He'd really said those horrible things to Alexis, and she'd really said she needed space again, and now she was telling people they'd *broken up.* But what else would she think? She'd broken his heart with her lack of faith in him, but he'd broken hers by not accepting her apology. And now they were officially broken.

"Also, what the fuck happened to your face?" Colton asked, leaning down.

Noah flipped him off.

"Seriously, dude," Mack said. "Get up. We can't help you like this."

"I don't need your help."

The guys snorted in unison and backed up. Noah tried to swallow and met only dry resistance. Jesus, he felt like shit.

"You didn't finish the book, did you?" the Russian asked.

"For fuck's sake." Noah tried to roll over, but a massive hand clamped down on his shoulder and held him back. He knocked it away. "I'm not talking to you about the goddamned book. In case you haven't noticed, it has caused nothing but problems."

"Fine," Mack said way too casually. "Then talk to us about this."

Noah cracked open an eye. It took a moment for his vision to clear, but when it did, he shot up so fast that he pitched completely off the couch. "Give that back," he ordered, trying to stand on legs that barely worked.

Mack backed up. "Not until you talk to us."

"Give me back the fucking letter," he growled. "I'm not messing around, Mack."

He'd never shown it to anyone before, not even Alexis.

"Why?" Mack asked. "Is it something important? It must be, because we found it on your chest while you were passed out."

Noah's hands curled into fists. "Give me. The fucking letter. Mack."

Mack held it aloft and out of Noah's reach. "What happened with Alexis?"

"Are you fucking kidding me right now? Give me my god-damned letter!"

"Malcolm," Mack said. "Why do you suppose this is what Noah turned to after apparently fucking things up with the woman he loves?"

"I don't know," Malcolm said, leaning in the doorway to the living room. "Maybe because it holds the key to his entire life and the reasons why he keeps pushing her away."

"I didn't push her away," Noah shouted. "She—" His voice gave out, and he sank back to the couch. He was officially all out of fight. He was nothing but fuck-its and whiskey.

"She what?" Colton asked, sitting next to him.

Noah ground the heels of his hands into his eyes and then propped his knees on his elbows. "You know what they call those letters?" he asked, looking up at Mack.

Mack shook his head.

"*If I Die* letters. They write them just in case they don't make it back. How fucked up is that?"

Mack didn't answer, probably because he knew Noah didn't really expect him to. Instead, he handed the letter back to Noah and sat down on the floor in front of him.

"They found this in my dad's things after he was killed," Noah said, unfolding the letter along well-worn creases. "He wrote one to each of us."

The guys fell silent as he scanned the words that he long ago memorized.

Son,

If you're reading this, it means I broke my promise. I'm not coming back. I'm sorrier about that than you could ever know.

I love you so much. Those words don't even seem adequate. The day you were born changed my life. I thought I knew what it meant to be a man, but that all changed the minute the nurse set you in my arms. My whole life flashed before my eyes as I looked in yours. I was a warrior, but in that moment, I was as scared and intimidated by a six-pound baby than I'd ever been by the enemy. Was I enough? Was I up to the task of raising a child? Was I man enough to raise you to be a man someday?

I wish I could be there to know the answers to those questions. I wish I could see what you accomplish with that computer brain of yours. I wish I could be there to put my arm around you when you get your heart broken for the first time (it will happen, but you will survive), pat you on the back when you finally meet the one (that will also happen). I wish I could see you become a father. I know you'll be a good one. I wish I could be a grandfather. I'm damn sure I'd be a good one.

There are lessons I haven't had a chance to teach you yet, so I'm going to convey them the best I can now.

Stand for something.

Life is a gift, an opportunity. Don't waste it on the sidelines. Be brave enough to go after what you want. Do something with that genius brain of yours.

There's no shame in failing. Unless you don't get back up, learn from your mistakes, and keep trying.

I'm sorry to leave you, son. I'm sorry I broke my promise. But I need you to be strong. Your mom needs you as much as you need her.

Be happy, Noah. Be at peace. Be the man I know you can be.

This will be hard. You're going to feel a lot of emotions—anger, sadness, betrayal, fear. But I promise you—and this is a promise I won't break—that a day will come when you feel at peace again. When it won't hurt to think of me. When you think about your old man and laugh at the good times we had, when you can remember me without all those bad emotions.

Know that I am okay, and you will be too. Someday, you will be too.

Love,
Dad

Mack leaned forward in his cross-legged position. "Tell us what happened."

Noah knew he wasn't asking about his father, so he did his best to explain it all—the leaked documents, Alexis's suspicion that he'd been the one who leaked them, her apology, his refusal to accept it. He even told them about the fight with Marsh.

They listened, for once, without interruptions. Without cracking jokes. And even when he finished, they remained silent for an unusually long, respectful moment.

"I can't imagine what you've been through in your life, the things you've had to endure," Mack said. "You've come so far and achieved so much, so it must have been really hard when she accused you like that."

Noah shifted uncomfortably on the couch.

"She didn't just accuse you of leaking documents, though, did she?" Malcolm said from his spot in the doorframe. "She accused you of not being good enough. Of not living up to your father's expectations."

Adrenaline surged through Noah's veins on a wave of pain. "One thing has nothing to do with the other."

Colton nudged him. "Then why did you drag out this letter as you drowned your sorrows over her?"

"And why did you finally have the fight with Marsh that you should have had years ago only after Alexis broke your heart?"

Noah felt something rising in his chest, a choking sensation that forced him to suck in a giant breath. "They have nothing to do with each other."

The Russian sat down on the other side of him and slung his arm around Noah's shoulder. "He broke another promise, didn't he?"

Noah cleared his throat. "Who?"

"Your father," the Russian said. "He made a promise in his letter."

Noah should have been offended that the guys had apparently read it, but he couldn't summon enough energy.

"He promised that you'd find peace someday," Colton said. "But you haven't, have you?"

Until you get over that anger. Marsh's words came back to

him, unbidden and unwelcome. And just as unwanted, his own response. *You're right. I never got over the anger. I hope I never do.*

But that was a lie. He was tired of being angry. Tired of fighting a war he never asked for, a war he was dragged into without his permission, a war that had cost him everything. Including Alexis.

"No," Noah whispered, the word scraping past a thousand others that longed to be set free. Words that had been inside him for so long. "I'm not at peace."

"It must have felt like a betrayal for Alexis to believe you leaked those documents."

Noah nodded, throat closing.

"Betrayal can make us do really stupid things sometimes," Mack said. "It blinds us to reason and logic. Makes us do things we know are wrong. Things that will only hurt us worse in the end."

"Things like pushing away the woman we love even when she's trying to apologize for her own mistakes," Colton said.

"Or like using that computer brain of yours to commit crimes," Malcolm added quietly.

The Russian squeezed his shoulder. "Who are you really mad at, Noah?"

"Him." The word tore from Noah's chest, breaking things and shredding things like only a reluctant admission could. Jesus, he was mad at his father. All this time. And he'd never been able to see it or admit it until now. Until that anger had nearly cost him everything.

The Russian tugged Noah closer, and Noah couldn't have fought it even if he'd tried. And not just because the Russian was built like a Sherman tank, but because Noah was weak and drunk with the release of such long-festering truth.

"I'm so mad at him," Noah rasped. "I'm mad at him for staying in the military. He could have retired. He made the choice to stay, to keep being deployed. He left us. He left me. I needed him. And he left."

"He broke his promise," Colton said quietly.

"So you broke yours." Malcolm said it softly, but it exploded in Noah's brain. Because his entire world became clear. Just like that, a veil was lifted.

"I didn't become a hacker to defend my father," he choked. "I did it to get back at him."

"And there it is," Colton said, lightly patting Noah's back.

Noah tried to hold back the sobs that were desperate to get out, but he couldn't. So he did the next best thing. He turned his face into the Russian's barrel chest and let them come.

"It's okay, man," Colton said. "Cry. Let it out. Cry until you're okay."

Until you're okay.

God, how he wanted to be okay. Not good. Not great. Not even happy. For the first time since that chaplain had appeared at his door, he was ready to just be *okay*.

The front door suddenly burst open, and Noah jumped. He sat up, wiping his face, praying to everything holy that it was Alexis, because God, did he have a lot to tell her. After he kissed the shit out of her and begged for forgiveness, of course.

But the woman who appeared in the doorframe was not Alexis. Noah's mouth dropped open. "Mom?"

"Good," she said, hands on her hips. "You're not dead."

Mack winced. "Sorry, Mrs. Logan. We should've texted you again to let you know he was breathing."

Noah gaped at him. "You called my *mother*?"

"Dude, you looked really fucking pathetic. We were afraid this was going to be a bigger job than we could handle on our own."

"You were right," his mom said. "Will one of you go out to my car and bring in all the food I brought and also my suitcase?"

"Suitcase?" Noah dragged his hand down his face. "Mom, I'm fine. The guys are morons. You didn't have to come."

"I got it, Mrs. Logan," Colton said. He winked for good measure, but it had little effect on her. She rolled her eyes instead.

"The rest of you make yourselves scarce for a few minutes. I need to talk to my son."

Nothing could make a man of any age move faster than *that* tone of voice from a mother. The guys vacated the room in five seconds flat.

"Have you been icing your cheek?" she asked, crossing the room to stand in front of him. She didn't give him time to answer. "Of course you haven't."

"It's fine, Mom."

"Here's what we're going to do," she said, jumping over his words like he hadn't even spoken them. "We're going to get you cleaned up, get some food into you, and then you're going to tell me the truth about Alexis. And then we're going to figure out how to fix it."

He'd be lying if he said his chest didn't flood with warm relief at her words, her presence, and her unmitigated confidence that he could be redeemed. Sometimes a man still needed his mother. This was one of those times. Didn't make it any less embarrassing, though.

She smiled and cupped her hands around his jaw. "You're so much like him, you know."

"Like who?" If she said Marsh, he was going to throw himself into traffic.

"Your father." Her hands smoothed over his unruly hair.

"So tough on the outside, but inside you're nothing but gooey goodness."

A snort of laughter from the hallway was followed quickly by the sound of a fist hitting an arm. Followed immediately by a heavily accented, "Ow, why you hit me?"

Noah pinched his nose.

"He was so, so proud of you," she continued. "He used to watch you doing your homework and just shake his head. He'd always say, *How did a guy like me create a brain like that?* You were the light of his life."

Pressure began to build in Noah's chest again. "Mom, I—I miss him."

Her face softened into a smile that spoke of regret but also hope. "I know you do."

"I'm afraid I'm forgetting him."

"Oh, Noah . . ."

"I don't remember what we did the day before he deployed the last time. I don't remember what we said to each other when he left. I don't remember . . . I don't even remember the sound of his voice some days. I've wasted so much time being mad and never dealing with the anger that I've started to forget the good things, the things that mattered."

"You haven't forgotten. It's all still right here." She rested her hand over his heart. "You just have to clear away all that bad stuff to let the good stuff out."

This time, the noise from the hallway was an unmistakable sniffle.

His mother smiled. "You have some very good friends."

"They have their moments, but right now I kind of want to hurt them."

She patted his chest. "Let's get some food into you to soak up that whiskey."

He watched her walk toward the hallway. "Mom?"

She turned.

"About Marsh."

"What about him?"

"You should call him. He was pretty devastated when you kicked him out."

His mom tilted her head quizzically. "Are you defending him?"

"I think I finally understand him." He suddenly understood a lot. Like how wrong he'd been when reading that damn book. All along, he couldn't relate to AJ because Noah thought he was too much like Elliott. A selfish asshole who abandoned his kid. But he'd been reading the story all wrong. Elliott wasn't AJ. Noah was. A scared, broken man who was so terrified of losing the things that mattered to him that he instead lashed out and pushed those things away. He'd been trying to make up for his past mistakes with his money, paying off houses and college tuitions because he didn't know another way to apologize.

He was Beefcake, biting and clawing out of fear. Pushing people away before they could abandon him.

His mother stared at him so intensely that he squirmed. "He wants to be a good man," he said. "But he only knows one way to do things. He will need help to change, but I think he can."

"Hitting you was unforgivable."

"It doesn't have to be."

She smiled. "Are you playing matchmaker?"

"I just want you both to be happy."

"One thing at a time," she said. "Let's take care of you first, and in the morning, you can go say all the things to Alexis that obviously need to be said. Then maybe I'll call Marsh."

"Deal."

The next time he woke up, it was four o'clock in the morning, and the guys and his mother all stared at him with bleary-eyed panic.

He sat up in bed. "What? What's wrong?"

"Dude, she's going through with it," Mack said. "We have to go."

"What are you talking about? Who's going through with what?"

"Alexis," Colton said, as somber as he'd ever seen him. "She's going through with the surgery."

His mom dropped a stack of clothes on the bed. "Get dressed. If you drive fast, you can get there in time to see her before she goes in."

Noah grabbed Colton by the front of the shirt. "Tell me you can drive fast."

CHAPTER THIRTY

The room was cold.

Alexis tied the thin straps of her gown at the shoulder and held the rest of it closed with her hands. The material was crisp and clean. She shoved her clothes in the plastic bag the nurse had given her. Then she climbed into bed and tugged the blanket over her bare legs.

There was a knock at the door followed by Candi's tentative voice. "Can I come in?"

"It's open," Alexis called.

Candi wore one of her oversize university sweatshirts and a pair of black leggings. Her eyes were tired, her hair pulled back in a messy ponytail.

Alexis and Candi spoke at the same time.

"You ready?"

"Is Elliott ready?"

Alexis laughed. "You go first."

Candi approached the bed. "I just wanted to make sure you were okay."

"Good to go. Elliott?"

"He seems good. He keeps trying to make us all laugh because we're all nervous."

Alexis reached out her hand. "Everything will be fine."

Candi's eyes shimmered with tears as she let Alexis wrap their fingers together.

"Hey," Alexis squeezed. "No crying."

Candi smiled and shrugged. "I can't help it. I'm sorry. My father and my sister are about to go into surgery together."

Alexis waited for the normal resentment at the word *sister*. It didn't appear. "We're in good hands, Candi. It'll be over before you know it."

Cayden walked in next, shuffling nervously. "Can I, uh, can I come in?"

Candi tensed and darted her gaze back and forth between him and Alexis.

"Sure," Alexis said.

He gulped. "I'm sorry about how I've been treating you. About everything."

Alexis tilted her head. "And you feel bad because I might die saving our father's life?"

He blanched.

Alexis laughed. "I'm just messing with you."

Cayden's face blazed red. "I deserved that."

Alexis didn't disagree because, yeah, he did. It would take a little longer for her to forgive him than even Elliott, because at least Elliott was willing to own up to his mistakes. Cayden dug into his pocket and withdrew a folded piece of paper. He handed it over. "She made you another picture."

Alexis opened it. It was a scribble of wavy lines in red, yellow, and blue. At the top, someone had written, *To Aunt Alexis*.

"It's a rainbow," Cayden explained. "I can hang on to it for you, if you want."

"No," she blurted. "I—I want to keep it."

"When this is over, I hope we can—"

"Maybe." Alexis cut him off because she was afraid of what her emotions would do if he finished the sentence.

He nodded. "I'll, um, I'm going to go back to Mom. She's kind of a mess."

"See you on the flip side."

He blinked again and then left the room.

"He's trying," Candi said.

"I know. So am I."

Candi did that nervous lip-biting thing. "So, Noah . . . ?"

Alexis felt another kick in her chest. She shook her head but had to breathe in and out before speaking. "I don't think he's going to forgive me for doubting him."

"But he loves you."

Tears burned her eyes. "I hurt him too badly."

"I don't believe that," Candi said, resting her hand on Alexis's arm. "I promise you. He will be here."

Noah had thought the worst moment of his life was when Alexis walked out the door of his house, but that moment had already been eclipsed. She was about to go into surgery, and her phone was turned off, and if he didn't talk to her, she'd go into surgery without hearing all the things he should have said if he hadn't been such a fucking selfish asshole.

"Drive faster," he growled at Colton for roughly the ten thousandth time since they'd left his house. They were still fifteen minutes away from the transplant center, and if things were on schedule with the surgery, then she would be going into pre-op soon.

And once that happened, he wouldn't be able to see her until afterward.

The thought of her going into surgery without knowing how much he loved her made him want to puke. Or maybe that was Colton's driving stirring up the remnants of last night's liquid dinner. He grabbed the *oh shit* handle above the passenger door and held on as Colton screeched from lane to lane to get around traffic.

The Russian moaned in the back seat. "I am feeling carsick."

"Open a window," Mack said next to him. "Breathe in and out through your nose."

"If he pukes in my car, I will kill all of you," Colton said. He whipped into another lane and back again. A minivan blared its horn.

"There's no point to any of this if we die before we even get there," Mack grumbled.

Noah closed his eyes. "Just fucking get there."

A nurse walked into the room and introduced herself. She ran through the standard safety protocols—verifying Alexis's name and birth date, quizzing her on why Alexis was there and all the things that were meant to prevent the wrong person getting the wrong organ removed, or something. She explained that they'd be moving into pre-op soon with Elliott.

Candi bit her lip, hands knotted at her waist. Alexis opened her arms, and Candi let out a relieved breath as she leaned down into the embrace.

"Thank you, Alexis. I won't ever be able to repay you for this."

"Just get me something good for Christmas."

Candi's surprised laugh broke the tension in the room. She gave a final squeeze and then straightened to leave. "See you when you wake up."

An orderly wheeled Alexis's bed down a long hallway and through a set of automatic doors. Down another short hallway, they turned the corner and then backed into a room twice the size of the one she'd been in before.

Elliott was already there. He was half reclined in the bed, arm extended as a nurse checked his blood pressure. He hadn't shaved, and the salt-and-pepper whiskers made him look older than his years.

He smiled when he saw her. "There she is."

"Were you afraid I wouldn't show?"

"Not for a minute." He held out his hand. Alexis stared at it for a moment, speechless and emotional in a way she never expected. She reached over and let him wrap her fingers within his.

Colton screeched to a stop in front of the hospital entrance. "Get out. I'll park the car."

Noah was out and running before Mack and the Russian had even slammed their doors.

"We can't run in a hospital!" Mack argued, catching up just before the double doors slid open.

Noah flipped him the bird over his shoulder. "People run in hospitals all the time. There are emergencies."

The Russian's feet sounded like cannon booms on the floor. "And this is grand gesture! We always run for grand gesture!"

Noah's sneakers skidded on the slick floor as he came the end of the hallway and turned the corner. He careened into the wall, rattling a framed drawing of some dude who'd donated a bunch of money to have the wing named after him. Mack grabbed Noah and tugged him upright before giving him a shove to keep moving.

An orderly pushing a cart of dirty towels yelped and jumped out of the way. "Hey! You guys can't run in here."

"It's grand gesture," the Russian said, panting. "We have to run for grand gesture."

"We need to get to the fourth floor," Noah said, racing past the elevator because it would take too long.

Mack whined when he realized they were taking the stairs. "Dude, really?"

Noah took the stairs two at a time. Behind him, he heard someone fall, and the Russian swore in his native language. Mack wheezed as he tried to keep up.

At the landing for the fourth floor, Noah threw open the door and stumbled into a bright hallway.

He flattened his palms on the counter and tried to catch his breath. "Alexis Carlisle," he panted. The nurse typed something into her computer, and Noah bit his tongue to keep from cursing. He knew before she even looked up that it was too late.

"I'm sorry. She's in pre-op. No more visitors."

Noah's knees went weak. "No. You don't understand. I have to see her."

Mack finally caught up, sweaty and out of breath. "It's true," he wheezed. "He screwed up really bad because he's total tool and he has to tell her he's sorry."

The nurse's mouth dropped open. "Well, I'm sorry to hear that, but I can't let you see her." She pointed to a large waiting room on the opposite side of the nurse's station. "You're welcome to find a seat, and we will provide regular updates."

Mack grabbed Noah's elbow and tugged him away from the counter. "Come on. We might as well sit."

The elevator dinged, and when the doors opened, Colton walked out holding an ice cream sandwich.

He approached the group, oblivious. "Dude, they have an ice cream vending machine." He blinked at everyone's silent stare. "What? Were we too late?"

Noah clenched his fists at his sides. "Yeah, we were too late."

"That sucks. We should've taken my helicopter." He once again blinked at the silence. "Now what?"

"You have access to a helicopter?" Noah barely recognized his own voice.

"Yes," Colton said slowly.

"And you're just fucking telling me this now?"

"You asked me to *drive* you."

Noah's expression must have been murderous, because Mack immediately stepped in front of him. "Why don't you go eat your ice cream over there," he told Colton, pointing to the far opposite corner of the waiting room. "Or better yet, go buy the Russian some ice cream."

The Russian's face lit up. "Ice cream."

Mack pushed Noah toward an open chair and then sat down next to him.

Noah braced his elbows on his knees and lowered his face into his hands. "I can't believe I was too late."

"It's okay, man." Mack patted him on the back.

"It's not okay. I should have been here. She was *alone*. I promised her she wouldn't have to go through with any of this alone, and I couldn't even keep that promise."

"Noah?"

He lifted his head. The Vanderpools—minus Elliott—had just walked into the waiting room. Candi walked over, smiling much more brightly than anyone should at that early hour and certainly not before a family member goes into surgery.

"You are here," she gushed. "I knew you'd be here. I told her you would."

He shot to his feet. "You saw her?"

"Just before they took her back for pre-op."

"How was she? Was she okay? Was she scared?"

"She was okay. But I know she'll be better when she wakes up and sees you here."

"I want her to see me now," he groaned, running his hands over his mop of hair.

And then his own words brought him up short as a memory invaded. *I want you to see me.*

"What's wrong?" Candi asked.

He shook his head and looked down at Mack. "I need to find a barber."

CHAPTER THIRTY-ONE

Someone was touching her.

That didn't make sense, though, because Alexis was swimming. Floating in thick, dark, warm water that lapped over every limb and dulled her senses in the most soothing, soundless way.

But someone *was* there. Touching her hand and speaking softly.

Alexis heard a moan, and suddenly the water was gone. One eye peeled open, and then the other, and she found herself thrown from warm, dark silence into cold, stark brightness. She squinted and rolled her head.

A nurse with a wide smile and gray hair stood next to her bed doing something with an IV bag. Her name badge read NINA B. The woman looked down and smiled. "Hi, Alexis. I'm Nina, and I'm going to be taking care of you while you're in recovery. How's your pain?"

Alexis braced her palms against the mattress and attempted to shift higher on the pillows. A stitch in her side made her wince. Nina tut-tutted and told her to hold still. "Too soon for that, honey." She pushed a button on the arm of Alexis's bed to lift the upper half a few inches. "Better?"

Alexis nodded and tried to swallow. It hurt. Bad. "Is it . . ." She swallowed again. If anyone had told her a sore throat would be the worst part of donating an organ, she never would have believed it, but her throat was on fire. "Is it over?"

Nina smiled again. "It's over. On a scale of one to ten, can you tell me how your pain is?"

Alexis tried to focus. Things hurt, but she was still too fuzzy to know where and what and how badly. "Six, seven. I don't know."

"We're going to take care of that for you, okay?" Nina said.

"Elliott?" Her voice was a croak.

"He's good. Everything went fine."

She winced at a sharp pain in her gut.

"Okay, honey," Nina said. "I've given you some more pain medication."

"Noah . . . ," Alexis whispered.

The warm, dark water washed over her again. But just before she went under, she heard Nina's voice. "He's here, and he loves you."

The next time she woke up, she was in a private room and alone. Long shadows stretched along the wall and bathed her white blanket in an orange glow from the sinking sun.

The fire in her throat had eased only to be replaced by a painful cramp in her gut. Both paled, however, to the ache in her heart. *He's here, and he loves you.* Nina's message had been a dream. Her imagination. Wishful thinking.

Alexis let her eyes drift closed again, not from the pull of pain medications but the tug of regret.

They flew open again at the sound of a toilet flushing. Alexis turned her head to the right as the bathroom door opened. A man emerged, silhouetted in the bathroom light. Alexis squinted and tried but failed to sit up. Who the hell—

He stopped short. "Shit. I'm sorry. Did I—Did I wake you up?"

The heart monitor recorded the skip of her heartbeat. "Noah?"

He stepped out of the shadows, and Alexis gasped. It *was* Noah. But not.

His beard was gone, revealing a youthful smile and baby soft skin. And his long hair was now short, cropped and styled tightly against his scalp. But his eyes were the same—warm and soft—as he stopped at the edge of her bed and gazed at her.

A tear rolled toward her temple. "Oh my God."

His smile slipped. "That bad, huh?"

"No," she choked. "You were right. It *is* too much male beauty." A suppressed sob broke free, and she clutched her stomach against the assault of emotion on tender incisions.

"Shit." Noah looked panicked. "Did I hurt you? Should I get the nurse?"

Alexis shot out her hand and grabbed his arm. "No. Don't go anywhere. I'll just think I'm dreaming."

Noah bent over the arm of the bed and lowered his brow to rest on hers. "I didn't mean to upset you. I just wanted you to see the real me when I groveled for forgiveness."

A watery laugh escaped her sandpaper throat. It quickly became a cough, which caused another sharp pain in her stomach. Alexis winced. "Don't make me laugh."

"I wasn't trying to." Noah stood and reached for a disposable cup with a lid on the table next to her bed. He brought the straw to her lips. "Here. The nurse said you'd need it."

She sucked down the cool drink with a sigh. "Thank you." She blinked. "What happened to your cheek?"

"It's a long story that I'll save for another time." Noah returned the cup to the table, and then his finger traced a gentle line from her ear to her jaw. "How do you feel?"

"Better now that I know you're really here and I'm not just hallucinating."

His eyes pinched at the corners. "I'm so sorry, Lexa. I tried to get here. I had a big grand gesture planned to swoop in just in time and tell you how sorry I was before you went in, but I was too late." His throat worked against a swallow. "I didn't know . . . I didn't think you were going through with the surgery. I should have been here with you."

"You're here now."

His lips thinned. "That's not good enough."

Alexis turned her face into his hand and kissed the tip of his thumb. "It is."

"You're interrupting my groveling."

She met his eyes. "You don't need to grovel, and I don't want you to grovel. I want you to kiss me."

Noah lowered the arm of the bed and gingerly sat down next to her. He reached one arm across her body and pressed his hand into the mattress. "I have to say this first."

Alexis sighed and settled into the pillow beneath her head. "You really don't."

"The things I said to you were cruel and inexcusable."

"Are you forgetting what I said before that?"

"It doesn't matter. You tried to apologize, and I threw it back in your face. And when I did that, I not only betrayed you, I betrayed our friendship."

His words were a skewer through the thin membrane that remained around her emotional stability. Tears turned his face into a shimmery blur.

His jaw jutted sideways. "I let my own anger blind me to the fact that you were hurting and you needed me. And so I hurt you worse."

She cupped a hand along his smooth, clean jaw. "Okay, what do I have to say to get you to shut up and kiss me?"

He blinked. "I'm being serious, Lexa."

"So am I. You're obviously not going to stop all this unnecessary apologizing unless I say something in response—"

He managed to look offended. "Unnecessary? I practically threw you out of my house!"

"Because I accused you of doing something you didn't do."

"But you had every reason to think I'd do that!"

"Are you seriously going to argue with me right now? I just had an entire organ sucked out of me through a hole smaller than my belly button."

His skin turned ashen.

"If you want something to be upset about, consider the fact that we can't have makeup sex for, like, six weeks. So you'd better kiss me before the nurse gives me more pain meds and I pass out again."

The smooth contours of his face softened. "God, I love you."

"I know. And I love you too. I've loved you since the day I met you, and I will love you until the day I die. You are my best friend, Noah Logan. Forever."

He gave up the fight, bent his head, and covered her lips with his. Gently at first. Wet and soft against her dry and scratchy mouth. But then a groan emerged from deep within his chest, and she wrapped her hand around the back of his neck to hold him, cradle him, *forgive* him.

He pulled back and hovered atop her mouth. "I'm sorry, Lexa. I'm so sorry."

"Shhh." She tucked his face against her neck. He arched over her, careful not to press on her tender abdomen. "Everything is okay now. The surgery is over, and you're here, and that's all that matters."

A knock at the door brought him upright, but Noah remained on the bed, one arm draped across her. "Come in," he responded, voice suspiciously thick.

Tentative shoes squeaked on the linoleum. Candi appeared a moment later. She hovered a few feet from the bed, smiling as she looked back and forth between Alexis and Noah. "I told you he loves you."

"How's Elliott?" Alexis asked.

"So far so good. He's asking about you too."

"Tell him I'll come see him tomorrow."

Candi nodded and got that hesitant, shy look on her face that Alexis now recognized. "What is it?" she asked.

"My, um, my mom wants to come see you. Is that okay?"

"Sure, um . . . yeah." Alexis looked at Noah. "Can you help me raise the bed a little?"

Noah found the remote attached to the bed and pressed the button that lifted her top half into a semi-sitting position. A moment later, Lauren walked in looking as undone and disheveled as Alexis had ever seen her. Her makeup-free face bore the traces of too little sleep and too much worry. Her hair, normally a perfect bob along her shoulders, was now twisted atop her head in a messy bun.

Her smile was forced, but not in the way Alexis had come to

expect. This was from pure weariness, not insincerity. "How are you feeling?"

"Not too bad. Tired."

Her footsteps inched closer, and that's when Alexis noticed that she held something in her hand. A small red box. "I have a present for you."

Alexis traded a surprised look with Noah before returning her gaze to Lauren. "You didn't have to do that."

Lauren extended the box, and Alexis accepted it with trembling fingers. As Noah hovered at her side, she lifted the lid. And then blinked, holding her breath. Nestled in the velvet cradle was a ring—a deep emerald surrounded by a spray of tiny, sparkling diamonds.

"Lauren, this . . ." Alexis looked up. "I don't know what to say. This is too much. I can't accept this."

"It belonged to Elliott's mother. Your grandmother." Lauren glanced at Candi. "We want you to have it."

Alexis shook her head. "I appreciate the gesture, but this is a family heirloom. It should go to Candi."

"It should go to family," Candi said. "You're family."

Tears pricked her eyes again, and Alexis sought the comfort of Noah's hand. He wrapped her fingers in his and squeezed. "I—thank you."

Lauren hugged her own torso. "Nothing I say will ever be enough to tell you how sorry I am for everything and how grateful I am that despite it all, you did this for him. For us."

"Lauren—"

"It would be disingenuous of me to say that everything is going to be normal and fine after this. I can't promise that. I'm . . . I'm still reeling from all of this, just like you are, I suppose."

Empathy flared. Alexis didn't resent it this time. It was part of who she was, and it always would be. "It couldn't have been easy for you to find out about me the way that you did."

Lauren smiled in thanks. "I don't know what happens now, or if you even want anything to happen now. But I hope that you will give us a chance."

The last part came out weak, uncertain, as if she was afraid how Alexis would respond. Alexis looked up at Noah. His smile was reassuring, strong, and it healed her fully. No matter what, he would be there. He would always be there. And they could get through anything together.

"Well," Lauren said. "I should . . . I should get back to Elliott and leave you two alone."

Her shoes squeaked as she turned to leave, Candi right beside her.

"Lauren?"

She stopped and turned around.

"I'd like that," Alexis said. "I'd like to give all of us a chance."

Lauren nodded, her smile real and grateful. "I'm glad."

After they left, Noah returned to his seat alongside her on the bed. "That was a nice gesture."

Alexis set the ring on the table and settled again against her pillow. "It was, but just so you know, *you* are my family." She stifled a yawn as fatigue made another run. "And my answer is yes."

He brushed his thumb across her bottom lip. "Yes, what?"

"Yes, I'll marry you."

He laughed thickly. "Did I propose? I don't remember."

"You will. And my answer will be yes."

He dipped his head and whispered against her lips, "You're not supposed to make any major decisions in recovery. Didn't you read the fine print?"

"Then ask me again when the drugs wear off. My answer will be the same." She tugged him close and kissed him. "But I promise not to make you pick out the flowers."

"Why not? I've gotten really good at it."

Alexis let her hand drift down his chest and stop just above the waist of his jeans.

He groaned. "Six weeks, really?"

She sighed and closed her eyes. "I was exaggerating to get you to kiss me."

Noah chuckled in that low, warm way of his. She felt the tug of the blanket as he pulled it higher to cover her torso and then heard a soft hum as he lowered her bed flat again. She wanted to open her eyes but couldn't. The warm, dark water was too tempting.

He kissed her forehead. "Go to sleep. I'll be here when you wake up."

She hmm'd a quiet *thank-you* as darkness dragged her under.

But just before it closed in fully, his lips found hers once again. "What're friends for?"

EPILOGUE

"You promised not to laugh."

Alexis peered up from the table where just moments earlier, she'd dropped her forehead out of pure desperation. She might have actually burst an incision. Noah rested his hands on the back of her chair and blocked her in as he bent to kiss her.

"You should have warned me," she breathed against his lips. "I had no idea what I was promising."

Mack and his attendants had just finished their surprise dance routine, complete with hip thrusts, an over-the-head toss of their tuxedo jackets, and a booty smack.

"I'm glad you enjoyed it, but I've never hated anything as much in my entire life."

"You had fun. Admit it."

"I had fun making you laugh." He kissed her again, lingering just long enough for her to start looking forward to the end of the reception. They were getting naked tonight for the first time since the surgery.

Noah dragged an empty chair close to hers. He sat down and hooked his arm over her shoulder. "You doing okay?" he asked, nuzzling her hair. His softer tone meant he was serious this time. He'd been hovering over her for weeks like she was going to break. He wouldn't even let her carry her own coffee mug in the morning, and he'd damn near tackled Mack at the rehearsal dinner when Mack tried to pick her up in a bear hug.

"I'm perfect," she murmured, burrowing her nose into his neck. His skin smelled warm and tangy from exertion, but so uniquely Noah. She ran her fingertips along the hard, smooth line of his jaw. She was still getting used to the clean-shaven version of the man she loved.

With a contented sigh, she leaned her head on his shoulder. "I can't believe Mack pulled this off. He should seriously become a wedding planner."

"Dear God, don't tell him that. He'll make all of us join him."

"But you guys did such an amazing job. I've never seen such a beautiful wedding reception."

"Ours will be better."

Alexis leaned back so she could peer up at him. "Noah Logan, did you just propose to me?"

"You tell me." He winked when he said it.

"I think you did. And the answer, as you know, is yes."

He dropped a kiss on her upturned lips. She smiled, because she knew someday he'd propose for real, and she'd say yes for real, and they would live happily ever after.

A disgusted noise to their left brought them apart. "God, you guys are as gross as them."

Sonia dropped into a chair at the table and waved her hand toward Liv and Mack, who were so wrapped up in each other on the dance floor that the rest of the room might as well have disappeared.

Colton suddenly jogged over and leaned down, hands pressed to the table and color high on his cheeks. "Holy shit, you guys. You are not going to believe it."

It must've been something really big, because this was the first time he'd left the side of Gretchen all night. Something was definitely brewing between them, and Alexis planned to get the full story out of Gretchen as soon as possible.

"What won't we believe?" Noah asked.

"She's real."

Alexis scrunched up her face. "Who is real?"

"The Russian's wife!"

Noah stood and looked over Colton's shoulder. "Holy shit."

Alexis peered around him and followed his gaze. A tall, impossibly gorgeous woman stood just inside the entrance to the ballroom. Next to her, looking both shocked and slightly pitiful, was the Russian.

"I thought she couldn't come to the wedding," Noah said.

"Looks to me like he wasn't expecting her," Alexis said.

As if on cue, the woman turned on one dangerously high heel and began to walk out. The Russian raced after her.

"Uh-oh," Noah breathed. "That doesn't look good."

"Maybe we should follow them," Colton said.

Noah shook his head. "Leave them alone. Something's obviously wrong."

"Oh, I hope not," Alexis said, leaning on the table. "He's so tenderhearted. It would destroy him if he's having marriage trouble."

Colton smirked at Noah and left the table. Noah returned to

his seat, and Alexis once again rested her head on him. "How long should we stay?"

"If that's an offer to leave so I can finally get that dress off you, then my answer is now."

She laughed and brushed the tip of her nose against his jaw. "Looking forward to that, are you?"

Noah's long fingers slipped inside the back of her dress. "You should too. I have some fun stuff planned for you tonight."

"Fun stuff we've done before?" Her voice was suddenly breathless.

Noah caught her earlobe with this lips. "And some that we haven't."

Alexis tilted her head and sighed as he kissed behind her ear. "And where did you learn these new fun things?"

He turned her face toward his. And just before lowering his mouth, he murmured, "The Bromance Book Club, honey."

ACKNOWLEDGMENTS

This was a very personal project for me because it tells a story I know well. Shortly after I married my husband, he donated a kidney to his sister in an emergency, fast-tracked donation. Just two months after finding out he was the only genetic match in his family, the surgery was successfully performed at the Mayo Clinic in Rochester, Minnesota.

So my first thanks has to be to the doctors, nurses, and entire transplant team who cared for him then—and the amazing health care professionals who continue to take care of transplant donors and recipients today. Every donation experience is unique. And though I had to employ some creative license in a few details in Alexis's kidney donation for the sake of the timeline, the heart of the story is based on firsthand experience and a simple fact: living-organ donation can save lives. For more information, including how to become a kidney donor and the donation process, please visit the National Kidney Foundation at kidney.org.

As always, enormous thanks to my agent, Tara Gelsomino, for the reassuring patience and unwavering belief in the Bromance boys. Equal gratitude to my editor, Kristine E. Swartz, who knows how to talk a panicky writer off the edge. And to the entire marketing, publicity, and sales teams at Berkley Romance—you are the best in the business.

Thank you to my friends—Meika, Christina, Alyssa, Victoria, and all the women of my beloved Binderhaus. I couldn't do this without you.

And finally to my family. Thanks for putting up with me. You're the reason I do this.

Photo by Lauren Perry of Perrywinkle Photography

Lyssa Kay Adams read her first romance novel at a very young age when she swiped one from her grandmother's stash. After a long journalism career in which she had to write too many sad endings, she decided to return to the stories that guaranteed a happy ever after. Once described as "funny, adorable, and a wee bit heartbreaking," Lyssa's books feature women who always get the last word, men who aren't afraid to cry, and animals. Lots of animals. Lyssa writes full-time from her home in Michigan, where she lives with her sportswriter husband, her wickedly funny daughter, and a spoiled Maltese who likes to be rocked to sleep like a baby. When she's not writing, she's cooking or driving her daughter around from one sporting event to the next. Or rocking the dog.

CONNECT ONLINE

LyssaKayAdams.com/newsletter

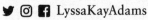 LyssaKayAdams

Ready to find
your next great read?

Let us help.

Visit prh.com/nextread

Penguin
Random
House